Elizabeth Horrocks is a retired teacher of English literature and former BBC Mastermind Champion, also appearing in several anniversary programmes. Born in Wales, she has always been fascinated by fantasy, myth and legend, and answered questions on Tolkien, and Arthurian Literature, on Mastermind. This interest provides a starting point for much of her writing.

Living in the legend-haunted village of Alderley Edge in Cheshire, Elizabeth is involved in Girl Guiding, and in the local church, particularly its youth drama group, as well as the Macclesfield Quiz League.

Married for nearly forty years, she has two grown-up daughters, two grandchildren and a cat.

The Edge of Doom

Elizabeth Horrocks

The Edge of Doom

Vanguard Press

VANGUARD PAPERBACK

© Copyright 2010
Elizabeth Horrocks

A CIP catalogue record for this title is
available from the British Library.

ISBN 978 1 84386 593 3

Vanguard Press is an imprint of
Pegasus Elliot MacKenzie Publishers Ltd.
www.pegasuspublishers.com

First Published in 2010

Vanguard Press
Sheraton House Castle Park
Cambridge England

Printed & Bound in Great Britain

The Edge of Doom

"Love's not Time's fool, though rosy lips and cheeks
Within his bending sickle's compass come,
Love alters not with his brief hours and weeks,
But bears it out even to the edge of doom."

William Shakespeare

To Olwyn, Barbara, and Tracey, without whom Olwen
would never have flown

Acknowledgements

I am indebted to all the writers of the many books dealing with the Matter of Britain, which I have read over the years. In particular, whilst writing *The Edge of Doom*, I found 'King Arthur, Dark Age Warrior and Mythic Hero', by John Matthews, most helpful – especially the list of names, on which have been based the names and relationships of many of the Circle of Companions.

Thanks to all those who have helped me with research, reading, suggestions and encouragement: the helpful people at Pegasus Publishers, Olwyn and the members of our Creative Writing class; Barbara and Tracey; my family, and especially my patient husband, Shaun.

Contents

Prologue: College.   17

Book 1: The Clearing.   25

Interlude 1: Cave.   82

Book 2: Country House.   103

Interlude 2: Causes.   154

Book 3: Camp and Conflict.   165

Book 4: Caverns.   251

Epilogue: College   289

Prologue: College

3.30 pm, a Friday in November 2006, at the Winsford campus of Mid-Cheshire College. Elli rammed her notebook and pen into her large handbag, on top of her mobile phone and a large block of Dairy Milk and heaven knows what else. Friday afternoon. Time to go home, perhaps have a quick cup of tea with her mother before helping with the evening milking, proving to her father that doing a full-time college course didn't mean she wasn't able to help on their struggling farm. Her improved IT would be good for the farm in the long run, she knew, and deep down her father did. He must do. It was only for one year, for heaven's sake!

"Go on, ask her!" she heard from the other side of the computer room.

"Who? Elli the Odd? She won't come."

"Yes, but she might like to be asked. Your 18th birthday bash will be a night to remember!"

Elli knew who were talking and about what. Carly was the nicest of the girls, the one who tried to be friendly. Megan wasn't too bad, but her other friends were nasty cows – except that the cows on the farm were much sweeter natured. And yes, she'd love an invitation to a party she wouldn't go to, and probably wouldn't enjoy if she did. All the girls who'd come straight from school to college seemed so young, although they were only a year or two younger than her nineteen years – and yet they seemed so sophisticated She tried to hum, so as not to hear, but the words still slid into her ears. More girls had joined in now.

"Go on! I dare you! Ask Miss Tollet! Tollet the Toilet!"

"Stupid name – even if she says it's an old Cheshire one…!"

"Do her good to meet some lads of her own age – stop her mooning around that aged army weirdo."

"Ex-army. And he's not that old – and I think he's rather fit!"

"He must be 35 if he's a day…go on, ask!"

Elli flushed red. Bad enough only being asked as a dare. To hear them mock Lance, and know that to retaliate would make things worse, was intolerable. She zipped her bag shut and went to walk out, only to find the whole gaggle of girls between her and the door.

They pushed Megan forward. "Like to come to my party tonight, Elli?" Megan asked.

"No thanks, I have to get home!"

"Got a date with a sheep have you?" one of the others asked.

"We don't have sheep."

"Sorry – it must be a cow!" Now everyone was trying to outscore the others in wit and cruelty.

"Don't show your ignorance – it'll be the bull!"

"Oh, Elli, no wonder you're not interested in the lads… or perhaps it *is* the cows. Either way, I'm not sure you're up to their standard of beauty…"

"Excuse me," came a quiet, masculine voice from the door. "I believe Elli, Miss Tollet, wants to leave. You seem to be in her way."

The girls stepped back a little and looked. The voice belonged to a dark-haired man, a little under six foot in height, in his mid-thirties. He was wearing chinos and a leather jacket, which was, Elli thought, unspectacular yet of very good quality, like its owner.

"Oooh, it's the soldier – come on, soldier, why don't you come to the party?" one of the bolder girls said.

"Thank you, no. I have a more satisfying evening planned, with a book and some music – although watching paint dry, or even having a tooth extracted, would be preferable to your company, I feel. Now shouldn't you lot be getting ready for the big occasion? I'm sure it will take most of you a long time to make yourselves beautiful – or even presentable!"

Such was his quiet authority that the girls were halfway through the door before they realised how much he was insulting them. Carly turned back. "Sorry about that, Elli – it got totally out of hand. It won't happen again, I'll see to that. What about a coffee, Monday break?" Then she too was gone, and Elli was alone with her rescuer. He spoke first.

"Not a bad kid, that Carly. She'd be better off sticking with you, than those others."

Elli was looking for a way to thank him without embarrassing him with emotion. She had known him for about two months, since their course started, and that was long enough to know that open emotion was not something that Lance Poole liked. She reached round her mind and their common love of sci-fi and fantasy, which had first drawn them together, provided a way out.

"Thank you so much. My knight in shining armour!"

"Always ready to help a damsel in distress!"

"But where's your white charger?"

"Tethered outside, of course. No room for him in a computer room – have you time for a coffee?"

"It's Friday afternoon – the canteen'll have shut."

"It won't take us long to walk into town. I promise you that you'll be home in time for the milking."

Elli wavered. Mum could do with her company: she was even more isolated now Elli used the old runabout to get to college. On the other hand, she'd be home all weekend – plenty of time for mother and daughter chats.

"OK. If you let me convince you of the worth of Marion Zimmer Bradley."

"You can try. Like you did in the great Dr. Who/Torchwood debate. You didn't win then!"

Oh but I did, thought Elli. We missed the afternoon session talking. I had you all to myself. You seemed almost ready to tell me about why you left the army – although all I actually found out was that you were on our course to widen your IT skills before setting up some sort of business. I think you enjoyed my company – not on the level of thrill I get from yours, of course, but enjoyed being with me all the same.

Or perhaps, she thought, more realistically, you're just an old-fashioned 'gentleman', and being kind. Or we're spending time together because we're the odd ones out in the class.

"Right," said Lance. "I'll just drop my laptop in the car first. Mind you zip up that jacket – it's cold outside!"

"There's no kind of atmosphere?"

"Red Dwarf. You can't catch me out on that, young Elli!" and he reinforced the old-fashioned gentleman idea by opening the door for her and ushering her through it.

As they walked out, heads bent against the autumn wind, they didn't at first notice the helicopter.

"What's that?" Elli stopped suddenly and pointed.

"A helicopter. Obviously," said Lance, grinning to take the sting out of his dry response to her enthusiasm. He often did that, thought Elli.

"Yes, but what's it doing here?"

The army helicopter crouched like an animal on the car park, which seemed, in this part, to have been cleared of cars. To

Elli's surprise the other students turned aside from the huge machine, or walked under its tail, seemingly unimpressed by its sight and sound.

The opening of the helicopter door spared Lance from having to make a speculative reply to Elli – the sort of thing he hated, she thought, realising that her unanswerable question would not appeal. A figure leant out: the pilot, a man in his sixties by the look of it, with iron-grey hair, and a craggy face. He beckoned them over. Wondering, they went.

"You are?" he said, addressing Lance.

"Lance Poole."

This seemed to bring a fleeting smile to the pilot's face. He looked at a check-sheet on his clipboard. "Yes. Army, I see from this." The man had a deep voice, with a Welsh lilt to it.

"Ex-army – at least the final details are still being sorted out." A look of pain passed over Lance's face, to disappear almost immediately.

The pilot turned to Elli. "But I don't seem to have your details – yet I think that must be an oversight," he said.

"Elli Tollet," she informed him. "But why should you have my details anyway?"

Again the secretive smile. "Sorry," he said. "There **is** a note about you here – I just didn't understand it. But come on, let me help you in."

"In? Why should I get in? Or do you mean Lance here? Who are you? Military? You may have business with him, but what's it got to do with me?"

The pilot turned to Lance. "This is a top-secret military operation…" He broke off, and turned an angry face to Elli, who had unexpectedly snorted with laughter.

"I'm sorry," she said. "It just sounds so ... Ripping Yarns… James Bond-ish. I don't know if I can take you seriously."

Lance looked at the helicopter. "It's definitely military – although of a sort I don't know. The whole thing must be kosher, why else would the college allow it to land?" He turned to the other man. "But Miss Tollet is right – it sounds strange – and why do you want us?"

"You saw the helicopter, didn't you?" came the enigmatic reply.

"Get in. Ex-army Lance Poole is definitely the man I'm looking for – you'll be fed information on a need-to-know basis." He turned to Elli, who was again snorting at the use of what she had always assumed to be a fictional cliché.

"And Miss Tollet here, is," he paused, "an unexpected bonus."

Elli wavered. The barrenness of her weekend stretched before her. The chance of a journey with Lance beckoned enticingly to the other. She felt suddenly mutinous. All her life she had been the goody-goody. Teenage rebellion – what was that? The fact that she had never wanted to rebel momentarily escaped her. Why shouldn't she have a fling, do something unexpected, something unconventional? And a 'military assignment': surely that was safe enough? Wasn't it? And with Lance, as a bonus…

She was recalled from her thoughts by Lance's voice, saying, "Show me some form of ID!"

The pilot laughed. "Think I stole this to abduct you, is it? Well, I'm sure there are easier ways of doing that! But here's my pass."

Sure enough, in an official-looking pass bearing the royal crest, was the pilot's craggy face. His name was, it seemed, was Lyn Sayer. Rank, commander. Lance nodded. Commander Sayer was right: abducting of two insignificant civilians carried out by military helicopter would be ludicrous. However, being cautious and methodical by nature, he would still have hesitated except that Elli had reached up, and allowed herself to be swung into the helicopter. Belatedly she asked, "Mr Sayer, what about my parents – they'll panic if I don't arrive home soon."

"No worries – that will all be taken care of, I assure you. And it's Lyn – first names only on this expedition, please."

Lance made his mind up, and then, as usual, acted decisively. Whatever was going on, he couldn't abandon young Elli in this unlikely set-up. He reached up, saying, "Elli, come down, let's discuss this," but his hand was grabbed, and, with a surprising strength, Lyn lifted him up. Unbalanced, he hit his head, rendering himself, for the moment, unconscious.

Through the growing blackness, he heard Elli's cry of distress and the noise of the ascending helicopter.

Book 1: The Clearing.

Chapter 1

Gradually, sensation came back. First, sound: a sort of rustling, a flapping and the sound of wind. Then feeling – a dreadful headache, a rough, prickling sensation. Then, reasoning: he was lying on some form of straw mattress, and the rustling was caused by his moving about on it. Before he opened his eyes and let his new world flood in on him, memory returned. Crossing the car park with young Elli... the helicopter... the pilot, Lyn Sayer... Elli's impetuous entry into the machine... He had tried to persuade her to come back, but Commander Sayer had lifted him up so quickly that he had banged his head and fallen, unconscious.

Slowly, he opened his eyes and saw that the flapping noise was to be traced to a loose piece of canvas moving in the wind. He seemed to be in a makeshift shelter. One wall seemed to be of rock, and two poles stretched the canvas out at an angle. How the canvas was attached to the rock, he couldn't see – if the slope of the rock allowed it, probably stones held it in place.

Turning his head was painful, but gradually he did so and looked out. The view was of an open glade, with trees in full leaf clustered thickly round the edges. On the far side they seemed to thin and fall away a little.

Lance shook his head, and stopped suddenly as the action increased his headache tenfold. The bright green of the leaves and the ease with which the sunlight penetrated suggested the light of early summer, yet the dry, glowing leaves of late autumn had been swirling round in the draught of the helicopter as they had crossed the car park. There was no way he had been unconscious that long, and no way that, if he had been seriously hurt, he would find himself in a shanty in a wood, and not in an intensive care unit.

There was a noise of someone approaching and Elli ducked in under the awning, carrying a sports water bottle. "Oh, Lance, you're awake! I'm so glad! How are you feeling? I've just filled this – would you like a drink?"

Lance smiled, surprised at the pleasure the sight of her gave him, a familiar figure in a world that seemed somewhat skewed. "I've a headache to match the worst hangover I ever had in the Army, and I think my neck's a bit sore, but I'll live – and I'd love some of that water!"

Elli knelt down, and he saw a look of weariness and worry in her young features, making her for once look older than her 19 years. She was a pleasant enough-looking kid, he thought, as he took the bottle – or was, when she wasn't pale with shadowed eyes, as she was now. Not as tall as he was, but still on the tall side for a woman, rather skinny, but with surprising strength – farm girl's muscles, he presumed. Not pretty, although she could make something of those chestnut curls. Today, they were tied back from her face, and in her bomber jacket and jeans she looked workmanlike, and at home. Not a sight to stir the blood, but comforting and reassuring all the same.

"Good job I had this bottle in my bag," she said, "but the water's fresh today. I boiled up some stream water earlier to make sure it would be drinkable."

Lance drank gratefully, noticing that the water was quite cool, despite Elli's talk of boiling it. How long had he been out of things? "What time is it?" he asked. "And where are we?"

"It's mid-afternoon – you've been asleep ever since we got here, nearly 24 hours, I reckon, although my watch isn't working. But most of it's been sleep, not unconsciousness. Lyn

gave you something to help, I think. As to where we are –
Lance, there's something very odd going on. Oh, damn," she
exclaimed. "I wasn't going to bother you about it until you were
quite recovered."

"Don't worry," Lance hastened to reassure her. "I'm not ill
– if only I could get rid of this thumping head – and I'm
somewhat confused as to where we are, so carry on."

"Hang on a minute – I've got some ibuprofen somewhere –
should have thought of it earlier…" said Elli, reaching over the
end of Lance's bed, and producing her capacious bag, the usual
type the girls seemed to have these days, Lance thought, halfway
to a briefcase or overnight bag. She rummaged in it and
eventually proffered two foil-wrapped tablets.

Lance swallowed them gratefully, then put his hand on
Elli's arm. "Sit down, and tell me."

She settled down, drawing her knees up, and circling them
with her arms.

"It *is* odd. Have you noticed the trees?"

"Yes," said Lance. "They shouldn't be light green. This is
early summer. Yesterday was autumn."

"I know, I know. And that's not the only odd thing. Here
it's quite sunny –a lovely day, if you can get over the season.
But there's this thick mist surrounding us: I can't go more than a
few hundred yards in any direction. And it's not only my watch
– I can't get a signal on my mobile."

"Let's see if I can." Lance dug in his pocket, produced his
phone, and tried. "No. No luck here either. What does
Commander Sayer say about it? By the way – Commander –
Fleet Air Arm, I presume?"

"No idea." Elli wasn't interested in the niceties of military
nomenclature. "Lyn's comforting, but he doesn't really explain.
He knows so much more than he's telling me. Perhaps he'll tell
you – a man, and an army man at that. Lance, I'm so worried

about my parents worrying!" This burst out of her in a voice that was near tears, and it was, Lance realised, the core of her discomfort. Changed seasons, mysterious mists produced no more than a puzzled frown. But the thought of her parents' worry caused panic.

"Lyn says he told them last night that I'm likely to be late – but how? – and this is more than late: it won't stop them from worrying. And who'll help on the farm? We can't afford to pay another casual."

"What did he say about that? I notice he's become Lyn by the way!"

"That's what I said at the beginning." Lyn ducked in, and joined them, swinging a dead hare from one hand. "First names only on this trip. And, Elli, I sent a brief text to your parents on your mobile phone, when you were busy with Lance, just as we were taking off. I promise they will not worry. Trust me."

Elli looked far from happy with this, but, Lance thought, decided to push the worry away for the moment, as Lyn continued. "So pleased to see you awake and taking notice – how do you feel?"

"I've a terrible headache – although it's lifting somewhat, thanks to Elli's ibuprofen. Otherwise, not too bad. But, Commander Sayer, Lyn – what's going on? The season's wrong, Elli says she can't get beyond the immediate area, mobiles won't work – and why are we with you anyway?"

Lyn passed his free hand through his grey hair. "I promise that I will explain as far as I can in the morning. But I'd like us to use this evening and overnight to rest and recover. This much I will say: I am acting under orders, and part of these orders are that we should have a 'bonding exercise', I suppose you'd call it. However, the place and mode were decided by a minor accident with our transport. Don't worry, we'll be out of here soon." He shook his head as both Elli and Lance started to speak. He looked fixedly at them, one after another, and said deeply and clearly, "I promise that no one at home will worry. I will explain more tomorrow when you are rested."

Elli found detachment settle on her, and curiosity die away, while Lance, with no home ties, and the remains of concussion, found his emotions easily calmed, and, although his intellect told him he ought to insist on an explanation now, he felt that tomorrow would be soon enough.

"Good," said Lyn, looking at them. "Now, if this is a bonding exercise, we'd better get on with it. Elli, you were saying you're a farm girl – how are you at preparing animals for the pot?"

Remarkably good, for a twenty-first century girl, it seemed, Lance thought. As Elli said, most of their classmates, male as well as female, wouldn't have had a clue, and, indeed, would have paled at the very idea.

"I've had my share of rabbit to prepare – shot the odd one myself, from time to time – a regular menace they can be on the farm! And I've prepared Christmas turkeys till I was sick of the sight of them, every year since I was eleven. 'You're at senior school, now, Elli, you can do a senior's job,' my dad said!"

"Let me at least skin it for you. You may be a farm girl, but I've got survival training – and some practice as well!" They settled down companionably, using the sharp knives Lyn had provided before disappearing on some business of his own.

"Where did you use your Survival Training?" asked Elli, probing gently.

"Afghanistan," Lance said curtly, not inviting further questions.

"Before or after you were in the Gulf?" said Elli, ignoring the tone.

"Before. Transferred from the one to the other, with not much time between. Now, what else are we going to put in the stew – or shall we spit roast this hare?"

Realising the subject was closed for the time being, Elli thought about ingredients for a stew. "I think I saw some old turnips stashed under the rocky overhang over there – I'll go and look."

The rocky cliff that the lean-to was up against bent away from the camp. Round the corner it was undercut, and there, as she had half-remembered, Elli found a pile of old, somewhat withered, turnips. She gathered about half a dozen, and carried them in the crook of her arm. Returning past the awning a flash of bright colour caught her eye. On investigation, it proved to be two large nets of oranges. What are these doing here? she thought. Did we rescue them from the helicopter? Try as she might, she had only the vaguest recall of the evening before: Lyn carrying the unconscious Lance in his arms, and herself stumbling after them, worried somewhat about being left behind, but strangely detached and insulated against the panic that should surely have overtaken her. Anyway, a few will go well. Hare a l'orange! she said to herself. Fleetingly, she thought that the "insulation" was perhaps still in place. Shouldn't she be worrying, even panicking more? She shrugged. She didn't seem able to do so, and in any case, they needed to eat. She emptied some of the oranges out of the plastic net, and replaced them with the turnips, taking the net with her.

As she approached Lance by the small fire Lyn had kindled before leaving, she started to laugh. Lance looked up, surprise in his eyes, and a small smile on his face. "What's so amusing?"

"What are you doing, Sam?" she asked in reply.

"Sam? Oh, I see, Sam Gamgee, *Lord of the Rings*, Volume Two – 'Of Herbs and Stewed Rabbit'. Except of course, this is hare, and we haven't collected herbs yet!"

"Oh, Lance, it is good to have you around, picking up on what I'm talking about! And not just the films – the chapter headings in the book!" said Elli, and then, embarrassed and afraid of embarrassing Lance, she rushed on: "But you know what that makes Lyn, don't you? After all, he brought the hare!"

"Gollum!" said Lance, and joined in her laughter. "Young Elli, you're hardly fair to him!"

"No – it's not a comparison that bears close examination. But here, look what I found!" and she displayed the turnips and oranges.

"Good girl – you're a treasure!" said Lance, with fervour.

Delighted if somewhat nonplussed by his praise, Elli turned to the skinned and gutted hare. "You've been busy! Now, if we had some of those herbs, we could make a stew. I see you found the pot I brought the water in earlier… perhaps it's a cauldron – it's large enough – and we're not characters from Tolkien after all, but the three witches from Macbeth! But if we don't get herbs, we can always spit-roast it."

"Will these do?" Lyn had appeared down the slope as they were talking, and offered Elli some bunches of parsley, thyme and wild garlic.

"Great!" said Elli. "Now, Lance, I'll chop the hare, and you can deal with the oranges and turnips."

"There's lovely!" said Lyn. "I'm very fond of oranges."

"Lyn, could you get us more water from the stream?"

Lance and Lyn exchanged the helpless looks of men being organised by a woman, and, without a word, Lyn picked up a smaller pot and set off down into the lower band of trees.

"Oh, Lyn," Elli called after him, "near the stream I found some coarse bread earlier, on a large stone right near the edge of the mist. I didn't bring it as I was struggling with that potful of water. But if it's still there, it would just top off the meal…"

Even the long light of summer was fading before the meal was ready, but it was worth waiting for. Lyn produced three wooden bowls and some curiously old-fashioned looking spoons, and they all fell to eagerly, remembering how little they had eaten that day. Lance had not felt hungry until after his headache had lifted, and Elli thought that she had eaten no more than a couple of packets of crisps she had found in her bag, supplemented by a few withered apples Lyn had offered her, and some brews of tea. "Not many of these left," Lyn had said about the tea bags. He himself had not seemed to need food through the day, although he had accepted the tea gratefully.

The stew was tasty, and they mopped up the last dregs with the mysterious bread that Lyn had retrieved. It was coarse, and occasionally gritty, but proved well suited to soaking up the liquid. Lyn then brought out more of the apples for dessert, and Lance, somewhat shamefacedly, produced a hip flask full of good whisky. Using the water from the smaller pot Lyn had filled, and that Elli has insisted on boiling, they made a hot toddy, and poured it into the bowls. It must be admitted, thought Lance, that the promise of the toddy had helped spur them to wash up!

Relaxed, and still curiously unquestioning, Elli looked through the young leaves of the trees to the stars appearing in the sky. To her own surprise, she started to sing softly, a song she remembered from her childhood.

> *"Say goodbye my own true lover*
> *As we sing a lovers' song…"*

Although it was untrained, Elli had a true alto voice, not strong but surprisingly resonant. At the start of the second verse, she was disconcerted to hear Lance join in, singing in what her grandmother would have referred to as a pleasant light baritone.

Together they held the last note for a few beats, testing Elli's breath control, and she wondered if Lance, too, was having difficulty, as his voice did not seem quite steady. But after a moment of silence, he said, in a casual voice, "You're too young to know 'The Carnival is Over'!"

"One of my father's favourites, from his teen years, and Mum remembers it from her childhood – she's some five years younger. But you're too young as well – don't play that old man act with me!"

"True," he admitted. "It pre-dates me, but the record was still around in my youth, and it's still a favourite at regimental dances. And I'm glad of it – Judith Durham has a wonderful voice, I think."

"If you two are going to discuss your musical preferences, I am going to bed," said Lyn. "But the singing was lovely – thank you! I've re-rigged the blankets to make separate cubicles again, like last night. Good night."

"No, it's time we all turned in," said Lance. "The sooner we do, the sooner we'll have your explanation of what's going on. No, I haven't forgotten – it just hasn't seemed important tonight."

"But it will tomorrow," said Elli, banking the fire with turf. "And it had better be good, Lyn!"

The next morning, Elli was the first to wake. It was another fine day, it seemed. She wondered if she should wake the others first, or fettle the fire, or fetch water from the stream. Her bladder decided her – she would go to the stream via the privacy of the woods. Wrapping one of Lyn's bright, un-military looking blankets round her, she picked up the larger cauldron, and set off down the slope, into the woods.

Bladder emptied, she approached the small clearing near the river, where she had found the bread the day before. Today, the mist seemed somewhat thinner. Perhaps, later, they could push through it. But first, Lyn must give them his explanations. Last night's detachment still held – just – but she could feel the mounting pressure as worries and fears tried to break it down.

She slid the last few feet down to the stream. This time, she thought, as she tipped the cauldron to catch the water, this time she wouldn't fill it too full: a 'lazy man's load' was what her mother would call it. The noise of the water rushing into the pot filled her ears, and she found herself hoping that Lyn had more supplies of tea or coffee. But I'm not giving them a wake-up cuppa in bed! she thought frivolously. When the cauldron was half full, she tilted it upright again. Then, bracing herself, she lifted it from the water. The immediate bank was steep and slippery, but after that the clearing sloped gently and the way through the woods, though steeper, was easy underfoot.

With less water yesterday, she could have carried the bread. It would be too much to hope that there would be some bread on the same stone today…

When she had negotiated the bank, she put the cauldron down, briefly, to draw breath. There was a movement in the corner of her eye, over near where the large stone – like an altar – was. Turning, she saw a young lad, little more than a boy. She started and nearly slopped the water. By the time she had settled the pot on the ground and straightened, the lad was standing behind the 'altar-stone', half-turned to the trees, poised for flight into the mist. He must have come through that, Elli thought. Perhaps, if it's your home territory, you can manage it. But the boy had an odd look, almost feral, she thought. Surely he couldn't be living rough in these remote woods? However, as far as she could see, those of his clothes that were visible above the stone seemed to be a rough top, almost a tunic, a belt, and what looked like a pair of poorly-cut trousers, as if he had worn out the more usual tracksuit, and had dressed in anything he could find abandoned in farm buildings.

She called out, cheerfully she hoped, to stop him going. "Hello. Can you help me? We're lost, and my mobile doesn't seem to work. Have you got one on you?" Silly, she thought, if he's that destitute he'll have sold any mobile – after all, who would he have to ring?

The boy turned toward her. At least, he hadn't run away. But a look of total incomprehension seemed to flick over his face. Oh, she thought, foreign? Deaf? Daft? But he smiled and held something out toward her. To her astonishment, it was another loaf of the same rough bread. As she stood, he spoke, with a strange accent that took her ear some time to tune into. Even then, it seemed like listening to a badly-dubbed film.

"Greetings. Are you one of the fey?"

"Fay? No, my name's Elli."

"An elf perhaps? I saw you had taken the bread from yesterday – I hoped it pleased you?"

Did he say elf? She looked nothing like the tall stately beings in *Lord of the Rings*. And what boy, however obsessively into fantasy or role-playing, would start a conversation in such a way?

"The bread was most welcome. Thank you."

"We always like to please your people. And especially now, when we hope you will help to keep us safe from the pestilence."

"The pestilence?"

"The dreadful black pestilence, that's spreading north from London. Even in your elvish halls, you must know of it. Even in our poor hamlet, even here in Gradbach, we know of it...and fear it!" He sounded genuinely afraid.

She had been right in the first place. The boy had obviously overdosed on fantasy. But at least she now knew where they were. Gradbach was not too far from home, in a remote corner of the Peak District. She'd stayed in the Youth Hostel there on a Guiding weekend, and walked through the steep woods up to the moor and the strange, haunted chasm known as Lud's Church. However, if the mist didn't clear, it would be risky territory to walk through. Perhaps the lad could help, but then again, he was definitely odd. Better secure the bread first, in case they had to stay longer.

She threw back the blanket which she'd fastened, cloak-like, onto her shoulders. The movement disturbed her hair, which finally escaped from the hair-bobble she had been using, and tumbled on to her shoulders. She reached her hand to push it back, and said to the boy, "Have you brought us some more bread? That was kind of you!" But at that moment a stray sunbeam illuminated her chestnut curls and the slight but definite curves of her body.

The boy gasped. "You are not an elvish man – you are a woman! Or at least, you have a woman's form – but you wear man's apparel – unnatural, foul! And appearing out of the mist... Go now! I fear you are of the devil come to tempt and maybe torment... Go!" With that, to Elli's astonishment, he made the sign of the cross, followed by the spread fingers that she believed to be the evil eye. Then, before she could respond, he turned and ran, the mist rapidly swallowing him. As he went, to Elli's astonishment, she noticed that his feet were bare.

She lifted the water pot, and noticed that the boy, in fleeing, had thrown away the bread, which had landed on the altar-stone. Collecting that as well, she walked briskly through the trees, thinking furiously. Various unrelated happenings of the last two days seemed to be fitting together, but she was unwilling to believe the picture they formed.

As she reached the clearing, she saw that Lance and Lyn were awake, and, to her amusement, she saw that Lyn, newly shaved, was finishing shaving Lance with what looked alarmingly like a cut-throat razor. She paused, waiting till the razor had been safely put down, and Lyn had emptied away the water which must have been heated on the newly-awakened fire.

Then, taking a deep breath, she moved forward. Seeing her coming, Lance smiled a welcome, and her heart flipped. But she was determined not to lose focus. Smiling briefly in return, she set down the water and bread. Then, turning to Lyn, she put the question she had been formulating: "Lyn, *when* are we?"

Lance turned toward her and frowned. But Lyn straightened up, reached out his hands toward her and smiled. "My dear Elli! How clever of you! It saves me a lot of explanation: I was just bracing myself to tell you – and for your disbelief. But what made you see it?"

Now Lance was on his feet and had come between them, laying a hand on each of them. "Elli, what on earth are you talking about? You're making no sense! Lyn," he appealed as man to man, "don't encourage her. But do explain!"

Lyn turned to Lance. "Elli is quite right ... she's not fantasising. The question that needs to be asked is not *where* we are, but *when*. I am a time traveller. And, now, so are you."

"What? But this is a military operation – one with a slight hiccup, which has led to a rather unconventional bonding exercise. Don't ask me to believe in time-travel – or is this role playing?" Lance hovered between scorn and annoyance.

"No role playing. Believe me. I *am* on military attachment. I didn't say which military. We had a small accident to our transport, so we had to set down unexpectedly. I used my small powers to protect us with that mist, and ..."

"And used something like hypnosis to calm us, until we were accepting enough of the situation that we could be able to listen to what you have to say," said Elli.

"Precisely. Please, Lance. Give Elli and me a few minutes. Listen." Lance nodded silently, and sat down by the fire. Lyn and Elli followed suit.

Lyn turned to Elli. "Elli, how did you work it out?"

Elli wasn't totally sure. "I felt there was something strange, something you weren't telling us. I couldn't think what. And then, this morning, less than an hour ago, I went to the stream..." and she recounted her meeting with the strange boy.

Lance was forced to admit to himself that time travel would make sense of Elli's encounter. He applied his training and experience and tried hard to think of another explanation, or at least to approach the evidence with an open mind. He kept quiet, whilst Elli and Lyn discussed her story.

"You say you know *where* we are?" Lyn asked.

"Yes – he mentioned Gradbach – it's a hamlet on the edge of the Peak District. In the hills near the centre of the country –

not far from where I live," she added, realising that the modern names might not mean anything to Lyn.

"So, we're not so far, geographically speaking."

"But Lyn, have you no idea *when* this is?"

"Describe the boy again."

"Roughly-woven tunic, loose – britches, I suppose you'd call them. Bare feet."

"Not a lot of help," Lyn mused. "The poor wore clothes like that for at least 1000 years, I should say!"

"He thought I was an elf – a Tolkien type of elf, I presume." (This to the still silent Lance.) "But when he noticed I was a woman, he decided I was a devil instead!"

"Again, not much help, but, as far as I can gather – and you must realise that I have not travelled to every century – that is more likely to be thought in what you call, for what reasons I'm not sure, the Middle Ages."

Elli suddenly remembered a detail she hadn't mentioned in her first telling. "He talked of a pestilence spreading from the South: the Great Plague or the Black Death?"

Lance decided to suspend his disbelief for the moment. "The clothes you describe, elves, and the devil – surely the Black Death – 1349 or 50?"

Elli looked at the trees. "Early summer – it must be the later year if the pestilence is coming so far north. But this is silly – why do we need to know? What are *we* doing here? Or should I say, now?"

Lyn looked rueful. "As I said, we suffered a misfortune. Our transport needs some minor – restoration. I had been told to take some time to forge a relationship with you, Lance, and, now I come to think of it, with Elli as well, although I didn't realise it from the way it was put to me. I had arranged a place, and a time – my own – but this will have to do."

Lance's mind had been working on the question of their transport since he had woken up, and, he felt, in his sleep before then. This was a puzzle in whatever time they were in. "That helicopter, where did you get it? It seemed a very modern machine – or is it yours? Are you from the future? But whatever, where is it? There's no sign of it, no wreckage, no indication of why you expect it to be functioning in a few days. Especially now, when I am given to believe we are stranded in time – any help you could have expected from experts, technicians, whatever, in your own time – any help of that kind, or any kind, won't be available."

Lyn smiled. "I asked you to trust me before. I have proved as good as my word. I told Elli that her parents wouldn't be distressed. Now you can see why."

Elli looked puzzled, then sprang to her feet, eyes sparkling. "Oh, I see! If you're a time traveller, you can take me back to when we left – or soon after! So however long I travel, they won't know – unless I return looking about 50!"

But how is she to return, thought Lance, if Lyn's mysterious transport has malfunctioned and stranded us here? And if, while we are here, we have hostile villagers and plague to deal with? Then he realised, to his intense irritation, that he was starting to believe the ridiculous time travel explanation. He opened his mouth to say some of this, then looked at Elli's happiness, and shut it again. Time enough. And perhaps time soon to look for Lyn's mysterious time machine.

The morning passed in domestic duties: collecting wood for the fire, sorting the makeshift shelter, and, at Lyn's insistence, packing so they could leave suddenly if they had to. "I'm not sure I liked the sound of Elli's villagers," he said. "They might come to root out the devils!" To the others' surprise he produced two modern rucksacks and suggested they packed into them. "Lovely things, these – like oranges, something from your time I really like," he said. "And, like the oranges, I couldn't resist them – but I must be careful where I leave them, not to cause an anach – an anachronism to puzzle the future!"

"Time Team would love it!" said Elli, cheerful now. "But what are these?" And she produced two packs of M&S boxer shorts from one of the rucksacks.

Lyn had the grace to look embarrassed. "They're for Lance – remember I wasn't expecting a young woman!"

"Better something than nothing," Elli responded. "And after lunch I'll do some emergency washing!"

It was after lunch – a peculiar meal consisting of bread, oranges, weak tea and some chocolate, which had been found at the bottom of Elli's capacious bag. Lyn was busy with the fire, and Elli had departed to the stream to wash-up, and, she had insisted, to wash out some clothes. Lance saw his opportunity, and, murmuring something that he hoped would be taken as a polite explanation of his bodily needs, he slipped into the woods. When he had retreated far enough to escape any detection from Lyn, he changed direction and cut through the trees till he met what he reckoned was the path Lyn had used on his mysterious excursions. Then he struck uphill, away from their camp.

Soon he encountered the mist that had frustrated Elli the day before. Remembering that Lyn had said he'd thrown it all round the clearing (how? the analytical part of his brain asked), he determined that he would push through it. It wouldn't be that deep. Don't look at it, that was the answer. He dropped his eyes to his boots – thank heavens he had worn them to college that day, and not flimsier footwear – and focussed on his feet. One step at a time. He'd look up every twenty steps and see if he had cleared the mist. The first time he shifted his gaze wider, he almost wished he hadn't. The mist seemed to press on his eyes, and swirl into his nostrils, blinding him and making it difficult to breathe. Now there seemed to be a sound of pulsating, or breathing, all round him. Quickly, he dropped his eyes again, and stopped still, until his vision cleared, and he could breathe more easily. As this happened, the oppressive noise eased as well. Looking hard at his feet, he muttered, "Fifty paces this time!" and continued up the faintly defined path.

After fifty paces, he tried again. The mist was still there, but less suffocating. Ten paces should see him through it. Fixing his eyes downward again, he continued. When he stopped for the third time, the mist was reduced to a few wisps and the trees were back, with sunlight shining through them.

The pull-up was stiff but nothing extraordinary. The path wound and zigzagged, then, when the trees started thinning, turned left. To his astonishment he found himself at the entrance of a steep chasm, decorated with some fading bunches of late spring flowers, as would be seen at a wayside shrine in a Catholic country. He went forward, finding himself flanked by steep rock sides. The wind swept over the top of the rocky cleft, but inside it was quiet, and the quietness bent about his ears – it was the pressure found in churches and other places with centuries of spiritual input. Looking at the reddish walls, with ferns and mosses growing on them, Lance was reminded of a cave with its roof collapsed or removed. Suddenly, he realised that this was the place that he had heard of from friends when he had first moved to Cheshire: Lud's Church, the Green Chapel visited by Sir Gawain in a medieval poem. He had always meant to take time to walk in the area. Now time had taken him there. Uneasy, he felt that any villagers visiting this place – which they would surely regard as holy, or haunted – would identify him as another elf, or, more dangerously, a demon. Treading as swiftly as the uneven ground would allow, he moved quickly through, and scrambled out of the chasm at the far end.

He paused and looked around. The trees were sparse here, and he seemed to have walked up through them to the edge of the moors above. The space in front was not a clearing, but rather the start of a wide, open space, of turf and rock and blue sky. A hundred yards or so away was a green hillock, and he walked slantwise across the moor toward it.

The green hummock seemed to shiver slightly. Toward one end there was a more definite movement. A slit some two foot long appeared, but instead of the darkness that Lance expected, light seemed to grow– a brown, peaty light with a black polished centre. It reminded Lance of a large eye … in fact, it *was* a large eye. Lance retreated hastily and tried to refocus. With a fresh perspective, the hillock now looked different. It looked like a shape out of fantasy, of legend … it looked like a dragon.

Already mentally battered by the concept of time travel, Lance rapidly decided that discretion was the better part of valour. He avoided looking again at the eye, faintly remembering stories of dragon enchantment, of basilisks, and the like. Nor did he move more rapidly or let his movements betray his rising sense of confusion and even panic. Instead, calling on his military training and experience, he walked diagonally back across the moor, keeping a sideways eye on the dragon-hillock. The eye of the dragon narrowed to a slit – watching him? Closing? – but the green body moved no more.

Breathing deeply, to keep himself calm, he reached the opening to Lud's Church. Only when he had dropped to the floor of the defile did he pause, and then, checking that the creature was out of sight, and therefore could presumably no longer see him, he turned and went as quickly as was safe back down to the entrance. Then he hurried toward the camp. Soon he saw the mist. A hundred paces should do it, he thought, dropping his eyes to his feet and counting. It seemed that it *was* sufficient, and there were no further obstacles. He reached the camp, and, pulling aside the makeshift curtain, confronted Lyn, who was lying on his bed.

"I went looking for the helicopter...I thought there might be equipment we could salvage... I got through the mist, but I couldn't find it. But there's a green hillock out there... with an eye. I swear it. It's dragon shaped and I thought I saw it move slightly. What *is* going on? You know more than you're saying. How dare you be so... smug, so self-contained? How dare you bring young Elli into this... this... mess?"

Lyn sighed. "I'm not fully in control. I have some...Power... but Olwen – the dragon – is the time traveller. And I'm dependent on her whim, or her plan, or whatever it is."

Elli was standing in the doorway, returning from the stream. "Dragon?" she gasped.

"Yes. She comes from another dimension, another world. Things slip through from time to time. Half of this world's legends are based on such, what shall I call them? – seepages. Olwen seeped through when I was quite young. We understand each other somehow."

"Telepathy? ESP?" asked Lance.

"Not exactly. She can make me understand what she wants me to understand, but it's nothing as clear as talking mind to mind. She has other attributes, mind you..."

"Time travel." This was Elli.

"Yes indeed. She controls it. I thought it was random, but now I'm not so sure. She won't – or can't – let me visit in my own lifetime – fair enough, I suppose, and she's very wary in the eighteenth and nineteenth centuries: hard for people then to accept a dragon, or one disguised as a flying machine! And coming here, she had a wing tip struck by lightning – a million to one chance – and, I gather, she needs a week, to sleep, and for the tip to recover."

"Is she...safe?" Elli ventured.

"Safe? Of course, she's not safe! She's a dragon!" Lance exploded.

"There's your answer," Lyn said, amused. "But if you mean will she eat you, the answer is no. Dragons, it seems, can go many weeks without food – although clean water is always welcome. Every so often Olwen flies off and returns within a few hours – although I don't know how long it's been for her – sated. With all of history and at least two worlds to choose from, I believe she chooses carefully, a different place every time. I've seen her looking closely at our sheep and cattle, but she's never even taken so much as a lamb. So don't worry, she won't eat you. But treat her with … respect, all the same."

"Obviously." Lance was recovering his equilibrium. He allowed the military part of his mind to be sucked into the details. "The helicopter. How is that organised?"

"It's a sort of cabin I've arranged on Olwen's back – a bit like the pictures of howdahs I've seen. And between her and me we can cast a glamour, so people see what is acceptable to them. Sometimes, for a short while, we can arrange for most people not to see us at all – like in your car park. But it's hard work."

The shared love of science fiction surfaced. "So, better, as far as blending in goes, than the Tardis," said Elli.

"Only not so big inside. Obviously," said Lance, with a grin in her direction.

"Obviously," said Elli gravely.

Lyn shook his head, seemingly baffled. He continued: "Despite the difficulty, she's insisted on bringing us to your time over and over again. I couldn't see why, but now I think it must be so we could pick you up, and so I would be at home with you – she even made me learn your language!"

"Your language is Welsh, right?" said Lance. "At least, you certainly have a Welsh accent!"

"When *are* you from?" Elli asked.

"Yes, I'm Welsh. From quite some time ago."

"How did you manage before you learnt to speak our English?" Lance was curious.

"Olwen can act as a sort of translator..." Lyn got no further.

"Like a Babel fish?" Elli almost giggled.

"Only you wouldn't stick her in your ear. Obviously," said Lance, trying to keep a straight face. Then he gave up, and the two of them dissolved into helpless laughter, a safety valve after recent pressures.

Lyn waited patiently for them to finish. "What was that all about?"

"Sorry. If you're not from our time, you won't know the Hitchhiker's Guide...it doesn't matter," Lance said.

Lyn continued. "But Olwen finds translating a real strain. For one thing she worries that someone will notice when the shape of the lips speaking doesn't match the words they hear..."

"Oh," said Elli. "*That's* what happened when I met the lad. I knew there was something odd!"

"You were lucky Olwen was awake when you met the boy, and that she decided to translate – otherwise I doubt you'd have understood anything! Also, in general, the amount of energy needed to convert thoughts and words is immense. So if you find yourself anywhere near your own time, you have to manage. Just don't use too much slang or other 'modern' language."

"Right on!" said Lance.

"Cool!" said Elli. And to Lyn's annoyance, they started laughing again.

"Seriously, though," said Elli, after a minute or so, "that explains why the journey here was so ... odd."

"How do you mean?" asked Lance.

"Well, I told you about it a little, when you first woke up, but I didn't like to worry you – or, if I'm honest, give you cause to think I was a silly, hysterical girl."

"Girl can't be denied," said Lance. " But I've never thought you hysterical. Silly, now, that's a different matter ..."

Elli nearly rose to the bait, but she was learning. If Lance wanted to tease her, that was fine, and if she did nothing but glare at him, that might impress him with her maturity.

"As I was saying, the flight was odd. I sat by you, and tried to remember what to do for head injuries from the first aid course I did last year. As far as I could remember, I should have sent for an ambulance, but that didn't seem practicable! I did mention it to Lyn here, and he said it would be sorted out when we arrived: I assumed he would send a message from the helicopter... then he gave me something from his 'emergency bag' for you to drink ... I spooned a little into your mouth, but you wouldn't swallow properly and I was afraid of choking you. So I just tried to make you comfortable, and keep you warm with that blanket over there. Then Lyn offered me a drink – it seemed to be one of those 'magic' cans, which are self-heating ..." she broke off. "It didn't just seem to be magic, did it? It *was* magic!"

"Well, not quite," said Lyn, " But it did have certain herbs, and a little of my Power ... Its object was to calm you, to make you accepting of the situation, so I could concentrate on aiding Olwen by lending her some strength, such as I have."

"Yes," said Elli. "It worked, in some way. I was in some sort of trance-like state, I think. Everything seemed to be slightly distant. I thought at the time that I ought to worry more, but I also felt on the verge of sleep, and had those sort of thoughts which come to you then: not really logical, although they seem so at the time... Now I'm beginning to think they were real, and because of Lance being unconscious, and me drugged–"

"Not drugged!" Lyn protested. "Just calmed a bit!"

"Whatever," said Elli. "With us both not fully operational, you dropped some of the illusion you had created of the helicopter. It must be very draining, even for you and Olwen, and you needed your power for the flight."

"Clever girl you are!" said Lyn with appreciation.

"Anyway, it seemed that the noise of the helicopter died away bit by bit, and we seemed to be flying silently. The sky was black and I couldn't see any stars. We seemed to sweep and hover and rise and fall, as if we were riding a great bird of prey, who in turn was riding the thermals and air currents. Of course, I realise now that the 'bird of prey' was Olwen, but then, well, I didn't wonder – your 'potion' having put me in an 'accepting' frame of mind, to use your term for it.

"Then, just before I did go to sleep – for the whole experience had been very tiring, on top of the 'magic' drink – I seemed to hear a voice: well not quite a voice, but into my mind came the phrases 'We are riding the wind between the worlds...' and 'The torrent of time is taking us – let it, let it...'"

Lyn was looking at her with a mixture of respect and utter astonishment.

"My girl, I think Olwen has been talking to you, or at least you have caught some of her thoughts! Very sensitive of you, and very unusual for her to let you. Perhaps she's grateful for some female company! But seriously, I've tried to ask her about this time travelling of hers, and those are the phrases she puts into my mind. She doesn't use language the same as us – she thinks in pictures, I believe, but the part of my brain that is human translates this into speech, at least on occasion. But for someone who is a wholly human, twenty-first century person to hear the same words is... astonishing – and may prove helpful before we're through!"

Chapter 3

That evening, they ate grilled fish. Elli had helped Lyn manufacture a fish trap out of springy willow twigs and it had proved effective. Again, Lyn's love of oranges proved useful. He must be from a time before they were usual in Britain, Elli mused. But how long could the three of them live on Lyn's hunting skills and oranges? This would be a bad time of year for living off the land – autumn, with its fruits, would be much better. Olwen needed to recover soon, she thought, or we'll be eating nothing but that stash of turnips – last winter's cattle fodder?

Later, they sat round the fire again, more truly relaxed than the night before, because this relaxation was growing naturally, not imposed. Worries were not artificially excluded, simply put aside for a while. Lyn turned to Elli. "Your song last night was lovely – I know so little of your music, and most of it seems shouting – and very artificial. Have you any more like last night?"

Elli thought, recalling her father's repertoire. Then she started on one from his Joan Baez album:

> *"Plaisir d'amour ne dure qu'un moment*
> *Chagrin d'amour dure toute la vie...*
>
> *The joys of love are but a moment long*
> *The pain of love ... "*

She was interrupted by Lance jumping to his feet.

"For heaven's sake, girl, don't you know anything but these maudlin pseudo-folksongs?"

He stormed off into the woods, disappearing into the gathering darkness. Elli stared after him, hurt and open-mouthed. She turned to Lyn, who shrugged. "Don't ask me, I've only just met him, remember? But do you know something so cheerful he can't object to it?"

She thought again, and then started on the silly, extended version of 'Old McDonald', learnt at Guide camp.

"Old McDonald had a farm,

Down by the sea, where the water weeds grow…"

To her surprise, when she got to the 'big sheep, little sheep, little sheep, big sheep' part, she heard Lance join in. After several verses, touring the variety of animals on the farm, she caught sight of Lyn's bemused face, and collapsed, giggling.

Lance looked at her and smiled. "Sorry about earlier. I was a little on edge, I admit. But Old McDonald was much more fun!"

"Where did *you* learn that?" said Elli, concentrating on the last part of what Lance had said.

"School Scout group, before I joined the OTC."

There was a pleasure to be had in discovering mutual experiences, and a whole variety of silly songs followed. At length, Elli stopped recalling the many verses of Pizza Hut, and stood up. "Bed for me. I hope you enjoyed the concert, Lyn."

Lyn smiled. "A lot of it went over my head. But it reminded me of a soldiers' drinking bout – but with no drink!"

Lyn and Lance stayed talking by the fire. Sometime later, Elli thought she woke and could see them still there, faces occasionally lit by a flame sparked from the embers. Whatever they were discussing was obviously serious, and, unusually,

Lance seemed to be the one talking most. Putting the world to rights, no doubt, she thought, and went to close her eyes again. As she did so, she saw Lance get up abruptly and say something to Lyn in a low, intense voice. The only word she could distinguish sounded, oddly, like 'Gwennie', and, as he came past her, she thought she saw, by the light of a sudden flame, a look of total bleakness on his face. I'm obviously still dreaming, she thought. And, indeed, it must have been so, for the next morning all was as normal as it ever was.

The next few days passed in a strangely calm way. They fell into a routine, pleased that the weather remained fine, if sometimes cloudier than the first day. After their first attempts with the razor, the men gave up shaving and determined on growing beards, which, Elli reckoned, would look well enough, once they were through the stubble stage.

She had developed a knack for making fish-traps, and with the frequent success of Lyn's snares, they ate well enough, if somewhat repetitively. The fish grilled easily on a sharpened stick, the oranges, turnips and herbs made a good enough broth to cook the meat in, and, saved, provided a midday snack. Oddly, a loaf of bread still appeared every morning, supplementing their midday and evening meals. They took good care not to collect it till near lunch, so as to avoid any repetition of Elli's meeting with the village lad. Breakfast was the biggest problem. The day before's bread was hard and virtually inedible by that time. Lyn limited them to one tea-bag and one orange between the three of them, and for the first two days, Elli added to this with two pieces of chocolate each, but then her supply ran out.

They were busy enough during the day – water to fetch, firewood to gather, fish-traps and snares to make and set, food to cook. On the day after Elli had met the boy, she insisted on washing as many clothes as she could persuade the others to part with. They swathed themselves in blankets, corded with some leather straps from Lyn's stash. Fortunately, the day was warm and the clothes dried quickly. Lyn apologized: "I had clothing for where we were going – but we're not there!"

As soon as they were dressed again, Lyn produced two heavy swords, which he'd hidden under his sleeping mattress.

"Any experience of swordplay, Lance?" he asked.

"I learnt fencing at school, and did a bit in the army – but not with heavy monsters like these!" Lance said, looking disconcerted.

"Time to try – once you compensate for the weight it won't be so different."

An hour later, Elli concluded that Lyn must be regretting that statement. It wasn't that Lance was inept – in fact, Elli admired the way he soon became used to the weight and the size of the sword, and adapted his stance and movements accordingly. It was his technique that was all wrong.

"No, no!" Lyn said for the fifth time. He thought, and then added, "You cannot prance around as if your sword is a willow wand. These are serious weapons, boy! Use the flat of your blade most of the time, not the tip. When you want to cut, still don't use the tip, slice with the side!"

"Ah," said Lance. "You want me to play cricket with it!" and launched into a series of moves which did, indeed, owe more to cricket than fencing.

Elli watched. Lance was a pleasure to look at, she thought, strong and graceful. You've got it badly, girl, she said to herself. She mused that most of the qualities that made army personnel fish out of water in the twenty-first century were the ones that made them admired – and valued – in earlier ones. Physical strength, skill with weapons, ability to live rough, and, in the case of people like Lance, the use of intellectual ability to solve real problems.

The watching and musing were pleasant enough for a while, but gradually Elli grew restless. It wasn't quite time to check the fish-traps – give them as long as possible, she thought. There was plenty of firewood, the camp was tidy – and packed as far as possible in the two rucksacks just in case, and it was impossible to iron any of the washed clothes, even those few which had not been immediately put on again.

She began to lose her admiration for the attitudes of earlier times. If she wasn't careful, she would find herself relegated to the traditional role of women – watching and keeping the home for the heroes to return to – although she had to admit that home-keeping in her present circumstances was a lot more challenging than filling the freezer and putting the hoover over.

Eventually, when the men paused for breath, she interrupted. "What about me? Am I supposed to look on and applaud? A lot of use that'll be if those villagers, or some roving outlaws, decide they don't like us!"

"True," said Lyn, mopping sweat from his face. "I can't see you in a battle, but you should be able to defend yourself. Give me a few moments, then I'll show you. Lance, you can rest." Elli was impressed. Lyn must be at least thirty years Lance's senior, but he was less out of breath than Lance, who sat down gratefully.

Lyn produced a long knife, almost a dagger, in a leather sheath. "Can you fasten this to your trouser belt? Good. Now I'll teach you some moves to defend yourself. But we'll use a stick, not the knife."

Lance lay on the grass, closed his eyes, and listened to Lyn's voice. "No, girl, not like that – don't aim for my heart: it's protected by a rib-cage, remember! Slash my belly, or my private parts... better..." Five minutes later, he heard a cry of pain, and opening his eyes, he saw Lyn doubled over and Elli with her arm around him, apologising.

"Don't apologise," Lyn gasped. "I told you what to do! But I'm glad we changed the knife for a stick!"

Lance sat up. "Well done, young Elli. Have you ever learnt self-defence?"

"Judo and the like? No – only two Guide meetings ages ago, when a policeman taught us one or two basic moves, and how to avoid being picked on. I don't know if I could remember any of it now!"

"That's about all I know – I did a weekend course once. But we'll try it tomorrow and see if we can help each other remember."

Oh well, thought Elli, I'd prefer a more romantic close encounter, but beggars can't be choosers!

Tired by all the exercise, they went to bed early that night, more or less straight after supper, without any singing, maudlin or otherwise.

"Self-defence, early tomorrow," said Lance, as they left the fire.

Chapter 4

However, the self-defence session was to be postponed. In the morning, while Lance fetched water, and Elli looked ever further afield for firewood, Lyn departed on the upward track, to see Olwen. Elli and Lance had just got back when Lyn returned, walking briskly down the path.

"Come with me!" he said, with the closest thing to excitement they had yet heard from him. "Olwen would like to meet you. Now where are those leather straps? We'll need them."

"In one of the rucksacks, I think," said Lance. "I'll bring it." As he caught up with the others, having found the right rucksack, he stopped, and looked around. "Where's the mist?" he asked.

"Ah," said Lyn, slowing his pace till Lance caught up again. "I took it away, once you two knew about Olwen. It's a strain keeping it up, and there's no need for it here now. I threw the mist in a sort of figure of eight with Olwen in the top circle and us in the lower one. I was concerned not to disturb Olwen whilst she healed, so I made that circle the thickest – how did you get through, by the way?"

"Looked at my boots. Checked every so often."

"Well done! The suffocation effect would have been considerably lessened."

"It was certainly effective when I looked up!" said Lance, remembering.

"We've already seen one effect of my concentrating on protecting Olwen," said Lyn. "So that I wouldn't be too tired by all the mist, I kept it thinner in the lower circle. That's how that lad got through – although he must have been very determined. Leaving the bread for the fey must be important to their village. Presumably the birds are usually the ones to benefit!"

"And you've kept the mist thin, like that? So they can still get through? Why?" said Elli, as they approached the steep left bend leading to Lud's Church.

"I felt the bread was worth the risk!" said Lyn. "But I try to thicken it just from the time we collect the bread until after dark, so as to discourage inquisitive villagers. It is certainly a relief to have less to maintain!"

Suddenly the opening to Lud's Church was before them. They stopped for a moment to catch their breath, and because the strangeness of the place reached out to them. Lyn, coming on that way on average twice a day, was the least affected. Lance, who had only seen it the once before, in circumstances that increased its mystery, was again struck with the sense of the numinous it exuded. Elli had also seen it just the once, with a group of other girls walking from the youth hostel at Gradbach. Even then it had seemed mysterious. In this time it almost took away what little breath she had left. Slowly they walked through, the silence beating against their ears. They said nothing: idle chatter seemed inappropriate.

As they walked in the silence, Elli's mind turned to the encounter ahead. Unlike Lance, she had had no previous meeting with Olwen, however brief, to help her judge what it would be like. She hoped she would know how to behave appropriately.

They scrambled out at the far end, and on to the moor. Lance's eyes went immediately to where he had seen the dragon on his previous visit. The 'hillock' was still there, but changed in outline – it was longer and flatter now, as if the dragon was more relaxed, less hunched. Suddenly one end moved, and the dragon swung its head toward them, opening peaty brown eyes. Lance heard Elli gasp. Moved by instinct, he stood smartly to attention, and saluted, a new recruit meeting a senior officer.

Elli felt a wave of approval, presumably for Lance's salute, flood in their direction from the huge creature. Unsure of what she should do, she managed a sort of curtsey – more of a bob – that she had seen servants give on TV costume dramas. Again a wave of approval, this time unmistakably tinged with amusement. What happens next? she thought with one level of her mind, whilst another was chanting in fear, and excitement, and, almost, joy: "It's a dragon! It's a dragon! It's a dragon!" Knowing about it was one thing. Seeing it was... immeasurably more, exciting, and... yes, frightening as well.

Lyn and the dragon seemed to be consulting. Then Lyn turned to them. She would like me to use words, so she can hear us speak. "Olwen, this is Major Lance Poole, and Miss Elli Tollet. Lance, Elli, this is Olwen, or at least that is the name she is happy for us to use." Again, they saluted and curtseyed. And again, Elli felt the approval and amusement.

"Now, said Lyn, "would you move to the left?" They did so, wondering why. They soon found out. The far end of the 'hillock' moved, and a large green tail with a knobbly ridge down the centre swept toward them, stopping when it lay reaching down the slope pointing roughly towards Lud's Church.

"You see," said Lyn, "your own personal staircase!"

"You want us to climb on her back?" said Lance.

"No, she wants you to! If we have to leave suddenly, this will be the best way – in fact it's the best way of climbing onto a dragon's back in any circumstances! You climb up the spine ridge and gradually you'll find yourself on her back, a long way further from the ground. Sit between two of the knobbly bits, and you'll find her back is narrow enough either side of the ridge for it to feel a bit like a saddle." And, fitting action to the words, Lyn demonstrated, nimbly scaling the living ladder.

"You next," said Lance. "I'll come last and push you if you get stuck. No, I'm not being a chauvinist pig – you're a bit smaller than me and haven't spent countless hours in mind-numbing physical training!"

"Farm work isn't exactly light housework," she retorted, but saw the sense of what he was saying, and put her hand on the tail.

It was tricky, and sometimes she had to stretch to work her way up the spine, but only once did Lance have to help her with a hearty shove. She was pleased to hear, from the frequent quiet cursing behind her, that Lance was not finding it too easy, either. Every so often she would remember the unlikely and, indeed, fantastical, nature of what she was doing, but mainly the reality of negotiating the bony, knobbly ridge kept her mind concentrated on the physical. Once her foot slipped and she found that below the spine ridge, the scaled skin was smooth and slippery.

Eventually, she found herself just behind where Lyn was sitting and stopped. It's like a ride at Alton Towers, she thought – will he have safety devices to fix us in our seats? As if in answer, Lyn called to Lance to pass the leather straps from the rucksack he still carried. "Riding straps – reins, I suppose you could call them. You'll need one for yourself, and you can pass two more forward for Elli and me. Thank you. This is how we'll travel when we fly. I had to dismantle the 'howdah' to make our shelter, and, anyway, as long as we don't have to carry too much, this is far more efficient."

Looping the strap round the protuberance in front of her as instructed, Elli tried hard to remember that first night and found she couldn't. Lyn must have worked through the night whilst she and Lance slept. How physically strong *was* he? How much could he achieve with his magic or Power as he preferred to call it? She remembered that, when she had woken in the morning on the same straw mattress that she was still using, the shelter had been more or less as it was now. And Lyn was there, bright-eyed and bushy-tailed, after a night spent tending Olwen, deconstructing her cabin, removing it to their clearing, and rebuilding it. Her opinion of him, already high, rose even more – although he was an exasperating, secretive and occasionally self-righteous man!

After she had put the strap in place, she knotted the ends, and wrapped the strap round her waist, as Lyn instructed. Then she looked down, and saw that she was about twelve feet off the ground – higher than she had realised whilst climbing.

Lance admired Elli's composure. Younger, untrained, she seemed to take the climbing of a mythical creature in her stride – or rather scramble. Perhaps it was the confidence of youth, believing itself invincible. Or perhaps, given what he knew of her background, the sheer novelty, the enjoyment of change, had overcome her fear. He himself was very uncertain of the whole process, and, as he seated himself behind Elli, and fastened the straps as directed, he cast around for something small to occupy the top of his mind, to stave off panic.

He looked round the moor, with its covering of heather, and its small trees. More trees than he would expect in his own time – fewer sheep to grub them up, he supposed. Below, he thought he could see the glint of the small river or stream they used for water, and also the white snake of Lyn's mist. Nearer, half under one of the bramble thickets, he could see a square-ended bag, very modern for this environment. He focussed on it, wondering what on earth it could be, and why it seemed familiar. Then he recognised it – his laptop, that he had been carrying coming out from college! Well, he wasn't going to leave *that* in the fourteenth century – he'd need it when he got back to the twenty-first. His files, both of the present course and some from his army days, were important to him. It was strange, though, seeing this reminder of the other life, and he felt a wave of embarrassment, almost shame, that he should be so concerned about an artefact of so little use in their present situation. He wouldn't want Lyn's bemusement or Elli's laughter.

His musings were interrupted by Lyn. "Olwen isn't going to be ready to fly for another day or two. But we think it would be a good idea to see how good your balance is, and she needs to try how well she is healing. Hold on. Olwen is going to spread her wings."

Lance heard Elli gasp and he felt the huge body ripple under him. Then he heard himself gasp in turn, as the dragon stretched out vast wings, scintillating where the facets of her scales caught the sunlight, yet shadowing the moor beneath them. Then he had no more time for amazement, for the movement reached him, and he had to cling on to the riding straps and press hard with his knees to remain upright. This is what riding a bucking bronco feels like! he thought, and pulled the straps tighter so he could lean and use the forward knob for extra stability. Elli, lighter than him, seemed to move more, but showed no sign of falling. The glimpse he got of Lyn showed him sitting easily. In fact, he was turning around to check on Elli and himself!

Olwen stretched and shook her wings for what seemed an eternity, but was, Lance reckoned, was not much more than five minutes. Then she folded them again, and subsided, a little more stretched out than before. Lyn twisted round and spoke. "Well done! When Olwen is actually in flight it's a little smoother than that, but landing and take-off – and unexpected air and time currents – produce turbulence. You two managed pretty well, considering. Now you need to get down."

Elli turned and looked at Lance and mouthed "How?" and, indeed, it was a good question. Going down was going to be tricky, whether they turned and descended forward down the precipitous way they had come, or tried treating the tail as a ladder and went backwards, Lance thought. "Lyn, what do you want doing with the riding straps?"

"Undo yourself from them, wind them – neatly, mind – round the protuberance they're attached to, and tuck the ends in so it won't loose itself, but can be pulled out quickly."

"Right!" Lance spoke to Elli. "Wait there and fasten your strap as suggested." He unwound his rein from around his body and used it as a climbing rope, and descended to within feet of the ground before he jumped onto the turf. "Now, can you do the same for my strap?"

Elli hauled it up and neatly fastened it so the end was facing where Lance had been sitting. "Now jump!" Lance said. "I'll catch you!"

She was obviously unsure, but refused to give herself time to think. She flung herself toward him and was well caught, although the impact knocked them both off their feet. As they scrambled up, they saw Lyn weaving his way in and out of the spiny ridge, walking as if this descent were no more than a walk down a steep path.

"Well!" said Lance. "What d'you think of that?"

Before Elli had time to answer, Lyn was with them. "A rather spectacular way of getting down! But unnecessary – if you had turned, you could have come down as I did, using the knobs to steady you. We'll practise tomorrow." And he turned, bowed to Olwen, and set off back the way they had come.

Elli and Lance looked at each other, eyebrows raised, rather disconcerted at the thought of Dragon Descending Practice, as Elli called it later. At the time they said nothing, and Elli, after bobbing a curtsey, set off in pursuit of Lyn. Lance, seeing them go, made a quick move toward the briar patch he had seen from the dragon's back, retrieved his laptop and pushed it into the rucksack he still carried, in place of the riding straps. When he got back to camp he'd place the stuff he'd removed earlier on top, and there would be no need to mention it at all. Then he, too, saluted Olwen and followed the others.

They did try some self-defence that afternoon, using the slope of the land and a straw mattress to minimise the impact. Neither Elli nor Lance were very good, but eventually they both managed to use their opponent's weight to their own advantage, thereby completing a basic 'roll-and-shoulder-toss' as Elli called it.

"Would you like to try?" Lance asked Lyn.

"No thank you! The idea is good, I can see that, but I think it would take a lot of practice to implement – and I don't think my old bones would stand the exercise – even if I had the time to give it!"

When Lance and Lyn moved on to sword practice, Elli started on a project of her own. She gathered straight pieces of wood, and broke them, or used the knife Lyn had given her, until she had a dozen or so pieces about two foot long. Then she used some of Lyn's twine to lash them together into a rough clothes horse, or clothes maiden, as her mother would call it.

Before supper, she announced: "We're all getting into our blankets and I'm going to wash clothes again. Look, they'll dry by the fire on this!"

Lyn and Lance shook their heads at the peculiar ways of women, but neither protested, and that evening they prepared the food whilst Elli washed the clothes in warm water at the edge of the clearing. As she did so, she noticed, for the first time it seemed, Lyn's clothes – loose drawers, fine wool drawstring trousers, and tunic top – vaguely hippyish in overall effect, but just as much at home in any time from the Bronze Age to early Middle Ages – were they from his own time? And why hadn't she noticed before? She'd washed them before – she knew that. Of course, the twenty-first century uniform they'd first seen must have been part of the original illusion, and she supposed Lyn had managed to keep them unquestioning about what he was wearing until they had fully accepted the bizarre situation. Certainly she could see them clearly enough now. Could Lance, she wondered? Men were notoriously un-noticing as far as clothes went, but soldiers were trained to see details, weren't they?

Returning, to hang the washing on her improvised clothes horse, she heard Lance say in a companionable way, "So you're not Fleet Air Arm after all."

"Fleet Air Arm? What's that?" Lyn asked.

"It's the airborne arm of the Royal Navy – uses naval ranks. That's what made me think you were from them. I did wonder, though – Commander is a naval rank, all right, but it's a rather more lowly one than I would expect you to have!"

"Ah," thought Elli. "He's admitting that this is real, at last."

"All this is news to me," Lyn said, with a chuckle. "I chose Commander because it sounded...well, commanding." They laughed softly, in the manner, thought Elli, of old friends.

She paused, feeling suddenly unwilling to join them, to break up this comfortable male companionship. The age-gap didn't seem to matter: she could hear Lance giving Lyn a comprehensive rundown on the ranks in the various British Armed Services – the sort of subject men found fascinating, for some unfathomable reason.

She felt not jealous, but envious. She had never had a close friend, someone of the same sex to share jokes and secrets with. She remembered the night that Lance and Lyn had been talking so seriously by the fire, and now they were in an easy relaxed conversation. The only person that she talked to like that was her mother – and, recently, Lance – and in both of these relationships there were undercurrents and aspects – blood-ties, sexual attraction – which meant that simple friendship was not on the agenda. Perhaps if the demands of the farm had not meant that she had had to leave Guides: that had been the place where she had felt most at home, most likely to find close friendship. But that was, it seemed from the perspective of her nineteen years, half a life ago – and, indeed, it was more than a third!

Unbidden, into her mind came a sudden clear picture. She saw a woman, nearer her mother's age than hers, but with a much younger air about her. She was short, and inclined toward plumpness, with long black hair, which carried some grey in it. It was caught into a loose bun at the nape of her neck. But her clothes were extraordinary: she had a long dress of a deep red colour, cinched with a golden chain at the waist and with golden embroidery on the bodice. It almost looked like a dragon. Her dark eyes seemed sad for a moment, and then sparkled, and her mouth smiled – her response, it seemed, to someone Elli could not see. Then, just as suddenly, she was gone, and Elli was back between the shelter and the two men at the fire. She shook her head. What was that all about? she said to herself, and walked over to join Lyn and Lance.

Chapter 5

The next day, early, they did indeed have Dragon Descending Practice, and, moreover, grew quite nimble at it. Olwen stayed still, and only once, mischievously it seemed to Elli, twitched her tail to see how they coped. Neither of the novices fell off, although it was a close thing. Late in the morning, after more sword and self-defence practice, Elli and Lance rested, watching the sunlight filter through the trees. Elli was reluctant to break the companionable silence, but, equally, she did not want to waste this rare moment of the two of them being alone to discuss the situation. Eventually, she said, "This is all very well, but what happens next?"

"We wait for Olwen to be fully recovered."

"And what happens then?"

"I think we move on to the next place…time."

"Why? When? Where?"

Lance smiled. "You sound like a five-year-old! But seriously, Lyn, or Olwen, or both, obviously have something in mind. Lyn is very close – he only lets us know exactly as much as he wants to…and then in very small…increments."

"Lance, does it frighten you? Or excite you? Or worry you? Or puzzle you? I know all of it does all of that to me, at different times. But what's most frightening is how often I don't feel any of this: it just seems …everyday."

"Well, you remember what Atwood says in *The Handmaid's Tale*? 'Ordinary is what you're used to.' It sounds comforting, but it isn't – especially considering what's happening in the book. At least, at the moment, we're having a bit of a holiday – a survival special, so to speak!"

"But Lyn didn't go to all that trouble just to widen our experience!" said Elli in frustration. "There must be some point to it!"

Lance turned, and briefly put his hand over hers, to comfort. "There will be. Lyn's working on the well-established military principle of 'need to know', and although we're in the middle of things, it seems we don't qualify. But we are being prepared. And we *will* find out – in fact we may find out something now!"

Lyn was hurrying down the path, looking pleased. "Olwen thinks she is ready to fly! She is aiming to try a short flight – not one in time – tonight, when it's quiet. Then, tomorrow night, she and I may try a time one, if she's not too tired. The day after we'll prepare for the next phase – we'll have to risk some daylight take-off and landings then. And that night we'll be away!"

Elli glanced at Lance. He nodded slightly in encouragement. "Lyn," she ventured, "we'll be away...where? When? What *is* the next phase?"

Lyn smiled, infuriatingly. "What is it the Holy Book says? 'sufficient unto the day is the evil thereof?' Well, the day is tomorrow. We'll talk about it then. Now, has anyone seen if the bread is there today?"

No more could be got out of him. The day progressed as the others had, and that evening, by the fire, they tried singing again. This time Elli and Lance were endeavouring to teach Lyn some traditional songs, many of which they themselves knew only slightly. They had progressed from Molly Malone to The Black Velvet Band, when suddenly the moonlight, which had been shining into their clearing, was cut off. Looking upward, they could clearly see the black silhouette of a dragon passing overhead.

That night, Elli dreamt vividly. Unlike most dreams, it seemed coherent and logical. She was standing in a room with about a dozen other people, all of whom were dressed in what she thought of, vaguely, as late-Victorian style. It was clearly an upper-class occasion, and the room was expensively, if rather heavily, furnished. Her attention was drawn to a photograph on the wall, which showed a group of cheerful, slightly dishevelled people. The writing underneath read: 'Celebrating the Relief of Mafeking, May 1900.' A voice said in her ear, "Yes, my dear, that was us, this last May!" Then the scene faded, and, on opening her eyes for a moment, she saw only the flap of canvas, and heard only wind in the trees beyond. She turned over and slept, and dreamt, again. This time, the dream was less coherent, involving herself and Lance trying to squeeze Olwen through the doors of college so the dragon could attend their computer class.

When she woke, she found Lyn was already absent. Lance, emerging from the trees, smiled and said, with a touch of cynicism, "He said he'd tell us about the next step today. Perhaps that's why he had to go to see Olwen so early!"

"To be fair," Elli said, "he must be anxious to see how she is, after her flight."

"Obviously," said Lance. " But I think he's procrastinating, all the same!"

After the usual meagre breakfast, they collected some firewood, not daring to go for the water yet, in case they encountered someone from the village; and in spite of the now poor pickings there, not wishing to go out of sight of the clearing in case Lyn returned.

Eventually, he did.

"Olwen is fine, and keen to try a time flight. Tonight, she and I will return to our time, which will be a gentle introduction, and collect some things I left where we were supposed to do this 'team-building' exercise. However, I wasn't expecting Elli – although perhaps I should have – and that causes some…complications. Tomorrow I think we'll have to do more flights, harder ones. Then we'll be off!"

With a great effort, Lance kept exasperation out of his voice. "Lyn, can we possibly persuade you to let us know where – and when – and possibly even why – we are going? Surely there is no further purpose in not telling us, and every reason to do so?"

"True. I wanted us to concentrate on the here and now, as your idiom is. We needed to 'bond', to use another of your terms, to get to know each other, to work out problems together. You needed to become used to Olwen, and time travel, to become acquainted with certain skills. Also, I had no idea how long we would be here and I didn't want you to waste time thinking fruitlessly about what happens next."

He paused, saw Lance take a deep breath, and, anticipating a verbal explosion, hurried on. "But now it is indeed time you knew. I'm not sure myself why we're going or when we're going, but Olwen is very clear. We have to go there. It's about one hundred years in your past, I think. She's taken me there on 'familiarisation' trips and…"

Elli interrupted. "1900. Second half of the year. Some upper class place."

Lyn looked at her, astonished. "And how did you work that out?"

"I didn't. I had a dream – more like a video clip, last night." As she elaborated, she felt a rumble of amusement, and approval, and, from his expression, Lyn felt something similar. Lance's face, on the other hand, had a blank, bemused, look.

A slow smile spread over Lyn's face. He nodded his head, as if in confirmation. "This will make things so much easier. We were right – Olwen can communicate with you. If I'm not around, you and she can still keep in touch. She uses mainly pictures, right?" On Elli's nod, he continued. "She does the same with me, and it's grown over the years to be almost like talking. So if you need to show me something, rather than tell me ... we can do it."

"Ah! A video Babel fish!" murmured Lance. Elli glared at him, and he fell silent.

Lyn continued. "As I said, I don't know why. I know when, and where – a large country house in your county of Cheshire."

Lance spoke. "We seem to move times more easily than place! All these places are within fifty miles of each other – nearer, perhaps."

"Yes," said Lyn. "To move both draws on much energy, and, obviously, the less distance Olwen travels the less likely she is to be seen. I believe we will be there for only one or two nights – a weekend shooting party, so Olwen informs me. It's a tricky business – we have to hide Olwen, but not so far way that we can't call on her power, as we have to 'persuade' various people of our right to be there, and cover up any mistakes we may make. Don't expect translation facilities as well – just use your own language very... conservatively. Give it some thought during the day and we'll talk about it later on. Meanwhile, business as usual – anything left for me to eat?"

They went about the usual tasks, tidying the campsite, packing as much as possible into the two rucksacks, although they no longer really believed that the village would force them to leave in a rush. Elli found that her washing the night before had left them short of water, and suddenly filled with a longing to wash her hair, thought she would go to the stream and risk collecting the bread early. "If it's not there, I won't venture out of the trees," she promised the men, who were preparing for yet another bout of sword practice.

"Those swords are definitely *not* for 1900!" she thought as she walked downhill. "They must be for a third time – Lyn's own? And will that be the next stop? And the last?"

The bread was there, so she made her way with one of the pots to the stream, cradling in her spare hand the precious item she'd found earlier in her bag – a tiny wrapped bar of 'guest' soap. A quarter of an hour or so later, she stood on the bank, looking across the stream through the thin veil that was all that was left here of Lyn's mist. She rubbed her hair dry with a piece of cloth, feeling much better. Another thing she needed a female friend for – and preferably with her on this trip. The men had looked at her strangely when she had insisted on washing the clothes, and although they did wash regularly, it seemed to be a necessary chore with them, not a pleasure. They certainly didn't gain the kick out of it that she did. Washing her hair under these circumstances was, she felt, an almost spiritual experience. She realised that she was now walking up the path having forgotten to pick up the water-pot. That's the trouble with spiritual experiences – they can make you forget the practical stuff! she thought. She returned, and was lifting the pot she had already filled, when, out of the corner of her eye, she caught a flicker of movement on the other side of the stream. She looked again, and felt, rather than saw, a figure moving, fading into the woods. She lifted the pot and walked back, feeling now worried rather than euphoric. The villagers must be trying to spy on them, and she had been, at the least, foolish. Should she mention it to the others? What could they do about it – apart from charging her, quite rightly, with carelessness?

Sword practice was still going on. Each day it took longer, and each day Lance seemed to be more at home with the heavy blades. She sat down and watched until they drew apart, leaning on the swords, breathing heavily. Then, before she knew she had taken the decision, she found that she was telling them about the watcher at the streamside.

To her great relief, they seemed interested rather than alarmed, and more inclined to congratulate her on noticing the movement than to be annoyed at any carelessness.

"If they've been keeping watch all this time, and not moved against us, they are unlikely to now. And tomorrow night we'll be away!" Lyn said.

Lance looked more doubtful. Elli knew that he found Lyn's occasionally light-hearted approach difficult to reconcile with his underlying power and sense of mission. She felt no such difficulty; Lance was a dear, and desirable, but needed to lighten up on occasion.

They had been too optimistic, it turned out. They were sitting round the fire, with the last dregs of Lance's whisky. Lance smiled, thinking of Elli. She had been fierce in the rationing of his precious commodity, but these were definitely the last hot toddies they would be having. Fortunately, he felt that whatever else might be missing in the way of modern comforts in 1900, alcohol not would be one of them. Indeed, he was pretty sure it flowed freely at those weekend shooting parties. He almost laughed aloud, then, at the realisation of how calmly he was taking the whole business of time travel.

They had spent more than an hour, over the meal and after, working out a scenario for 1900. Lance and Elli were to be brother and sister. "Let's stick as close as we can to our real names. Lance is a fine Victorian name. Eleanor is the most likely full version of Elli, so that had better be my full name. What about Lyn? Where does he fit in?" Elli was enjoying the creation of their roles.

"My manservant. Former batman," said Lance decisively.

"Army servant," Elli explained to Lyn. "So we're to be an army family, are we?"

"Yes. Army life has changed remarkably little in the last hundred years – the order of command, life in the mess, the formal banquets, among other things. And if we could have been posted abroad, it might help cover up any slips."

"India," said Elli. "Lots of families weren't just posted there, they lived there – that should help with the slips even more. And you've served in Afghanistan –you could have done that a hundred years ago, and the scenery, etc won't have changed much." She paused, seeing the look on Lyn's face. "But Lyn will know little or nothing about all this. How will he manage?"

"I'm a servant. I know my place. I'll keep my mouth shut."

"So," said Elli, "what are all these journeys you and Olwen must make? What do they have to do with this?"

"Ah," said Lyn, smiling. "First I will go and collect the clothes I've stored for Lance and myself, back where we should have been. Then…"

"Then what?" asked Elli.

"Then, my dear, we need to find you something appropriate to wear!"

Elli gasped. "Do you know, I hadn't thought of that! How stupid can you be?"

Lance laughed. "Well, there's been a lot going on! However, you can hardly appear at a Victorian country house dressed as you are – or without clothes." He paused. "Obviously!"

"You'll have to help me," said Lyn, ignoring the by play. "I'll need to know what…" he broke off. "What's that?"

He had stood up, and was looking into the woods, along the path to the stream. Lance and Elli, facing away from the path, turned to see, and then also leapt to their feet. Through the heavy dark of the trees could be seen wavering red-gold light. Almost flame-like, Lance thought, then, quickly, "Almost be damned! They are flames –and moving, coming up the path."

"The villagers!" said Lyn – "They're coming to us – and, I fear, in no very friendly way!" And indeed, the growling murmur of discontent, and louder shouts, could already be heard.

"Why now?" said Elli, trying hard to keep her voice level.

"I've just withdrawn most of the mist – it's that time of the day..."

"I didn't mean that – it must be five or six days...since I met that boy. Why wait?"

"Are you two going to stand there, discussing why, while they burn us down?" said Lance angrily, and, diving into the shelter, he re-emerged carrying the two swords and Elli's knife.

Lyn stood for a moment, withdrawn. Then he seemed to come to. He grasped the sword, thanked Lance, and said, "I've woken Olwen. She feels we should be ready to go if we can't defuse the situation quickly. Elli – go and get those rucksacks and put anything still lying around into them. Quickly!"

Elli was soon back, carrying the two bags. "Does this mean we're leaving?" she said.

"Obviously," said Lance, curtly.

"In that case..." she said, and disappeared back into the shelter. In a moment she was back with her capacious bag, Lance's leather jacket and two of the blankets. "Can't carry any more," she said.

Lance looked somewhat witheringly at her, but Lyn said, "Good girl, well thought of!" and wrapped one of the blankets round his shoulders, making him look even more like a Bronze Age warrior. Elli did the same with the other, and Lance, not taking his eyes from the approaching lights, put on his jacket.

As they did so, they saw the first villagers emerge. They carried flaming torches, and many had sticks and staves. One or two had sword or knife or hunting bow. There were, Elli saw, some women there. Leading were three figures – a large strong-featured man of middle years – probably the village headman – a priest carrying a large wooden cross, and a young lad – the one she had met, she thought.

Lyn handed his sword to Lance and approached the villagers. He held his hands out, palms upward to show his open-handed, unthreatening intentions.

"Welcome, friends and neighbours. We wondered if you would visit us, but we have respected your privacy, especially in this time of pestilence. Thank you for our bread – it has been a godsend and a life preserver."

There was a fractional pause, as Olwen's translation took place. The lad looked relieved and the murmurs of the crowd grew less threatening. But the headman's face did not soften, and nor did the face of the priest. Elli stood still, hardly daring to move in case she should draw attention away from Lyn.

Then the leader spoke. "Fair words, stranger, but you do not fool me. We have been cautious and moderate. We sent Ned here" – and he indicated the youth at his side – "we sent him all the way to Leek, where we knew the priest was a man of learning. Not wishing to be discourteous, we continued our offering of bread, in case you were one of the good Fay. And Father Thomas has spared time to travel back with Ned because he thought this matter so important."

"Welcome, Father," said Lyn. "We are honoured you thought us worth it."

"You are indeed worth it," said the priest, and his face took on a glow – of fanaticism, Lance thought suddenly, remembering his days in Afghanistan. He tightened his grip on his sword, feeling that all of Lyn's words – and, indeed, any calming 'spells' – would have little effect.

"You are worth it because you give me, and these good folk here, the chance to fight for Our Lord against the forces of Evil, the emissaries of Satan! I have told them that in future they should have no dealings with spirits, even those they consider kindly" – and here he threw a blazing look at both Ned and the headman. The latter quelled a rising murmur from the crowd with a movement of his hand. The priest continued in a loud, ringing voice: "No bread! No Garlands! No celebrations to welcome summer!

"But you – you do not even try to pretend to be good! I can see her, hiding in the shadows! A brazen, female Devil, travelling with two males – for their carnal satisfaction, no doubt! And dressed in male attire...but her curls betray her... and their colour...almost red, the colour of Judas, the great betrayer!

"Come!" He raised the cross with one hand, beckoning with the other. "Kill them! Kill them! Strike a blow for the Heavenly Kingdom!"

The murmur grew to a roar, and Elli heard "Kill the witch! Keep the plague away! Slay the devils!" before it all merged into a rising chant of "Kill! Kill! Kill!"

Lyn stood at his tallest, a commanding presence. He raised his hands and, Elli and Lance saw the wisps of mist that had been surrounding them converge on the clearing. Then, to their amazement, as the white cloud formed a barrier between them and the villagers, it changed into a wall of flame.

The villagers gasped as one. The priest let out a cry of triumph: "I told you! The flames of Hell!"

Elli heard Lance's voice: "Obviously! Perhaps not one of Lyn's better ideas!"

She struggled to stay calm. "Obviously," she stated. "But it gives a breathing space."

At that moment, Lyn turned and said, "Now. Before they realise this is just an illusion; the rucksacks are here – packed? Good. Each of you put one on. Give me my sword back, Lance. Now go – up the path. Olwen is waiting."

Elli needed no further bidding. She set off, keeping to the shadows, being as inconspicuous as possible. Her heart was thumping and she noticed that she was trembling. Not cut out for high adventure, she thought. Nevertheless, she paused at the edge of the glade, waiting for Lance, whose instincts were, clearly, to stay with Lyn. She saw Lyn physically turn Lance round, and push him in her direction. As Lance reached her, she saw the priest try to break through the flames but be beaten back, presumably by the heat.

"He won't be able to keep that up for long," said Lance, arriving. "A moment's heat to help us on our way, that's what he said he could manage."

"What about him?" said Elli.

"He'll manage," said Lance. "In fact he'll have to!" for at that moment, a well-thrown hunting spear came flying through the crowd and passed through the flames without harm. Encouraged, the villagers pressed forward. Lyn could not maintain the heat on so wide a front, and some men broke through. Instantly, the mist was back, filling the clearing.

"I told you so!" said Lance. "But he's got to get out now – the mist will slow him as well, I think. Now, Elli, Let's go!"

They made their way as quickly as they could through the trees, thankful for what light the moon gave them. After a hundred yards or so, they stopped, for Elli was becoming tangled with blanket, rucksack, handbag and knife. Lance helped her fold the blanket, and tucked it in the top of his rucksack, while Elli thrust the knife into her belt, and secured her handbag tightly to her rucksack. All the time they glanced the way they had come, waiting for the mob to be upon them. But the confused noise came no nearer.

They arrived on the moor hot and, in Elli's case at least, short of breath after scrambling out of Lud's Church. Olwen had her head turned toward them, and her huge eyes gleamed in the moonlight. She swung her tail across the rough turf until it stretched toward them, a staircase for them to climb, a route to safety.

Climbing proved harder than in the practice sessions, encumbered as they were with sword, knife and bags. Lance was constrained to use only one hand, holding the heavy sword out, well away from Olwen. Elli, knife stuck in her belt, had to move very cautiously, to avoid stabbing herself. Eventually, they made it to the places they had used before, and then moved a little closer to the dragon's head, to leave space for Lyn. Lance swung his rucksack in front of him, and firtled in various side pockets, eventually grunting with satisfaction and producing two sword belts with leather scabbards. Further investigation produced the smaller scabbard of Elli's knife, which fitted on her belt.

"I knew I'd seen them somewhere!" he said.

"Life would have been easier if you'd thought of them earlier!" Elli remarked.

"Would you have liked to stop for even longer, to find these and put them on? No, neither would I! Anyway, we made it. Now, all we have to do is wait for Lyn!"

This proved a difficult and tense task. Vague noises could be heard coming up from the woods below, but not distinct enough for them to be able to work out what was going on. Then they heard someone climbing out of Lud's Church. Lance drew his sword, and twisted round, waiting. To their relief, it was Lyn who emerged, breathless and dishevelled, sword in hand.

As he drew near, Lance threw him the second sword belt and scabbard. "Thank you!" said Lyn, putting the sword down, and quickly buckling the belt on. "I got caught by my own wretched mist, would you believe! Couldn't find the path – as I feared! That's why I used the fire to start with – but they soon saw through that!" He wiped his sword on the grass before sliding it home.

Elli breathed in sharply. "Was that blood?" she asked.

"Only a little!" Lyn grinned. "One of the men blundered into me in the mist, and very bravely tried to hold on to me. I – dissuaded him – he has a cut on his arm, that's all." As he was speaking, he was climbing. "They may not be far behind – I hope the veneration they seem to have for... Lud's Church, you called it?... may put them off a little, but with that fool of a priest with them..." He broke off as the noise of raised voices broke in on them. "I feared as much – here they come! Are you secure with your riding straps? Then go, Olwen – find us somewhere safe and quiet!"

As he spoke, Olwen moved, and a huge ripple, like a minor earthquake, shook them. Simultaneously, the first of the men clambered out of the cleft that was Lud's Church, and, turning, helped the priest up. As the priest strode toward them, Elli realised they were airborne. Not in a graceful curve, as she had vaguely imagined they would move, but in a sort of scrabbling movement that seemed to remind her of something. To gain height, they circled, and she could see the astonished faces of the villagers. Some fell to the ground, cowering. Others turned and fled. But a few drew near the priest, who swept his wooden cross up, and stood, shouting inaudibly at them.

But it was too late. Having gained height, Olwen stretched her neck and her wings, and took off in what seemed to be a westerly direction, flying smoothly now, and gaining height with each rhythmic wing-beat. Elli suddenly realised what Olwen had reminded her of: it was a swan, elegant in repose, comically awkward during take-off, and then crossing the sky with a swift, fierce grace. Elated, and almost breathless with the wonder of it, she turned to share the feeling with Lance. To her surprise, he was sitting with hands gripping tightly, shoulders hunched, eyes shut.

"Lance," she said, "relax! Open your eyes! It's the most wonderful experience of my entire life! You must feel that, surely?"

His shoulders relaxed a little, and he opened his eyes cautiously. "No. I don't, young Elli! Only someone very young, or blindly optimistic could enjoy this! Aerodynamically speaking, a bumblebee or a plane shouldn't be able to fly – let alone a huge be-winged creature out of myth!"

Elli laughed. "Lance, you're not that old! Anyway, planes and bees do fly! So does Olwen – wonderfully, beautifully! Enjoy it." With that, she turned back and let the wind sweep past her. For the first time in weeks she gave herself to a pleasure that was not centred round Lance. Indeed, for a while, she forgot him entirely, as the dragon took them higher and higher, and further from the clearing in the woods.

Interlude 1: Cave

They never knew where – or when – they spent the next twenty-four hours. By the time Lance grew relaxed enough to look, a fine mist had veiled the ground from them. Elli seemed only to have recovered from what Lance thought of as her "first fine careless rapture" at about the same time, and knew no more than he did.

After about an hour or so, they began to lose height. Elli was by now chilled to the bone, as her bomber jacket was proving woefully inadequate to being on dragon-back. She had managed to fish out some gloves from her pocket, but thought longingly of the blanket safely and inaccessibly rolled in the top of Lance's rucksack. But still she longed for the flight to go on and on, and it was only when they drifted through the mist and saw the sea below that she started to wonder about what came next.

There had been no jarring and no feeling of dislocation, so, she assumed, they had moved in space, rather than in time. Talking about it later to Lance, she had made her case for the Lleyn Peninsula in North Wales. "Deserted, not too far for Olwen to fly. And there is a mention of 'things that came out of the sea caves at Criccieth, yonder', in a Robert Graves poem. Perhaps that was Olwen!"

"That would mean she'd been seen," Lance objected.

"Only from a distance – perhaps from over Harlech way. It doesn't matter. It's a good spot."

It was indeed a good spot. Olwen landed smoothly on a stretch of sand with the sea retreating in the distance. Lyn told them to stay put, and climbed down, disappearing toward the cliff face.

He was soon back, and seemed to be smiling. "Clever Olwen. She's taken us to the place I'd planned to use for our time together – although not in the same time, of course. Nevertheless it's still got all the things I chose it for in the first place. It'll do nicely for a short stay." Bidding the others to follow, he moved back toward the cliff.

Elli found she was so stiff and cramped that climbing down proved as difficult as it had the first time. But soon she was walking over the sand, following Lance, who seemed to be coping better than she was – military fitness or the warming effect of a leather jacket?

Lyn disappeared into a darkness, which proved to be the opening of a cave. "Wait!" he said, and picked up some driftwood. To their surprise, he produced a cheap plastic cigarette lighter and played its flame over the wood till it caught alight.

"Isn't that cheating?" said Elli.

"And don't dragons breathe fire?" said Lance.

"I wouldn't do anything which could seriously alter the balance of the world," Lyn replied. "Twenty-first century weapons, for instance. But a quick bit of flame, rather than using flint for an age, where no one can see...I don't think that matters. And, if any dragons do breathe fire, Olwen doesn't – her brothers could, now I come to think of it. It must be a gender thing. Now, come and see your new home!"

The cave was above the high water line, with a floor of soft sand, interspersed with slates of rock, and a small stream running down one side. It bent to the left, so the view of the sea was cut off. About fifteen feet further in, it came to an end with a broad shelf along one side, and a spring of fresh water, the source of the stream, bubbling out of the rock opposite.

"With the blankets on it, the shelf will be a decent enough sleeping place. There's fresh water to drink and we'll collect driftwood, and light a fire at the bend – but we must put it out as soon as it gets light. I must be away by then, anyway." Lyn sounded as pleased as a new house owner, thought Lance, but to him the cave seemed a poor substitute for the clearing and the shelter. However, it appeared that they weren't staying for long – just long enough for Lyn to collect what he thought of as 'costume and props' for their next destination.

Elli obviously had reservations too. "Lyn, why can't you do all the visits and return to the same time each time – if you see what I mean? Say dawn. Then we could be on our way very quickly, no need to stay. What will we do for food, if we're here long?"

"As to that, I'll bring you something to eat on my first return. And you won't be here long: just till tonight. And no, I'm not going to keep returning to the same moment of time – for one thing I might meet myself, and that's something I don't want to risk, and, for another, think how long that would make my day! And Olwen's. I aim to do this as close to 'real time' as I can."

They put the blankets on the stone shelf and busied themselves collecting wood along the beach in the half-light of the moon, diffused through the thin mist. The late winter storms had deposited plenty, but Lance could see that there would not be enough to last more than a few hours. They would be cold before dawn. Lyn used his lighter to set the fire going. By its light, the others could see uncharacteristic indecision on his face.

"Perhaps I should go now. You will have an uncomfortable time waiting: cold and probably hungry before I return. So, the sooner I start, the less misery for you! But I have had no sleep,

Olwen has already flown tonight, and this will be her first time-flight since the accident…"

Lance spoke quickly. "You must rest – if anything went wrong with the flight, Elli and I would be far worse than uncomfortable – we'd be stranded, hundreds of years adrift!"

Lyn nodded. "That's true. Let's get a few hours' sleep, then, and Olwen and I will be off just as it gets light. Easier all round."

With only two blankets between them, and just a small fire, the next few hours were not comfortable ones. They squashed together on the shelf for warmth, sharing the blankets. Propped up against each other, they couldn't move without disturbing someone else, and the heat from the fire was not always sufficient to ward off the cold of the stone walls. Every so often, one of them would jerk awake and notice that the fire needed feeding. This was impossible to do without disturbing the others, and then everyone would have to rearrange, and try again to sleep.

However, they must have managed to sleep eventually, for Elli, waking cold and stiff, saw the fire had burnt itself out, with some wood still unused. A faint pale light was filtering into the cave. She wondered if she should wake the others, one of whom was snoring softly into her left ear. She stretched gently and the movement woke first Lance, then Lyn.

They stood up and tried to move sluggish blood around their cold bodies. Elli moved past the remains of the fire toward the front of the cave. There seemed to be a large rock obscuring almost all of the opening, keeping most of the light out – and, she thought, keeping in what warmth the fire had generated. Her sleepy brain was just trying to get to grips with the question of where the rock had come from, when it moved aside, and she realised it was, in fact, Olwen. The dragon moved slowly, making room for them to emerge.

In the cold half-light of dawn, they could see that the tide was now well in, a wind whipping the wave tops. But it seemed that, for the moment, the good weather was holding.

Lyn laid a hand on Olwen, in greeting, and then turned to the others. "I'm going to my own time – we'll head back to here, which will mean travelling in one dimension only – time, not space. I'll collect the stuff I left there – here? – and then take the rest of our stuff to where it'll be safe. We're not going to need those swords and rucksacks in Victorian England! I'll bring you some food, too."

They used the reins to strap on one rucksack, and Lance's sword. Lyn wore the other one, and hoisted the second rucksack onto his back. Lance insisted that they keep Elli's knife and one blanket 'for protection and warmth'. Just as Lyn was climbing up, Elli had a thought. "What about these clothes – can't use them in Victorian times, either?"

"Do you want to give them to me now? Spend the day wrapped in a blanket – the both of you? No, I'm teasing," he said as Elli blushed. "I'll bring the sort of saddlebags we made for Olwen, when she doesn't carry a cabin. Oh well, the sooner we're off, the sooner we'll be back!" All the time he was talking, Lyn was climbing. Then, settling himself down on the dragon's spine, he waved, and Olwen set off along the beach, scrabbling as before, then moving gracefully, disappearing over the cliff top, so they couldn't see how she vanished from the time they were in.

"I hope the flight works," said Lance. "Otherwise…"

Elli refused to follow that line of thought. "We'd better try for some more sleep," she said. "Not much else we can do – no food, nothing to read, we daren't go for a walk…"

In her daydreams, Elli had imagined leaning closely against Lance, on a sandy beach, on a summer's day. Huddling on a rocky shelf in a damp cave, sharing body heat under one blanket, seemed to be lacking something. Even when Lance put his arm around her, and drew her close, his remark – "The last time I did this was with a sixteen-stone Geordie sergeant to ward off an Afghan winter" – was not calculated to instil a sense of romance. He could at least have said that the present arrangement was an improvement, she thought. Despite all of this, she couldn't suppress a shiver and a tumult inside. Eventually, she nodded off, warmth gradually making itself felt.

When she woke, some hours later, it was to find herself alone, her head resting on Lance's carefully folded leather coat. How he had managed that, she wasn't sure, but as she was stretching, preparatory to going to look for him, he came in, shaking himself.

"It's starting to rain – good for keeping the public away, but bloody unpleasant!"

"Unpleasant or not, I must risk it!" said Elli and dashed for the nearest rock. Although, with Lance in the cave, who's to see me, she thought as she ducked down. Relieved, if rather rain-spattered, she rejoined Lance. He had rebuilt the fire, and was searching on the rocks nearby.

"Do you know if Lyn left the lighter – ah here it is! Good!"

The fire flamed into life. With comfort and warmth came the knowledge that they were hungry. "Although breakfast has hardly been a major event ever since we left our time," Elli remarked.

"But we've usually just woken after a night's sleep – not spent half the night riding on a dragon!"

At that moment, they heard a whooshing sound, and, looking out, saw Olwen landing. The tide was now in retreat, but it seemed as if the great creature was worried about landing on the wet sand, newly exposed. She landed near the top of the beach, and folded her wings. Lyn leant over and extracted a bundle from one of the pannier type saddlebags that Olwen was now wearing.

"Catch!" he said and threw the bundle to Elli. This was followed by a small leather Gladstone bag from the other pannier, which he threw to Lance. Then he climbed down Olwen's spine ridge. As he grew nearer the ground, they saw that he had a small canvas bag slung over his shoulder, and, more surprisingly, he was now dressed in the sombre garb of a Victorian manservant.

"Right," said Lyn. "That went very well. Here's breakfast!" He firtled in the canvas bag and produced some parcels of a muslin-type cloth. Investigation showed them to contain thick chunks of brown bread, butter, cheese, dried meat and a few wrinkled apples. He then produced some small knives and small bowls. "Didn't bother with drink – the stream water is excellent. But these bowls will make it easier."

"Lyn, you're a marvel!" said Elli, fervently. "This is the best breakfast since we met you!"

"Shame we finished the oranges, though," said Lyn. "The last of last autumn's apples just don't have the same appeal!"

They perched on some of the rocks just inside the cave, looking out to sea, through the fine, slanting rain. Olwen seemed to be watching them peaceably.

"She drank enormously back home," Lyn said, "And she doesn't seem to be hungry yet."

"Let's hope not," said Lance. "I can't see the Victorian upper-class wanting to share their hunting and fishing with a dragon!"

Breakfast over, they turned to other matters. Lyn instructed Lance to take the bundle, "And do what you can with them." Elli and Lyn had gathered up the cloths from the food, and were standing at the entrance of the cave, looking seawards, when a slightly embarrassed cough from Lance made them turn.

Elli gasped and giggled. Lyn smiled with satisfaction. Lance stood there in a well-cut tweed suit, a late Victorian gentleman from his shiny boots to his matching tweed cap. "I'll need to shave this beard off, I think," he said. "There are some good razors and some soap in the bag, thank goodness!"

Elli, as if to apologise for her first reaction, smiled her approval, then turned to Lyn. "Lyn, where did you get all this stuff?"

Lyn looked slightly abashed. "I told you I'd visited that time before. The first time I had the usual difficulty – my clothes didn't fit in – but Olwen and I worked the 'un-noticing' trick very hard, to allow me to... acquire some. Then when I found out it was Lance we needed – same difficulty with your time's clothes, same solution – I looked for some clothes suitable for him."

"But how..." Elli repeated, and broke off as a series of images flashed into her mind: Lyn outside a shop labelled 'Gentleman's Outfitters', depriving an astonished manservant, walking behind his master, of several brown paper parcels; Lyn on what seemed to be a railway station taking a Gladstone bag from under a bench where it had been stowed; Lyn removing a cap from a display inside a shop; Lyn standing in the shadows whilst irate victims looked for him..."

"Lyn!" she said between outrage and amusement. "You've been stealing! Olwen has just given me a private viewing of your activities!"

"These people seemed very rich in possessions. I'm sure they could afford to lose some," Lyn said, defensively.

"And how many servants, or railway workers, lost their jobs, or had wages deducted, to pay for them?"

"Ah."

"You're not to use those methods to get my clothes!"

"What do you expect him to do – pay for them? With what?" said Lance.

"As to that…" said Lyn, and paused.

"What?" said Elli and Lance together.

"Well, I… acquired… a small amount of coin from those times, and then… well, I'm quite good at games of chance…"

Lance's face showed a similar mixture of alarm and amusement as Elli's had.

"I'm not surprised, given your Powers! Really, Lyn!"

"Yes, it's true that I'm forbidden to gamble in my own time, but needs must when devil drives, as you say."

Elli said, "But Lyn, if you have money, you must *pay* for my clothes. Pretend that you've been sent to collect them for me – 'persuade' the shops that I *did* order them."

"Would you send a manservant to collect undergarments?"

"Good point. OK. Take those from a laundry or somewhere, but you must leave some money."

"Moral little lass, aren't you? Very well. But you must tell me what to get you."

Elli thought hard. "You've only got Lance one outfit and one small bag – not enough for a weekend. And a woman would need masses…"

"We'll say there's been a mix-up on the railway and the rest of your luggage has gone elsewhere. Is that likely?" Lyn asked.

Elli and Lance laughed. "More than likely," Lance explained. "Good idea!"

"Right," said Elli. "I'll need travelling stuff then. And it's a shooting party, so say, late summer, early autumn?" At Lyn's nod, she continued. "Shall I describe some possibilities?"

"Do you know what you need?" said Lance in some surprise.

"Yes. *The 1900 House.* On BBC. Wonderful programme – I was only young, just into my teens, but I got the video and the book as well. Of course they were of a lower class than this but I read round. Now let's see…"

"Don't describe it to me," said Lyn. "Picture it for Olwen!"

"Oh yes! What a bright thought!" Elli was enthusiastic. She thought, then visualised, giving a running commentary to help herself.

"A walking suit – long skirt and jacket – nice leg-o'-mutton sleeves …a blouse to go with it…good leather gloves…smart hat, with a flat brim…boots…stockings…someone's travelling bag – like Lance's but a woman's one – might have some good stuff in it, with a dressing case, if possible, with toiletries…"

"Underclothes?" said Lyn.

"Oh, you wouldn't believe how many!" said Elli, and rapidly visualised combinations, corset, chemise, knickers, and petticoats. "Good quality, mind, if we're going to a posh country house!"

"She had the satisfaction of seeing Lyn's look of stupefaction as he received the pictures from Olwen. Then he climbed back up the dragon's spine. He threw more parcels of food down from the panniers, and then said, "We'll spread our visits around – don't want to be too obvious. And I'm not sure if we'll return here between trips or not. Either way, you've got food now. I'll be back before evening at the latest!"

As he and Olwen rose into the air, Elli shouted, "Be sure to pay your way!" Lyn nodded, and then they were gone, flying over the cliff and out of their sight, as before.

Time moved slowly for Lance and Elli. They sat just inside the cave, their view restricted by the misty rain. After a while Elli wearied of discussing where they were and what would happen next and asked Lance about his childhood. Reluctantly at first, he started to talk. Then, as Elli thought to herself, there was no stopping him.

"We were an Army family – father, both grandfathers, back into the mists of time! My parents married late. I'm an only child, and I think they never quite adjusted to having a child around – they loved me, but it was as if I was an exotic pet: something quite outside their experience. They were abroad with the Army a lot – I went to boarding school early."

"You only saw them in the holidays?" said Elli.

"Often not even then!"

"Who did you live with, then?"

"My grandmother – my mother's mother. She was the central figure when I was growing up. An amazing lady – vigorous and talented – an amateur painter of high quality. It meant I was isolated during the holidays, but that's me looking back at it. Then, I loved it."

"What did you do in the holidays?" asked Elli.

"It was like an Enid Blyton or an Arthur Ransome, but played by a solitary child. I rode. I explored the country. I swam in the river. If it was wet, I tried painting with Grandmother, or read. One wet summer I read through her whole collection of John Buchan. And we played cards."

"It sounds…idyllic… but rather…unusual."

"You mean old-fashioned. Odd. Weird."

"I didn't say that!" Elli protested.

"No, but I saw your face. Don't worry – the army is hardly in the forefront of social reform, and even there they called me the Anachronism – or the Dinosaur."

"Oh, that's not fair!" said Elli.

"I'm not so sure – but I can't change now, whether it's fair or not. I can alter on the surface, but underneath I'm still living in the first half of the twentieth century. It'll be a change to be the one with the modern views if –or when – we land in 1900!"

"I don't think you're fair to yourself – you're great at IT and you were good at your job."

"I'm not talking about ability, or even interest. It's more basic. Attitude perhaps. How I react instinctively, before my brain kicks in. But enough of me – what about Elli Tollet?"

"There's not much to tell. Bred and born and brought up in Cheshire – on our farm near Winsford. A bit like you in some ways: not a lot of my spare time spent with people my own age. They usually don't have the same…priorities as I do. I loved Guides, but the work on the farm grew too much, especially when we couldn't afford as much hired help, and I couldn't spare the time."

"I know you're close to your parents. You were almost out of your mind when you thought they'd think you had disappeared."

"Yes." Elli smiled. "In lots of ways, Mum is my best friend. We talk, and watch TV together, when we've time. And we giggle a lot, and Mum tries to …shield me from Dad."

"Why? Does he hit you?"

"Oh good God, no! Nothing like that! It's just that he's so absorbed with the farm, it's the most important thing in his life…and I try my best, honest I do…but…I'm a girl."

"Obviously," said Lance. "So?"

"So I'm not as strong as a lad. So I might marry and move away. I might marry and stay and be deflected into bearing babies and bringing up children. Or I might never marry. Either way, the family name would be lost – or the family would die out."

"So, he thinks, why aren't you a son?" Lance grinned.

"It's worse than that. I'm not my brother."

"Brother? If you have a brother, where's the problem? But you've said before you're an only child."

"My brother died when he was four – some sort of twisted gut. Before I was born. I was the replacement, and I've not been a satisfactory one. He loves me dearly, and takes such pride in what I *do* do, but he does feel – at the level you were talking about – that I'm a disappointment!"

"Oh my dear, I'm so sorry!"

"Don't worry! I don't think of it for months on end. It's just now, with time to think and you asking – I don't think I've ever talked of it before."

"There are very few who know my background, too. But I find you easy to talk too, Miss Elli Tollet!"

"What about your grandmother – is she still alive?"

"No – she'd be well over a hundred by now! She died when I was 15 – she was nearly eighty-five. At the time I was devastated, but by then I was old enough to spend the holidays with my parents, even if they were stationed abroad. And I was old enough for them to like having me with them. I was quite sorry when they died, within six months of each other, about seven years ago. But it was nothing like losing Grandmother!"

"Well," said Elli, "we're a weird pair, and no mistake. I wonder why Lyn wants us, of all people?"

"I expect we'll find out!"

"Obviously!" said Elli, and grinned.

Conversation lapsed. It was companionable, in a way, but it was also boring, Elli decided. The rain was easing, becoming a warm and clammy mist, the sort that often presages hot weather. The sea, at low ebb, was inaudible and invisible behind the grey, which occasionally had the golden tinge of hidden sunlight. The occasional seagull called loudly, but apart from that, and the small noise made by the cave stream, all was silent.

After a little, Elli felt she had to speak. Lance felt quite comfortable with the silence and inaction – she remembered the definition of war as nine parts boredom and one part absolute terror. He must be used to the state of suspended animation. But she wasn't.

"I wonder about Lyn," she said.

"Obviously."

"If you say that much more… Anyway, what do you think?"

"I don't know what to think. I've never met anybody like him before."

"Obviously," said Elli solemnly, and dodged as Lance made to push her off her rock. "But, for example, when do you think he calls home? Any idea?"

"Something quite old?"

"Bronze Age? Iron Age? Romano-Britain?"

"If I ever could make that sort of distinction, I've forgotten it ages ago. You're near your school years, you read. What do you think?"

"I don't know," said Elli. "I can't distinguish them either – but I think he referred to the Bible once…"

"Which would mean…?" asked Lance.

Elli was prevented from answering by the swooshing noise that heralded Olwen's arrival. This time, however, the dragon spared herself the trial of landing and takeoff by hovering briefly while Lyn threw down a large bundle wrapped in what seemed to be a sheet. "Hope to make one or two more shopping trips," shouted Lyn. "I may be back here after the first…or not." Then he flew off again.

Elli picked up the bundle and went back into the cave. "I got almost used to him this last week. I forgot how…strange he is. And now…"

"Now you've remembered that time travelling and dragon-riding are somewhat unusual?"

"No, it's more that we got used to him, and now he's doing something *differently* odd again. After all, as you said, 'Ordinary is what you're used to!'"

"True, young Elli. It seems we can adapt to the most peculiar, even unpleasant, situations."

"Yes. Margaret Atwood got it right. As did you, Major Poole!"

"Don't call me that. I'm not Major any more."

"So, don't call me Young Elli. I'm not young any more."

"Yes, you are!" Lance insisted.

"And you're still Army through and through, as you were saying earlier!"

They glared at each other for a moment, on the verge of a quarrel. Then Lance looked away and said, "So what's in that bundle?"

Elli untied it, glad of the diversion. "Oh, my goodness! Victorian underwear! I hope Lyn left some money in return – there's masses of it!"

"Are you going to put it on now?"

"I've nothing to go over it, and some of it looks very uncomfortable – so no. But clean clothes are a great temptation!"

"I put my Victorian gear on the shelf when I changed back," Lance said. "You do that as well, and make sure it's covered to protect it!"

"Yes, sir!" Elli saluted, and did as he said, bringing the food parcels when she returned.

"My watch hasn't worked since college, but my stomach says it's lunchtime!"

The mist had grown lighter in colour, as if the sun was up there somewhere, but it hadn't thinned at all. However, it was warm, and Elli, wiping sticky hands on her much ill-treated jeans, was swept with a sudden longing for cleanliness. She jumped up, rolling the small remains of cheese, meat and bread into one of the cloths.

"Come on, Lance, let's swim!"

"Swim? Aren't we meant to be keeping a low profile?"

"Who's going to see us in this mist? But it's warm, and I do so want to feel clean!"

"Are you suggesting skinny-dipping? Remember, I'm the conventional dinosaur!"

"Certainly not! My underwear would pass as a bikini on any beach, and I bet you're wearing boxers, which would do the same."

"What, pass as a bikini?"

"No! You know full well what I mean – they look like swimwear. Oh, come on!"

She pulled off her rugby shirt, having already abandoned her jacket with the heat of the day. Then, kicking off her trainers and socks, she climbed out of her jeans and ran down the beach, wearing, Lance had to admit, a very passable imitation of a neat black bikini. She turned around and shouted, "Bring that soap," and then was swallowed up by the mist.

Silly child, thought Lance. I'd better go after her and make sure she's all right. And yes, I will go in my boxers, so I can swim!

When he was ready, he looked around for one of the few remaining sticks by the fire and used it to make a groove in the sand all the way down to the water, fearing that the currents might otherwise shift the two of them, all unknowing, all along the beach. Reaching the waves, he stuck the stick upright in the sand as a further marker. Then, abandoning all sensible behaviour, he ran, splashing into the waves to where he could hear Elli splashing in delight.

Elli was floating on her back when he found her. She registered his approach by a flurry of vigorous kicking, splashing him liberally with water that was far too cold for his liking. In retaliation, he dived, passing underneath Elli and, emerging on her far side, tipped her, face down, under the water.

"Lance Poole, I'll get you for that!" Elli spluttered as she emerged. "On second thoughts, I'll forgive you if you've brought the soap!"

"Your wish is my command," said Lance, and produced a bar of soap from the pouch-pocket of his boxers. "Catch!"

"Oh, wonderful!" said Elli, soaping vigorously. "Just don't try anything like that again!"

Even at the sea's lowest ebb, there were waves and currents to make pure swimming tricky. But, Lance thought, Elli was right: to float on the swell, in sea that seemed warmer now you were used to it, was worth the effort.

Elli threw him the soap. "Clean yourself up, Major! We need to be respectable for our next assignment." With that she swam into the mist with a sturdy, if not particularly speedy, backstroke.

About fifteen minutes later, they found that the early summer sea was gradually chilling them, so, finding their way back using Lance's trail, they set off up the beach.

"Shall I call you Hansel in future? As in Hansel and Gretel, leaving a trail to follow?"

"You do, and I'll find something far worse to call you – unfortunately, all the female sea creatures sound far too flattering – mermaid, siren…"

Elli was about to respond in kind, when she stopped and pointed. "What's that?" A large carpetbag lay at the top of the beach.

"I think we missed Lyn," said Lance. "Here's your luggage."

Elli was already looking inside. "Oh, wonderful!" she said. "Brushes, combs, hair pins, hat pins, perfume, rouge…and this." She held up a shawl of fine cashmere wool, dyed a delicate sea green. "How lucky – Lyn can't possibly know that this is cashmere, or the link with India, but it'll help with our story. And it's a beautiful thing in itself."

"Now," she said, folding the shawl and restoring it to the bag. "I'm going to rinse the salt out of my hair in the stream and dry myself with the blanket."

"You're dressing twenty-first century again?"

"Certainly not! I'm clean – those clothes aren't. I shall put on something comfortable from my selection of underclothes, and wrap the shawl round me. Oh, and dry my 'bikini' on a rock!"

They looked an odd couple, thought Lance. He had on his Victorian trousers and shirt, but the latter was open at the neck and collarless. Elli was wearing knee-length knickers, and a chemise, both of fine linen with embroidery round the edges, and the cashmere shawl over her shoulders. How was she going to manage to climb and ride Olwen in full 1900 regalia?

"It's warm," said Elli. "I'm going to sun-bathe," and, spreading the blanket on the sand by the cave's entrance, she lay down, regardless of the fact that the sun was hidden by swathes of mist, and was soon breathing deeply and evenly. Lance sympathised – it was warm, and the swim had left them pleasantly tired. Add to these the excitements of their disturbed night, and it would be all too easy to sleep. But a soldier who slept on duty could – and should – be court-marshalled. The question was – was he on duty? Or, perhaps, even, was he a soldier? No longer with the British Army, certainly. But in the present circumstances? More to the point, how risky would it be to sleep: what were the dangers? Only discovery by some wandering peasant or fisherman. Given the weather, and the location it was unlikely. But if it happened, and they were taken from here, would Lyn ever find them? And could his staying awake prevent it, anyway?

He suspected that some of these musings were happening in a semi-conscious state, by the way he jerked awake at the sound of the arrival of Lyn on dragon back. This time he unloaded a number of brown paper packages, most meticulously tied with string or sealed with red wax. By the time Elli woke up, disturbed by the noise around her, her view of Olwen was partially obscured by the heaped parcels.

"As you can see, Miss Tollet," said Lyn gravely, "I paid good coin for these – how else would they be wrapped thus?"

"Thank you, Lyn," said Elli sincerely, ignoring the note of irony. "Let's see what I have... gloves...boots...I'm glad you measured my feet – nothing more uncomfortable than ill-fitting shoes...oh, I like the hat," she said, holding up a black straw hat, roughly boater-shaped, with a bunch of roses on a broad green ribbon. "And this is beautiful," unwrapping a fine cotton blouse with a thin primrose stripe, matching the roses. Finally, she opened the largest parcel, and held up a well-cut suit of dark green, with a long jacket and leg-of-mutton sleeves and a narrow skirt, which gradually widened to a small flounce at the hem. She held the skirt up against her. "It's a bit short."

"Yes. You're a bit tall for a Victorian woman. Olwen and I will have to 'distract' people from noticing. But how is the stuff in general?" If Elli hadn't known better, she could have sworn Lyn was anxiously waiting for her approval. She gave it without reservation.

"Lyn, it's all lovely! It'll be a challenge to wear, though, and I think it'll be uncomfortable. And how am I to ride Olwen in it all?"

"Leave off those underskirts and the suit skirt and put them on when we arrive – if we manage it without people noticing a dragon, your state of undress will hardly cause comment, I imagine," said Lance.

"Good thought," acknowledged Elli. "Lyn, when do we go?"

"During the night. We'll travel to the area in this time and then transfer – it'll be still dark. So, night flight to minimise the chances of Olwen being seen and distance travel in the Middle Ages, when people might just accept a dragon overhead. Now we must settle down: we have hours to go, and sleep to have. Oh yes, and this food to eat." He fetched some more parcels that he'd left near Olwen. They proved to contain a large pork pie, a jar of pickles and three bottles of beer. "No bottle-opener though – we'll have to use the rocks!"

When the evening grew cooler, Elli decided to have a full dress rehearsal. Modestly clad in the combinations, she hooked the corset down the front and asked the men to pull her laces tight at the back. The result was interesting – she liked the uplift of breast and the narrowness of waist it produced, but it was unbelievably uncomfortable. As rapidly as she could, she put on the whole outfit, except the hat, and reappeared in the cave mouth, and coughed, self-consciously.

The men had been looking at the sea – the tide having come in about an hour earlier, and the evening was finally free of mist. They turned, and Lance gasped. "Elli Tollet, you look marvellous!" He turned to Lyn. "Is that acceptable 1900 speech?"

"I believe so," said Lyn. "Although I'm no expert. But I agree with the comment, in any case. Elli, you look every inch a lady."

Elli, unused to compliments, asked, "But what am I to do with my hair? There's no way I can do it as a lady's maid would – and even a lady would have more idea than me!"

"Use the clips to shove it under your hat and pin it in place. Make sure you don't take off the hat off until you can do it in private. Then brush it out and get a maid to put it up."

"Could work," said Elli. "I'm not sure what will happen about maids anyway – I'll think I'll be offered a share in one!"

"Right, Elli," said Lyn. "Get back to what you were wearing before – we need to keep your stuff clean. We must sleep early and it's going dark now. And, as we need to save the last of this food for when we get up, we might as well turn in now."

"What's the plan for tomorrow, after we arrive then?" asked Lance.

"When it gets light, I'll do some reconnoitring to check things out. I believe we need to be at the railway station for about two in the afternoon. We'll be picked up as part of a group coming from London. As I don't know what else Olwen has in mind, that's as much as I can tell you."

Book 2: Country House

Chapter 1

It was just before moonrise when Lyn roused them, huddled as before under the blanket. Outside the cave, however, the mist had finally cleared and there was soon bright moonlight to help Elli struggle into all her extra clothes with the multitude of laces and buttons. She had decided to pack her petticoats, skirt and hat, and travel in the rest, so that she could straddle the dragon spine ridge. Lance donned his jacket, and tied his tie from memory, hoping the knot would be an acceptable one. Everything else they packed into the saddlebags.

Then they climbed into their accustomed places – Lyn nearest Olwen's head, then Elli, then Lance. Elli silently bid farewell to the Middle Ages, then took a deep breath and fixed her mind on the immanent, exciting, prospect of time shifting.

However, that thought soon got swallowed up in the intensity of night flying. To Elli, it seemed even better this time, when there was no cloud or mist, but instead, the silver brightness of the rising moon, the luminous pinpricks of the stars, and the shadowed darkness of the ground below. Very occasionally, a tiny orange flicker could be seen, from people ignoring the curfew, and once or twice there was the suggestion of a large lighted building – a castle, Elli speculated. But generally, they flew on, eastwards, over the dark land, in silence, except for the beat of giant wings.

When it happened, the time shift was vaguely disappointing. Nothing great occurred. There was a slight movement, almost sideways, it seemed, and a feeling in the stomach like going over a humped-back bridge, only magnified. Then the stars rearranged themselves from the patterns of early summer to those of early autumn – at least that was what Elli, no astronomer, assumed.

Then they began to descend, and soon Olwen was wrapping herself round a small hummocky hill, a barrow from ancient times.

Stiff and tired, they climbed down. Elli reached up and took the rest of her clothes from Lyn who was unloading the saddlebags, and shook them to remove the creases. Olwen made a green cave of her wing, and yet again they slept shaded from view, this time on the sheet spread on the grass, with the blanket over.

When they woke, light was filtering in, and Lyn was nowhere to be seen. Before they were fully awake, however, he reappeared. "I've brought you some fresh drinking water, but only a few stale bread rolls for breakfast, I'm afraid. And we'll need water to shave and wash – if there's any left in our bottles we'll use that." He refused to say more until they were dressed, washed, and in the case of the two men, shaved – an awkward business, this, with only cold water to go with the soap.

They stood on the hill, outside the cave that Olwen had made. Once they were clear, the dragon shook her wing and folded it close to her side.

Elli looked properly at their surroundings for the first time. And drew in her breath. "I know where we are," she said, surprised, and paused to look further.

"Well, where are we?" Lance was impatient.

"Not far from my aunt's market garden –or rather where it will be. On a barrow or tumulus, near the Knutsford-Macclesfield road. At least I think so. It's called Sodgers' Hump, I believe. It's either on the Capesthorne Estate, or very near it.

Oh no, Lyn – we're not staying there, with the Bromley-Davenports – I'll never be posh enough!"

Lyn smiled. "No, we're staying in the other direction – towards Chelford. It's a small estate – no tenant farms, just gardens and some good shooting in woods that adjoin Capesthorne's. Sir Edward Bairstow and his wife, Lady Anne. I don't know if the estate survives into your time."

"I don't think so," said Elli. "At least not in that form – but there are several good houses round here, so I can't be sure."

"Sit down," said Lyn, "and I'll tell you what I've found out, both from Olwen, and, in particular, from my investigations this morning."

It seemed that Lyn had approached the rear of the house just after dawn. The kitchen was in a wing on the east of the house, and was already stirring. Using his 'self-effacement' power, he had slid into the scullery and then stayed, unnoticed, just inside the kitchen door. Olwen, who was partly occupied with maintaining her own anonymity, spared some power to help Lyn hear, and, occasionally, see, the occupants of the breakfast room.

He discovered that this was one of the four big parties held annually by the Bairstows. The Christmas celebration was always held in their London house – a fact appreciated by those of the kitchen staff who were thus freed to spend the season with their families. One big spring party was held for neighbours such as the Bromley-Davenports, and the Stanleys of Alderley Park, and this was followed by the summer weekend, mainly for Lady Anne's friends – 'your blue-stockings and artists', as Sir Edward had called them, half-jokingly. "I gather she has a fine library of books both old and new, and a great interest in many academic subjects – especially literature, history and where they meet – myths and legends. I gather, also, that she is wealthy in her own right, and considered a little eccentric – she loves gardening, and often gets her hands dirty, rather than just directing the gardeners," Lyn said.

He continued: "This weekend is mainly for Sir Edward's shooting friends – according to what I overheard, Lady Anne doesn't always get on with the wives," Lyn said. "But then Sir Edward feels the same about the husbands – and wives – of her friends. The staff think they're an oddly-matched couple, and rather eccentric, but good to work for, and very happy together, perhaps because neither is the usual class-ridden socialite. Sir Edward likes the company of his gamekeeper – and of the footman who is teaching him photography! Lady Anne is more concerned with intellect than class."

"That should help," said Elli. "But how are you going to wangle us in there?"

"If by 'wangle', you mean: 'ensure our welcome'," said Lyn, "well, if you must know, I used a method I seldom use, and don't really approve of. I slipped a memory into Lady Anne's mind, which suggested that she had heard from a friend living near Preston, saying that her niece and nephew were home from India and were to visit her soon. I heard Lady Anne talking of this friend to Sir Edward, which made it easier. So she told him that she had invited the two young people to break their journey by joining the shooting party."

"False memory syndrome," said Lance.

"Lyn, you shouldn't have!" said Elli.

"What else should I do?" asked Lyn. "Oh, your aunt is called Helen Astbury – she is your father's sister, and a talented amateur artist. She and Lady Anne are friendly when they're both in London, but they don't see a lot of each other. And Lance – I hope you can shoot!"

"Naturally – it was part of my job description. But I've virtually no experience of pheasant shooting. Never mind, I expect it'll be OK."

"That reminds me," said Lyn. "No twentieth century colloquialisms, if you please!" Then he turned to other matters. "As I'd sort-of-gathered from Olwen, the London-based guests are arriving on a train at quarter past two this afternoon. We'll be amongst them, and from then on we'll play it by ear."

"Which station?" asked Elli. "Alderley Edge?"

"No," said Lyn. "They're stopping the train especially at Chelford Station," and waved in a westerly direction.

"How are we getting there? We can't risk Olwen."

"No indeed. We're walking."

"Lyn! It must be a good two miles – and I've got new boots on! Why didn't Olwen drop us there last night?"

"How – without risking being seen in the village, or scaring the livestock? And then for me to maintain a 'self-effacement effect' solidly for hours on end, whilst we waited? No thanks! So it's walking for us – if we pass anyone, they won't see us, I promise you!"

So, in the mid-morning, they left Olwen, and walked westward. When they reached the road, and looked back, she had melded and moulded into the barrow, so as to be virtually indistinguishable from it, even to those who knew she was there. She had even arranged herself so that the view of the trees on the top of the barrow was undisturbed.

It was another fine day, this one hovering between late summer and early autumn, perhaps late September or early October, with a hint of crispness in the air. A few leaves were starting to turn colour, but the rest still had the heavy look of the very end of summer. There had been rain recently – there were puddles at the side of the road – but all this had done was to refresh the green countryside, which would otherwise have looked dusty and tired.

The road itself was lined with more trees than Elli thought were there in 2006. Certainly the elms were no longer gracing the landscape. Many fields looked smaller, and the road, missing its tarred surface, puffed small white clouds of dust when the occasional carriage or farm worker went past. These did not, as Lyn had promised, give them a second glance. It was quite easy, he said, to get people to fail to notice them for the few minutes they were in sight of each other. The occasional cottage along the road received the same treatment, in case there were any eyes watching.

Soon they passed a long wall with an impressive pair of gates, half-open, between tall pillars – the entrance, Lyn said, to their destination. Elli, a sore spot already being rubbed by the newness of the boots, wished Lyn had thought of a scheme which enabled them to arrive there without going to Chelford first.

But, sore spot excepted, it was a pleasant walk, and after the strange, isolated life of the last week, it was good to be walking openly through surroundings that approximated to normality, and have strangers passing with no more than a casual nod, as Lyn kept their profile low and unremarkable.

Eventually, they arrived at the station, on the outskirts of the tiny village. They found a side entrance, and emerged on the platform where they sat on a bench. Lance consulted the half-hunter watch that had come with his outfit. "If you gave me the right time when you came back this morning, it must be around noon. Over two hours to wait – well, I suppose we're used to it – like war, there seems to be an awful lot of hanging around on this adventure!"

As he spoke, they heard the clock on the station-building behind them strike twelve. "Your watch is right then," said Lyn. "Good. And talking of watches…"

He reached into his pocket and produced a couple of small packages, wrapped in tissue paper, and handed them to Elli. "Not enough, really, but they'll have to do."

Elli unwrapped them, and felt a rush of pleasure, and, simultaneously, a pricking of tears. In her hand lay a small fob watch, a cameo brooch, a delicate filigree silver bracelet, and a ring with what looked like a small emerald. "Lyn, they're lovely," she said. "But where did you get them?"

"I bought them in a pawnbrokers," said Lyn. Lance felt he was rather pleased with his grasp of the mores of the time, but Elli was too wrapped up in the objects and their story to notice anything. "They had been there for over a year, I gather, so no one will come back for them, and miss them."

"Oh." Elli felt her response was inadequate, but she was alarmingly close to tears – the thought of a woman having to part with such things, and the gradual dying of hope that they might be recovered, seemed to her unutterably sad.

She was roused from this by Lance saying speculatively, "I wonder if the pawnbroker's the local fence – disposing of stolen articles," he added for Lyn's benefit. Men! Elli thought, but acknowledged to herself that her reaction was probably excessive – but life was excessive these days.

"Thank you, Lyn," she said and squeezed his arm. "I'll go and see if the ladies' room has a mirror to help me put them on. My hands aren't ladylike enough to do the ring justice, though, I shall have to wear gloves as much as possible."

"More work for me, deflecting people's interest," said Lyn. "Never mind – I'm glad you like them!"

After that, they settled on the bench, and, eventually, in response to their disturbed night, the fresh air, exercise, and boredom, they dozed, awaking with a jerk from time to time as a train went through, or, occasionally, stopped. No-one bothered them, or tried to sit on the bench. Lance supposed they were not invisible, just unremarkable.

A little before two, Lyn woke them. Had he, too, been asleep? If so, thought Elli in a muddled way as she surfaced, that would mean that this Power worked even when he was asleep – very impressive. Lyn was speaking: "We need to be ready soon, and at the moment we look rather dishevelled, even for people arriving after a long train journey. Elli, you'll need that mirror again – your hat's at a very odd angle!"

"I'll go and re-pin it now," she said and went off, while the men brushed each other down and straightened jackets and ties.

They were ready when the train slowed and stopped. From a first-class carriage six well-dressed middle-aged people were emerging when a puff of smoke enveloped the platform. Taking advantage, the three of them moved from the shadow of the building and positioned themselves as if they were coming with the others who had alighted from the second-class carriages. This had been Elli's idea. "We may be well connected, but we're here mainly on Lance's soldier's pay, so we won't be extravagant," she had said as they sat waiting.

Lyn spoke quietly. "From now on, until we leave, remember I'm your manservant. Don't be rude – that's not good behaviour in any age – but we're not friends."

"But as you've been my batman, I may be excused if I'm a bit more friendly than they're used to," Lance responded, as Lyn lifted his 'master's' bag. Elli kept hold of hers.

They followed the six first-class passengers through the station building, past the un-noticing man collecting tickets, to the yard beyond. There was an impressive array of vehicles drawn up, waiting: a closed carriage, two open dogcarts, and another one, which had, instead of a horse, a large box-like structure. "Wow!" said Elli. "You can see why they called them horseless carriages – that's exactly what it is!"

One of the dogcarts, it transpired, belonged to a local man, the forerunner of the local taxi service. Into this was piled an astonishing amount of luggage and four people – the two men and two women who were presumably servants belonging to the three couples, and who had emerged from the second-class part of the train.

Two quiet men stood at the horses' heads, whilst from the proto-car, a stocky man – a little above average height and of middle years – jumped down. He greeted the others as old friends and then turned to Elli and Lance, standing apart, with Lyn one step behind. "Welcome," he said, "you must be the young people Anne has asked to stay – Helen Astbury's family. I'm Edward Bairstow, Anne's husband. You must be Eleanor – and you, Lance."

"Yes," said Elli, "Although I'm usually called Elli."

"Right, young Eleanor, Elli it shall be. Where's your luggage?" he said, looking round.

"There's a problem," said Lance, smoothly. "We sent two trunks to Aunt Helen's, but we discovered on the way here that our weekend stuff seems to have gone as well." He looked at Lyn, as if for confirmation. Lyn nodded, maintaining a smooth face, behind which, Elli could almost feel, the calming, unquestioning power was working away.

"Wretched railways! Oh well, my wife will fix you up – I think, with a bit of luck, our offspring will have left stuff to fit you." He then regarded them with a look of mixed apprehension and appeal. "You're young people," and then said in a rush, "would you like to venture into my new toy? I tried to persuade my dear friends over there, but they turn out to be regular stick-in-the-muds. Do say you'll give it a go – I have veils and goggles – and some capes."

Lance and Elli looked at each other. "Yes, Sir Edward, we'd love to," said Lance. "And perhaps my man, Sayer, could ride as well? He was with me in the army, and loves new mechanisms."

"Certainly," said Sir Edward. "No maid?"

Elli started to explain how she would be sharing her aunt's, and had therefore dismissed her London one – with the undertone, she hoped of cost-cutting – but Sir Edward broke in. "No problem – not too much room for too many servants, anyway. The Bennetts and the Johnsons are sharing, I see. Don't worry, my wife'll fix you up." Lady Anne was going to do a lot of fixing up, thought Elli, amused by Sir Edward's endless faith in his wife's capabilities.

Chapter 2

So they travelled in one of the earliest motorcars. Lance reckoned that this one might well be the first in Cheshire. He and Elli, duly kitted up against the dusty rigours of the road, sat in the back, while Lyn, deferential, assumed the seat next to Sir Edward, shielding the others somewhat. "I only hope Sir Edward doesn't ask him to drive," muttered Elli.

"Although it might be easier to control than a dragon with a mind of her own," returned Lance, quietly. Just then, the engine clattered into life, and speech became pointless, as it would have been inaudible.

The journey back along the road was quicker, noisier, and in many respects, more uncomfortable than their walk, rubbed foot notwithstanding. However, they were soon turning in at the gates they had seen earlier. A circular driveway led to a few steps up to the front door of a mellow, redbrick Queen Anne house. Elli, looking with interest, saw three storeys with beautifully proportioned windows, and reckoned that there were attics behind the balustrade, and cellars below – in fact small cellar windows were just visible.

To the left, eastward, there was another brick wall, parallel to the front, but set back, pierced by a graceful archway – the stable yard, she presumed. To the left, this was balanced by a two-storey wing, probably built a hundred years later than the main house.

As they had started before the carriages, and maintained their lead, they were the first to arrive. Perhaps alerted by the noise of the engine, a woman appeared at the top of the stairs – a tall thin woman in skirt and blouse, with untidy dark hair. Lady Anne, for this must be she, waved in an energetic fashion, quite unlike the ladylike behaviour they were expecting. Sir Edward brought the car to a juddering halt and leapt out, offering his hand to Elli whilst Lyn did the same for Lance.

Their host raised his voice and addressed his wife. "Anne dear, these are Helen's young people: Eleanor, who likes to be Elli, and Lance. One servant – Lance's batman – and no luggage. Idiot railways have sent it all to Helen's."

While he spoke, he ushered Lance and Elli before him up the half a dozen steps.

As he reached the woman, he ran out of information. His wife shook her head. "He never will learn to behave as he should – but perhaps that's just as well or he might object to some of my behaviour! Lance, Eleanor – no, Elli – how nice to meet you! Life in England must seem strange after so long in India. I'm Anne Bairstow, as you must have gathered. Teddy persuaded you to ride in that contraption? How brave of you! Come in, come in, and recover from your journey. The others will be here soon, but we won't wait for them – in fact, you might like some recovery time without them. The weather remains unseasonably warm, so I've had cook prepare lemonade." Still talking, she showed them into a well-proportioned hall, where sofas and chairs were placed round a large fireplace with windows looking west on either side of it.

"Would you like some refreshment now, or would you prefer a wash and brush-up first?"

Elli nodded at this, and Lady Anne swept them up the staircase which faced the door. At the top, she turned left, and then, shortly, right, where there was a long corridor with windows on its right and an array of doors on the left.

"Guests are usually in the west wing, or on the floor above," their hostess said, "but we're a little pushed for space, and, fortunately neither of the children are home – John's a barrister, you know, living in London, and is far too busy for this weekend. And Alix – well, she was so ragged last September about being at Oxford that she persuaded us to let her visit a college friend – a vicar's daughter in the depths of Somerset."

Elli and Lance, having failed to break into the torrent of words, exchanged amused glances. Lady Anne was obviously a talker, which might help them avoid gaffes – the less they spoke, the better.

"So I've put you in the children's wing," she said. "The corridor looks over the kitchen yard, but the rooms have a lovely view east. The children still use the rooms when they're here, so the rooms are comfortable, if a little small. There's a bathroom at the far end of the corridor, Elli, but I'm afraid the nursery itself is full of my painting stuff – I had to move it when we needed the drawing room for this weekend – and Nanny's room is now Teddy's darkroom."

She opened the second door on the left. "This is Alix's room. I hope it suits. I'll come back in a moment – let me just show Lance to his room – does he like horses?"

Elli decided that Lady Anne's mind had a logic of its own and it would be revealed in good time. "Yes," she answered.

"Good – his room overlooks the stable yard!" And with that she was gone.

Elli looked around her: a smallish room, certainly, but far from a monkish cell. The bed throw and curtains were of an art nouveau design in flame and deep green, and the rugs picked up the forest colour. There was a cast iron grate, an armchair, a small dressing table, and a large wardrobe. She went to the window and looked out. The lawns, smooth and green, fell away gently, with beds of large bushes – rhododendrons, she thought.

Then they merged with the woods. Looking over the treetops and slightly to the left, she thought she could make out the distinctive outline of the haunted hill of Alderley. She turned round as Lady Anne knocked and entered.

"Lance's man has found his way up the back stairs, and he and Lance are looking through John's wardrobe. Now, let's see what I can do for you." Elli had taken off her gloves, and now, forgetting the state of her hair, her hat. Most of her bun promptly tumbled to her shoulders.

"I tried to fix this myself, on the train," she said, hastily. "But I seem to have made things worse!"

"Oh, my dear, you should see what mine looks like if I get at it! Never mind, I'll send Ward to you very soon – she's my maid, and was my mother's, so she's very experienced. We'll share her for your stay – but can you ready yourself for bed without help?"

"Yes," said Elli, getting into her role. "I've done so often in India, especially when we went up country." Whatever that means, she added to herself. "But why?"

"Ward is so good, but becoming elderly – I usually say I can manage myself, so she can go to bed."

"That would be fine, Lady Anne. I'm not too comfortable with other people's maids, if I'm honest." Elli tried to imagine any servant she would be comfortable with, and failed.

"Now let's see what you can borrow of Alix's," Lady Anne said, opening the wardrobe.

"Your daughter is at Oxford University? Isn't that unusual?"

"It is, but she longed to go, and I longed for her to do it – something that had been impossible for me when I was young. And Teddy loathes convention, so it was all fine. John, who is five years older than Alix, is embarrassed by it, but that is because lawyers tend to be extremely conservative. We live in hope that she may even be awarded a degree – if they allow women to graduate before she's in her dotage!"

Elli was looking at the clothes displayed in the wardrobe. She lifted out one, vibrantly coloured. "This is beautiful."

"It is, indeed," agreed Lady Anne, "but not for this company, I fear. The wives of Teddy's shooting friends – and most of the men – are very conventional about such things. A Pre-Raphaelite dress would shock – but come to my summer weekend, and you can wear one then!"

"So what should I choose? Indian dress follows different conventions – the heat, and so on," said Elli vaguely, grateful for the all round usefulness of India.

"An afternoon dress – I think there's one in white with sprigs much the colour of your suit, if Alix hasn't taken it... ah, here it is!" and she placed a high-necked, full-sleeved dress on the chair. "But my dear, you look all in. Why don't you have a small sleep before bothering any further? I'll send up some lemonade, there's fresh water in the basin, or the bathroom is just next door, and I'll send Ward up in time for you to appear at afternoon tea."

Elli nodded, grateful for the kindness under the talk.

"That's settled then. Have a good rest, my dear." And Lady Anne removed herself, quietly, with no further chattering.

Elli looked longingly at the bed. How long was it since she had slept in a conventional one? She swilled water over her face, poured herself a glass of the cool drinking water from the carafe, and gratefully undressed to a minimum of underclothes. By the time a maid brought the lemonade, she was blissfully asleep.

She woke about an hour later to find a sturdy, grey-haired woman standing by the bed.

"My name is Ward, Miss Poole. My lady sent me to help you dress – she says afternoon tea will be served shortly in the morning room."

"Thank you," said Elli. "Why the morning room?" A stupid question, she thought, but the thing that came to her half-awake mind.

"So the men can wander outside and look at some of the shooting prospects even before they walk the coverts, I gather. And unless we have guests we do not use the formal reception rooms on this floor. Indeed, Lady Anne usually uses the rear room for her painting. Now, is there a dress that you and my lady selected?"

Elli found Ward reminded her of one of her primary school teachers – friendly, but rather intimidating. However, she nerved herself to ask: "Must I wear my corset? We often do not in India – the heat, you know."

Ward looked at her critically. "You young people! Miss Alix is the same – and even my lady, occasionally. Well, you are as long and thin as they are, so you can get away with it for an afternoon dress, but the décolletage will demand one this evening. And if you pardon my saying so, your bosom requires all the help it can get. And we must find you some mittens – your hands are as rough as my lady's – you must be a gardener, like her?"

Elli nodded, wordlessly. Less 'distraction' work for Lyn if there was a natural explanation – but she hoped her gardening knowledge wouldn't be tested too thoroughly!

Some twenty minutes later, Elli found herself on the landing feeling more glamorous than she could ever remember. Her hair was dressed simply in a knot at the back of her neck, and fortunately Alix's clothes, and even her low-heeled slippers, had fitted well enough. A waft of perfume accompanied her, and she thought that the pampered life of a Victorian gentlewoman had its compensations.

Made curious by Ward's conversation, she opened a door on the other side of the landing. She was in the smaller, rear reception room, separated from the larger front room by folding doors. The view was west over the gardens she had seen from the front, these more formal, with many flowerbeds, but again leading to woods. The room bore no trace of its usual function as an artist's studio, except for the faintest whiff of turpentine. The furniture was lighter and more sparse than she had expected from a Victorian room, but that would be Lady Anne's aesthetic taste. She pushed open the door leading to the front room, and went in. Here her eye was drawn to a splendid grand piano ensconced on the far side, beyond the fireplace. Approaching it, she pushed back the lid, and started picking out a tune. Before she even realised what it was, she was transported back to a green glade, a dying fire and Lance's voice... "Plaisir d'amour..." she sang, quietly.

"I wouldn't sing that!" a voice behind her remarked. Lance had come upon her unannounced. "I believe it became popular at around this time in French bordellos – or at least less-than-respectable night spots!"

"Really?" said Elli. "I never knew. It puts a different slant on some of the words!"

"Come!" said Lance. "Let me take my 'sister' downstairs to meet the company. I've talked to one or two of the men already. Why Olwen thinks we should be here is a mystery, but let us try not to 'blow our cover' as we might say a hundred years on!"

The next half hour or so was difficult, Elli had to admit. The women were pleasant enough, but, with the exception of Lady Anne, extremely condescending to her – young, and from India, and in borrowed clothes – although at least this meant she was not expected to speak much. She set a guard on her tongue and concentrated on eating the small sandwiches and cakes daintily. This was difficult, as she was ravenous, having eaten little for over twenty-four hours. Whilst the women sat and ate, and conversed, the men mainly stood, obviously restless, longing to be away, examining the arrangements for the following day.

Elli was temporarily without a companion, so she stood up and wandered over to a different part of the morning room – which was far more as she had pictured a Victorian room. She found she was looking at a photograph of her host and hostess with others she did not know – although the young woman with the look of Lady Anne was surely Alix – all smiling and slightly dishevelled. The writing underneath read: 'Celebrating the Relief of Mafeking, May 1900.' A voice said in her ear, "Yes, my dear, that was us, this last May!"

She turned and smiled at Sir Edward. "That was certainly a day – and a night – of celebration. All over the Empire." But as she spoke, a strange feeling swept over her and she held onto the table for support. Sir Edward was all attention and soon she was sitting, with Lady Anne and two other women making concerned noises.

"Please…I think I must be more tired than I knew from the journey. Perhaps I should just rest some more, so I can enjoy this evening fully?"

"Of course, my dear," said Lady Anne. "Will you be able to manage the stairs?"

"Oh yes. I feel better already. I'll just tell my brother what I'm doing."

"I think he's outside. Shall I fetch him?"

"No," said Elli. "The fresh air will do me good."

She found Lance, and drew him aside. "I just came over all faint, so I'm using it as an excuse to go to my room. But don't worry – I'm fine now. But Lance, do you know why I felt strange?"

"Tell me."

"It was like déjà vu – only I *had* been there before. It was how I knew where – when – we were going. It was what Olwen showed me – why, Lance? How?"

"I have no answers, Elli. But never mind. Go and rest. I'll walk the coverts with the men, and I'll see you when we all assemble before dinner." He gave her a brotherly kiss on her forehead, and turned her toward the room, where Lady Anne ushered her through the other guests and out of the room.

Reaching the safety of her own room, she took off the dress, lay again on the bed, and, despite everything, slept again until Ward came to ready her for dinner.

Lance, formally dressed for dinner, was one of the earlier guests to arrive in the fine reception room. The blue skies of the day had ensured a cool evening, and a fire had been lit in the grate. He cradled his second glass of pre-prandial sherry, and reflected on the pleasures of good alcohol, especially after days on short rations, and some without. He had already had a few mouthfuls of fine whisky from one of the men's hipflasks whilst they were walking the estate. Off-duty, the army was notoriously hard-drinking and he had a hard head. However, the trick would be to remember that he was not strictly off-duty. He must not make any mistakes tonight.

As he listened to Sir Edward extol the virtues of his motorcar, he was struck with a passing thought. Sir Edward Bairstow, whose wife calls him Teddy. In a few years he'll be plagued by people calling him Teddy Bear – and he looks rather like one! His lips twitched and he controlled himself with difficulty. Where was Elli with whom he could share this revelation? Most of the women had not yet joined the company, although there was one coming in now, a younger woman that he'd not met earlier.

With a start, he realised that it was Elli. Although no one had ever called her beautiful, the dress code of the day made her look elegant, and the liveliness of her expression, and the grace of her carriage, made her, for the moment, almost stunning – and a lot older. Her hair was piled up, and a small bunch of artificial flowers was attached to it. The dress, pale green with a darker pattern, revealed smooth shoulders before puffing out into short sleeves. Some miracle of uncomfortable corsetry had made the most of her small bosom, which peeped alluringly over the tight bodice, and the soft swirl of skirts completed the effect. Lady Anne had obviously lent the silver necklace and earrings, but the filigree bracelet was the one Lyn had acquired.

Excusing himself to his host, Lance moved across the room, and reached her, taking her hand and saying, as he moved her toward the others: "Young Elli, you look wonderful! I hardly recognised you!"

"And that, sir, is a back-handed compliment, if ever I heard one!"

"Oh!" Lance was embarrassed. "I see what you mean – but that wasn't how I meant it!"

"I know," said Elli, "I was teasing. I'm glad you like the effect – but 'Pride must suffer a pinch', and this corsetry is extremely uncomfortable!"

Sir Edward watched them approach and echoed Lance. "Elli, you look lovely. A breath of fresh air – I wish Alix was here to keep you company – we're a lot of old fogeys, except perhaps for Julian Meredith and his wife. They're near Lance in age, I think, so I'm sending you in with Julian, and Lance can take in Julian's wife – Katherine, her name is."

Julian and Katherine Meredith were standing with Lady Anne and another couple near the piano. After ascertaining that Julian and Lance had talked that afternoon, but that Katherine and Elli had not, the conversation turned to music.

"Can you play, Elli?" asked Lady Anne.

"A little. My mother…" she nearly said 'taught me', but remembered their cover story that their mother had died young, when Elli was a baby. "My mother was musical and my father made sure I learnt, but I'm not skilled."

"Do play for us now," urged Julian, a tall, friendly, if not very intelligent-looking man. "Let's see what music there is in the stool."

"No," said Lady Anne. "We go down to dinner in a few minutes – afterwards, perhaps. But can you play anything for us from memory, Elli?"

Elli nodded and sat down. As had happened that afternoon, her fingers played of their own accord, and this time it was the other song from that evening in the Middle Ages. As she recognised what she was playing, she hoped desperately that this one had no traps, but she thought she remembered that the tune was traditional, and the words from the late twentieth century. Anyway, there were no shocked faces, and, indeed, Lance had started to sing softly. Together they sang the second verse and reached the last two lines:

"Though the Carnival is over,
I will love you till I die."

Again she saw that the odd look was on Lance's face.

Lord Edward applauded. "A charming song," said Lady Anne. "I don't think I've heard it before."

Elli improvised wildly, seeing no help was forthcoming from Lance. "It was very popular last year in India – I think someone out there wrote the words to an old tune."

"It was lovely. But now we must go down for dinner."

Lance offered Katherine Meredith his arm, and Julian Meredith did the same to Elli. Lady Anne was squired by a red-faced gentleman and Sir Edward led the way with a woman who just topped him in height. Lance turned and winked at Elli, but she found a light-hearted response difficult. This, she thought, was going to be a trial.

As they walked downstairs, her escort made polite conversation. "You were feeling unwell earlier, Miss Poole. I hope you are fully recovered?"

"Yes, thank you. I was just overtired. And please do call me Elli. I'm not used to Miss Poole, yet." And that's true enough, she added silently.

"Not long out, eh? Very well, Elli, if you call me Jeremy. With being not quite the thing, I suppose you didn't have a chance to see over the house?"

"No, indeed."

"Well," he said, as they descended to the hall. "As you'll see, the dining room is on the right, to the front of the morning room. It's a fine room, but rather old-fashioned – oak panelling, and all, you know."

"And the rooms on the left?"

"Behind that rather jolly sitting area round the fire, Teddy's study. And behind that, mainly in the west wing, under the guest bedrooms, a perfectly enormous library, Anne's territory. She's a dreadful bluestocking – has probably read most of the books in there, and keeps buying new ones. If you're not careful, she'll talk for hours on anything from polar exploration to King Arthur or Robin Hood. And she even buys poetry – Tennyson, and all that," he added with a small shudder, in a mystified tone.

"Isn't this a rather unusual arrangement of rooms?"

"Yes, but they're a totally batty couple! I shouldn't say that, but they decided to swap the main rooms to the first floor as the children grew up and were seldom in that wing, and they entertain so little. It suits them, I suppose, but it's jolly odd!"

Elli was spared having to answer as they were now in the dining room, and all sixteen diners – eight men and eight women – were being shown to their seats. She was between Julian and an older man. Lady Anne was on the far side of Elli's escort, and Lance was towards the other end of the table, near where Sir Edward was sitting opposite his wife.

The room was impressive. The staff appeared noiselessly, and, starting with soup, placed course after course in front of the guests. It seemed to Elli that the wine flowed even more lavishly. The whole process was leisurely, and the others seemed to rate conversation as at least as important as eating. This led to long pauses between courses and cool food, thought Elli, and kept her eyes down, playing the modest Victorian maiden, in the hope that she wouldn't make an irredeemable mistake. She answered Julian's questions as briefly as she could, and plied him with her own, about his homes (in Derbyshire and London), his family (two children so far, a boy aged five and a girl, three), and his interests (mainly cricket and shooting, of which he was willing to talk at great length).

From time to time she glanced across the table at Lance. His would be the harder task – men were expected to take the lead in conversation. He seemed to be surviving: Elli could see him, head bent, talking earnestly to Katherine Meredith, and Sir Edward on her far side. As she watched, he drained his glass – instantly refilled by an attentive servant, and, in one of the sudden silences that occur at dinner tables she heard him say: "The North-West frontier with Afghanistan? Oh, yes, I've served there."

And so you have, she thought.

Conversation didn't immediately restart. Everyone was looking at Lance, and Sir Edward said, "Tell us about it."

"Yes, do, Major Poole," echoed Katherine.

Lance spoke, his eyes looking beyond the immediate. "It's a wonderful place, and a terrible. Full of extremes – it can be bitterly cold in winter, when the wind sweeps down from the high mountains, and burningly hot in summer. You can have your breath taken away by the beauty: you come over a hill and see a plain before you, with high peaks beyond, and a river winding over it, with puffs of dust from the road and smoke from the village fires. All the time there's an itchy feeling in your back that perhaps one of the Pathan – or another tribesman

– has his rifle trained on you. And the people are wonderful and terrible, too. Capable of great hospitality and loyalty – and cruelty and vengeance…"

Elli realised that his description was doubly valid, and held her breath in case he forgot the century he was in. She looked at him and he caught the glance. "My sister is trying to tell me that it is rude to monopolise the conversation. And, obviously, she is right. But that's how it is there." He forestalled any attempt to get him to speak more by applying himself to his wine glass, until, again, it was empty.

Elli tried to catch his eye again, this time to suggest he ease up on the drinking. However, the man sitting on the other side from Julian asked her how she found life in England, and she became fully occupied concocting a plausible answer.

The dinner continued, and, as it drew toward its end, Elli began to dread the time when Lady Anne would lead the ladies out and leave the men to their port. Her reticence would be harder to maintain in an all-female group. What on earth were they doing here anyway? Why had Olwen insisted on it? Lyn didn't seem to know, and, for that matter, had she really been riding through time on a green dragon? It seemed ridiculous, but here she was, and she knew things that would come in the next hundred years. It had happened… it was happening… but why?

Her reverie was interrupted by an over-loud voice from the far end of the table… "as the actress said to the bishop!" The voice, slightly thick with drink, was Lance's. Elli felt a constriction in her throat, and her stomach flipped over. What now? There had been a collective intake of breath from the far end of the table. One man laughed, but Katherine Meredith looked shocked, and Sir Edward embarrassed.

Seeming to realise that he had somehow offended, Lance half-stood up and turned toward Katherine. As he did so, he swayed slightly and, flinging out an arm to balance himself, caught her glass and sent its contents – a heavy dessert wine of which little had been drunk – straight into her lap.

For a moment, chaos reigned. Katherine Meredith shrieked, and Sir Edward came rapidly out of his seat toward her, on the way pressing Lance roughly back into his chair. Julian got to his feet at the same time and he and Lady Anne reached the shocked woman more or less together. Lady Anne put her arm round Katherine, and, accompanied by Julian, they started toward the door.

Elli stood up. She must get Lance and herself out of here before Lance said something worse, something impossible. "I am so sorry," she said. "The medicine my brother takes – for a condition contracted up-country – reacts badly with alcohol." (As does a short abstinence, she reflected bitterly.) She saw sceptical faces but ploughed on. "He should have thought. I think he had better retire now, and I will go and sit with him."

One of the servants came forward and helped Lance who had been sitting, slumped forward, to his feet. Elli made her apologies and accompanied them out of the room and along the hall.

When they reached the stairs, Lance gripped the banister with his left hand as a drowning man might grip a plank of wood. The manservant competently supported him under the right elbow. "That's right, sir, steady as we go!" Elli had the distinct impression this was not the first time he had performed this sort of operation. She followed behind and was surprised when, about halfway up, Lance swung his head round and winked at her. Perhaps he wasn't quite as drunk as he seemed – although he had certainly drunk plenty. But why should he be faking – or at least exaggerating his state? She had no idea.

At last they reached his room and James, the manservant, guided Lance to the edge of his bed. "Thank you so much," said Elli. "Could you find his man, Sayer, and ask him to come to us?" James nodded and went out, turning up the oil-lamp, and pulling the door to, although it did not entirely shut.

He sat on the bed with his head in his hands, not looking at her.

"Lyn will be here shortly," she said, trying to maintain a detached, even tone. "He should help you, if you're too far gone to help yourself."

He shot her a quick look, dropping his hands. "Elli, Elli, why are you so... angry... I think is the word?"

"Virtually the first alcohol you get to on this mad adventure – you make an idiot of yourself... and me... how am I meant to deal with it? It's hard enough pretending to be your sister, to be at home in 1900, without shouldering your part of the act as well! Is this why you got out of the army? The drink?"

Lance looked as if she had slapped his face. "Shut the door," he said in a low, intense voice. "You need to have some things explained to you, you... self-righteous young madam!"

Elli was shocked into compliance. As the heavy door swung shut, Lance stood up, steadying himself on one of the bed's brass posts. He looked, she thought, far better than he had downstairs.

"First, you silly young thing," Lance said, "I am not drunk – at least not drunk and incapable. I will admit," he said with the slightly overdone dignity of the verging-on-inebriated, "I will admit to 'having drink taken' as the Irish put it. The men of 1900 certainly can drink! And, perhaps it is affecting me... somewhat!" This as he swayed a little. "But I'm not as drunk as..."

"Thinkle peep you are?" said Elli, mischievously.

"Precisely. I thought it would be a good way of exrac...extracat...of getting us both out of that bloody banquet before we got something so horribly wrong that even Lyn and

131

Olwen couldn't cover it up, and we found ourselves imprisoned as con artists, or locked up in the local lunatic asylum!"

"That's a point," said Elli, slightly mollified. "But it's the sort of plan which might appeal to the already somewhat... inebriated!"

"And secondly – and secondly, my girl, don't you ever dare to talk in that way about why I left the army. You know nothing about it!"

"Exactly. I know nothing about it. You won't talk of it. Back in college or now. So what am I meant to do? Never refer to it, whilst all the time it's like the elephant in the room, ignored, but huge and getting in the way?"

She had left the door, and now stood close, blazing back. It occurred to her that her sudden lack of tact might be because she, too, 'had drink taken' although not to the same extent as Lance.

Lance turned away. His shoulders slumped and he seemed to shrink a little. For a moment, he stared at the blank of the window as if seeing into the heart of life. Elli saw with surprise that his eyes were wet. Straightening and pushing himself free, for the moment, from the befuddling fumes of the alcohol, he gripped her wrist with one hand, the other still resting on the bedpost.

"Elli. It wasn't the drink. But yes, there was a reason for leaving. I'm good at the job. I like a challenge, in a job which combines brainwork with the physical. My men liked me, and I liked them. And I got on well with the other officers. I enjoyed the social side. I was happy to put up with all the pettifogging rules and regulations, if it meant I could continue to live the life. Anyway, it gave me a framework to operate in...no need to spend time on moral or ethical choices: even in the Gulf, even in Iraq, it was possible to close your mind and just get on with the job in hand..."

"Then why?" asked Elli.

"I said I liked the officers. My CO was a terrific man, charismatic, a real leader, yet one of the lads…"

"So – what was the difficulty? You didn't fall for him, did you?" Elli tried to be as broadminded as the other college girls, although a cold weight settled in her stomach at the thought of a Lance permanently unavailable to her, to any woman…

"No. No. Not him – his wife." The words seemed forced out by an uncontrollable power and Lance looked faintly shocked to hear them.

"Oh my poor dear!" Shocked by the bleakness and the naked pain in his face, Elli acted instinctively and reached out, folding her arms round him. She was, some part of her mind noted, almost as tall as him, which made the operation easier.

Now he had said the unsayable, Lance felt a great need to carry on. He sagged in Elli's arms, as weariness, alcohol and loss nearly overwhelmed him.

Elli felt with her leg for the edge of the bed, and guided Lance to sit with her. He leant on her shoulder, and, unbelievably she found she wasn't mistaken in her former suspicion. She could feel the wetness of tears on his face. Loosing her arms, she took his hands in hers.

"Tell me."

"Little to tell. She was lovely: tall, like you, and with red hair – brighter than yours," he said, noticing Elli's hair for the first time, it seemed, as the flickering of oil light caught the chestnut curls. "And her smile lit up the world."

"And she never noticed you?"

"Oh no! She noticed me all right! Gwennie noticed me. The CO was away several times and I accompanied her to dances and the like. And she noticed me. She even noticed me noticing her, if you see what I mean. But half the regiment was going on tour of duty in Iraq, and the CO was too, and I wasn't, that was the problem."

"Problem? I would have thought it was an opportunity." Elli was determined to be sympathetic, even though her thoughts of this Titian-haired idol of Lance were far from kind. Well born, well bred no doubt, expensively educated, socially skilful – all the things she most definitely was not.

"The opportunity was the problem. We couldn't do that to him – it would have been hard at the best of times, but to distract him on active service – we could have had his death or the death of too many of the regiment on our consciences."

"Did he have to know?"

"He might have found out – it's a closed world and gossip flies through it – and anyway it felt so furtive, and guilty, sneaking about…"

Elli didn't dare ask. Did this mean that they ended it, or that they had decided not to start? And why should it matter? He was as firmly entangled as if they never had come together, perhaps more so. She was a silly kid with a crush on an unobtainable older man. Now she thought of it, he always called her 'young' Elli. If she was lucky, she might reach the status she was already pretending to – that of a favoured younger sister. Hope shrivelled.

Lance seemed suddenly to realise that he was sitting on the bed with Elli's hands clasping his. He jumped up, but emotion and alcohol took their toll and he stumbled. Elli leapt to catch him as he reached again for the bedpost. Almost without volition, his arms went round her. In the low light, the dark chestnut-red head was so like his Gwennie's that he almost – but not quite – forgot that it was young Elli. She was slighter, of course, and Gwennie's lifestyle had not led to her developing farm-girl's muscles, and the scent was different … but despair and drink made it difficult to distinguish…

Elli wondered fleetingly if she should protest, if she should be insulted by his sudden interest, so soon after the revelation of his love for someone else. But she decided against it. Instead she raised her face to his, and pulled his head toward her. Her gown slipped further from her shoulder, and suddenly Lance was assisting it, fumbling with the elaborate 1900 fastenings, kissing her all the while.

Lyn arrived, having been sent 'to attend to his master'. When he looked in, he hesitated at the sight of the entwined figures. He was stopped from entering by the strongest injunction he had ever received from Olwen. It was as if a sheet of glass had come down between him and the rest of the room. Stepping forward proved impossible. He searched round in himself for Power to counteract it, when he felt the warning from Olwen in his mind as a command: "Leave them!"

"Ah," he thought. "I wondered... that's why we came here then. Obviously, as Lance would have it." So thinking, he closed the door and went to send the message that his master was now sleeping, and his mistress had retired early.

Chapter 4

In the morning, soon as he heard the other servants stirring, Lyn rose, replaced the ridiculous garments he was forced to wear in the present present, and made his way to Lance's room, glad that custom meant that he would be the first to enter – if Olwen allowed. Wondering what he should find, he was relieved to see only Lance, half-dressed, sitting on the edge of the bed, staring blankly.

"Lyn, what have I done? Elli was here until an hour ago, you know – I think you looked in – but it's very difficult to remember the details. But Elli … that sweet child…how could I take advantage like that? How can I face her again?"

Lyn could not help thinking that an army career might lead to original thought but hardly to original modes of expression. However, he hastened to try to reassure. "Lance, look at me, listen to me. Yes, I looked in. And yes, I saw what was going on. But to me, it looked as if there was no 'advantage' being taken on either side. In fact, given the amount of wine you'd consumed before, I should say, if anything, Elli was the one taking advantage. And certainly, *she's* the one who's been pining after *you* ever since I met you both, and not the other way around!"

"Elli? Young Elli? Pining after me? But I'm years older than she is…and I never gave her any encouragement – or at least I never meant to…"

"Until last night," Lyn said dryly. "You both seemed to be very… encouraging, then!"

Despite himself, Lance smiled briefly. "Oh yes – perhaps I'd better stop calling her young! But, Lyn, however you look at it, it's a breaking of trust. I *am* years older, I *should* have acted differently. I don't quite know what happened. It was almost as if I was, no – not controlled, exactly – but, well, *fated* to act the way I did. And yet, despite the booze, and the despair – I told you about Gwennie that evening in our camp, didn't I? – despite all that, I could have stopped. I didn't want to. What happens now?"

Lyn had grown still. "Fated you say? There may be something in that. No, don't ask me – better if you work it out for yourself, I think. Maybe Elli already has: she seems a well-read young lady."

"Well read? What has her choice of literature have to do with anything?"

"I need to talk with her first. Get dressed, go down to breakfast. Apologise humbly and heartily for your behaviour last night – especially to Katherine Meredith. I think you'll find they've come across army officers on leave before! I'll try to find Elli. I hope she managed the clothes without giving herself away! I wonder – will she be breakfasting? If she's realised what's going on, perhaps she's seeking enlightenment from the books."

He turned and went out, leaving Lance, puzzled but less despairing than he had been, to fight the many buttons of the era's clothing by himself.

Lyn found her, surrounded by books, in the tall library. She turned to him, ashen pale and wide-eyed. "I must talk to you," she said, "but not here."

In reply, Lyn opened the glass door onto the terrace. In the garden below there was a bench, sheltered from the fresh breeze by a yew hedge. They sat down, and Elli drew her cashmere shawl round her shoulders.

"Last night ...last night ..."

"I've seen Lance," Lyn said. "He talked to me a little ... and I'm not surprised..."

"I don't suppose you were," Elli snapped. "You planned all this, didn't you?"

Lyn turned a shocked face to her. "No! Elli, my dear, you must believe me – that is not the case. I was as surprised as you when Olwen brought us here – and now! But the way things are developing ..."

"OK – sorry – very well, if you insist on nineteenth century language. I'll trust you so far. But even so, I know why you're not surprised. Last night...afterwards...Lance turned to me, and stroked my hair, and... and... called me Gwennie...Gwennie... I remembered that was his CO's wife...the one he left the army for. And it rang bells. At home, life's very quiet in the evenings, but we have a good number of books. I've been reading them since I was very young – not so much recently, which is why it's taken me so long. And so this morning I've been reading again. This is why we're here, partly...the books. Tell me I'm wrong if you dare. But: Lance...Lancelot. Gwennie...Guinevere. Elli...Elaine (that's my real name, anyway). And Lyn..." She paused, hardly daring to put her thoughts into words. "Lyn...Merlin?"

"Yes." His craggy face broke into a smile. "Such a relief to have it out in the open. But truly, many of the details I do not know. I told you of the seepage between worlds: have you read my story in books, in the library here, or in your own time?"

Elli pushed the questions about her own role to the back of her mind. If Lyn – Merlin – was about to 'come clean', she would let him lead. She would learn more that way. And if she didn't find out what she needed to know, then she would still ask. As if reciting a lesson in the manner suitable to the age they were now in, she started.

"Merlin was a boy wonder. King Vortigern of Britain wanted to sacrifice him, to stop his tower falling down. But Merlin showed him the underground lake that was the real cause of the tower's falling down. When they drained the lake, two dragons flew out, fighting ..." She broke off. "Dragons? Like Olwen?"

"Yes. I told you Olwen 'seeped'. So did her two brothers. But she is the most skilful of the three, or at least the one most concerned with us. Why did Vortigern want to sacrifice me – I mean me in particular? Do your books say?"

"I think you were the boy without a father they were told to look for – or your father was the devil. I'm sorry if that sounds impertinent."

"No, no!" Lyn dismissed politeness as irrelevant. "Yes, that was who the king was looking for. I was so frightened – I was only about nine years old – but when I saw that my poor mother, normally a courageous and dignified lady, was so much more so, I put my terror aside and listened to my inner voice. And then I knew what to say when I met the king. All that journey from what you call Carmarthen – Caer Merddyn, Merlin's fort – to the fastness of Snowdonia, I listened. Now I believe that voice, and my Power, my magic, such as it is, are my inheritance from my father. Not the devil, but someone – or something – from the other place, like the dragons. My mother never said who my father was, but once I glimpsed him, tall and dark, in the bronze mirror in her room. And when I met Olwen, I started to wonder...

"But this is of little concern to you. Tell me what you have found out, from your reading, from your heart."

Elli looked over the immaculate lawns. She fixed her eyes on a distant, spreading tree, and spoke, as before, as if reciting by rote. That way she could distance the pain, make believe this story had nothing to do with her, hold the frail sphere of calm inside her.

"King Arthur's best knight, Lancelot du Lac, fell in love with the King's wife, Guinevere, and she with him. Some accounts say they never consummated their love – especially these Victorian ones," said Elli, gesturing vaguely toward the library. "Some say they did. But, whichever, the strains broke the Round Table, Lancelot went away, and only returned for the last battle – and by then it was too late...

"But Lyn," Elli broke her calm recital and looked full at him. "What is all this? Lancelot du Lac – Lance Poole: Guinevere, Gwennie. And me ... Elli Tollet... that was a bit of the story I didn't remember, but I've been looking it up. Elaine, the Lily Maid of Astolat – or the other Elaine, the mother of Galahad. They both loved Lancelot, but he barely noticed them, because of his love for Guinevere. Elaine of Astolat, they say, pined away for love of him."

Lyn, drawn in, said, "I read the nineteenth century version last night. Lord Tennyson wrote a wonderful poem, but I barely recognised the story!"

"Lord Tennyson? Oh, good Lord, The Lady of Shallot! But then, there's the other Elaine. Lancelot 'lay with her' to use the polite, poetic, phrase, thinking she was Guinevere. Merlin laid the enchantment on her, because it was important that she gave birth to Lancelot's son, who was Sir Galahad – the odd, prudish one, who found the Holy Grail ..." She stopped, suddenly.

"Lyn, or in this instance, Merlin – *did* you lay an enchantment on her – or on him? If so, how dared you? Did you do the same to Lance last night? How...how...arrogant!"

"Elli, I swear that what happened last night was nothing to do with me. In fact, it was a surprise, although perhaps it shouldn't have been. But the echoes, the parallels... I've seen them ever since I found you were to come with Lance, there in the car park of your college. Olwen was definite."

Elli clutched at his arm. "I don't understand: is this coincidence... inheritance... reincarnation... re-enactment?"

Lyn shook his head. "I don't know. I don't even know what really happened in the end – I think I told you: I can't time travel in my own days. For some reason, Olwen won't even take me within hundreds of years of my own life. By the time I can visit, the accounts are so – approximate – I can't translate it into reality. Perhaps that's why she – Olwen – does it, of course. Keeps me distant, I mean. But there *is* a link, there's a purpose: how it works, I don't know. But it's there, it's there."

Elli interrupted him. "Elaine, the Lily Maid of Astolat – my full name is Elaine Lily Tollet, did you know? And Elaine, who slept with Lancelot, the mother of Galahad ... Which of them am I, Lyn?"

"Oh my dear, there was only the one. They seem to have been separated by the centuries, but there was only one. Elen, or to give the later form of the name, Elaine, of Astolat, in the sub-kingdom of Carbenic. Astolat was isolated, surrounded by marsh and forest. When Lancelot came past, on one of his desperate flights from court, one of his attempts to escape his desire, Elaine fell deeply in love, as only an isolated, romantic innocent could for an older, chivalrous man with a secret sorrow."

Elli gasped. She could feel her cheeks burning, and she leapt up and walked rapidly away. Lyn, sighing, followed and easily overtook her, slowed as she was by her unfamiliar, cumbersome skirts. He gently took her arm, and guided her back to the bench.

"You know!" she accused him. "What you've just described – it's how you see me and Lance, isn't it?"

"There are ... certain similarities," Lyn admitted, wryly. "But there are so many, so many. It doesn't matter, really it doesn't. But I was telling you what happened so long ago. Elaine enticed him, only half-deliberately, and, like most men, he can – could – be weak. He was half-mad with despair, and half-starved when he arrived – quite ill – and she nursed him, and… what you might call the inevitable happened. Then he recovered his health of mind and body, if not of soul, and rode back to torture himself some more. And she – she stopped eating and thus nearly killed herself. Then she discovered she was carrying Lancelot's child. So her father, a stern but loving father, sent her to some holy sisters in another part of the country. He also fabricated the absurd story of my enchanting them, as a second line of defence – defence of Elaine's reputation, that is.

"So, some people thought she'd passed away, but others knew she'd had a son, brought up, like her, in isolation, but with the holy sisters, so with a certain otherworldliness. I don't know anything about the Holy Grail, but young Galahad left on some sort of pilgrimage, a year or so back – in my time that is – and Lancelot went missing – he took his son's departure as a judgment. He left to be a hermit. And here we are with the battle looming…"

"But you know what happens," Elli responded, drawn from her dilemma by Lyn's distress. "So what does it matter?"

"Because Lancelot is the strategist, the planner, the one who Arthur needs. The accounts of the battle that I've read all vary: the earliest says only that Arthur and Mordred die…but who knows how the details will shape history? And anyway, Lancelot should be there. I found him, you know. He won't return…"

Elli looked at him with a sudden awful realisation. "I know why you've come," she said. "Why Olwen insisted. It isn't Lancelot who will be with Arthur. It's Lance!"

"Indeed. Olwen told me, when Lancelot left, that she would find a substitute. I have spent years in this last year, living in your time, living in this time, learning, preparing. And, yes, at times, I despair. This last battle – why all this work when the outcome will still be the death of Arthur?"

Elli remembered something. "You just said, 'Who knows how the details will shape history?' Arthur stopped the Saxon advance, yes?"

"For the last twenty years."

"And now Mordred has turned to the Saxons to help him?"

"Yes, the fool has learnt nothing from the example of poor Vortigern. He has far less excuse, too – just a desire to make himself High King in Arthur's place."

Elli said thoughtfully: "I read somewhere how the halting of the Saxons for some fifty years was vital in the way this land developed. They – the Saxons – became settlers, not ravishers. They became Christian – a religion which, despite all the wars fought in its name, is basically one of peace. They intermarried. Oh, the dispute between Celt and Saxon still goes on in some form – usually sport! – even in my day… but the basic tolerance – perhaps that's what this is all about."

"You mean Mordred must be stopped at whatever cost?"

"I think so. Both sides must exhaust themselves into a time of quiet."

Lyn looked at her with some admiration. "I told Lance you were a well-read young woman. I didn't realise to what good use you could put your reading. So we fight for that – a necessary, if rather depressing, end." He paused. "And this means we bear quite a burden, young Elli. We two must let no one know. The heart – and the hope – must not go out of them."

"You're right," she said. "What about Lance?"

"If he knows what happens already, and remembers, he must be silent as well. Otherwise we keep it from him. And now," he said, changing his tone, "I have spent far too long talking to you already, for a mere manservant. Have you breakfasted? No? Well, go now and apologise for last night. It won't be as bad as I see you fear. You will find Lance has already done so – I sent him! I'll find him and try to explain all this."

"Yes," said Elli, thankful that Lyn did not expect her to do the explaining. "It may come better from you – and you are his batman, so you can talk to him more than you can talk to me."

Helping herself to dishes from the sideboard in the morning room, Elli found that, indeed, the incident of the night before had subsided to an amusing anecdote. Katherine Meredith and Lady Anne were particularly emphatic that she had nothing to blame herself for. The men – and one red-faced, middle-aged female guest – were already preparing for the day's shoot, and the rest of the women were to join them for what sounded like a lavish lunch. Until then, they were very much to be left to their own devices, and Elli, faced with a morning to make mistakes in, suddenly had an idea.

"Lady Anne," she said, "your library is wonderful – so much above anything we have in India. That's why I was late for breakfast – I looked in, and was captivated. Could I spend the morning reading there – or would it be impolite?"

"No, indeed, my dear. After all, we're all so much older than you are, we wouldn't seem very lively company. But this afternoon, perhaps a walk and a look at my garden?"

Elli agreed, again blessing India, and its wonderful provision of excuses. It might also help explain her remarkable ignorance of 1900 gardening for a professed gardener. She applied herself to her kedgeree.

Lance found he had spent a lot of time sitting on the bed recently. First it had been because of the drink, then in shame, and now in pure astonishment. Lyn's explanation of what they were about had at first sent him into blank denial, but that soon moderated – the time travel and the dragon were equally impossible, yet were real. And the chance to be part of a military set-up again – to plan strategy and tactics, perhaps to feel the comradeship and the excitement of danger – was enormously attractive. Although he had a vague memory that this battle did not have a good outcome, it hardly mattered compared with the pluses.

"Oh well," he said, "I've learnt to believe in six impossible things before breakfast on this trip. But, Lyn, can we leave now? If the purpose…purposes… of our coming here have happened and we know what we're about, can't we just go? Avoid seeing more people after last night's fiasco? Just make us 'unnoticeable' along the road to Olwen. Then we can stay with her and leave tonight."

"Possible… but not advisable. As I said to Elli, an army officer becoming drunk at a lavish dinner cannot be an extraordinary happening. The servants didn't seem too surprised."

"No," Lance agreed. "I got the impression that the one who helped me upstairs had done it before."

"Well, if we leave at the usual time tomorrow, it will be far easier for me to have our hosts gently and gradually forget your visit than if we go early, unexpectedly and in a way that will cause comment. But we won't be this way again, so we could just leave, of course."

"No, that wouldn't be fair on the Bairstows: a poor return for their kindness. What about the other guests?"

"Even easier. A tweak, a confusion – who remembers, a year on, details of people they met fleetingly, even without my help?"

"Very well," said Lance. "If it makes things easier."

"And use it as the calm before the storm," said Lyn. "To gather your strength. Now, what are we meant to do today, exactly? How can we best prepare ourselves, so I have to use the minimum of Power?"

After breakfast, Elli went to her room to tidy up. In the corridor she met Lance and Lyn – the first time she had seen Lance since the early morning. He looked slightly embarrassed, muttering that he had to go and see about borrowing guns. As he left, Lyn made for the servants' stairs, but Elli stopped him, after following Lance with her eyes till he turned onto the landing and could be seen no more.

"Well?" she asked.

"He's accepted it. He said something about having had 'to believe six impossible things before breakfast' on this adventure."

Elli smiled. "I might have guessed he'd know his Lewis Carroll."

"But now I must go. Lance has been instructing me in the theory of loading his gun – I believe I will be called upon to load his – and I want to get some practical experience before I have to do it for real! But Elli, my dear, one thing more…"

"Yes?"

"Try not to look at Lance in quite that way. And if you… visit … each other, tonight, be very discreet. There are very few societies that condone incest, and I'm sure this isn't one of them!" With a smile at her shocked expression and reddening face, he left her.

The day passed, and it seemed a little easier than the day before. Elli was wary, however. She remembered that when, as a child, she had had a new bike, she did not fall off it on the first day, but about a week later, lulled into a false sense of security, into believing concentration was no longer necessary.

The morning she spent reading in the library – mainly Lady Anne's collection of Arthurian books, which suddenly seemed very relevant. They also accustomed her to the cadences of Victorian English and made her feel more confident to face the rest of the day.

At lunchtime, she donned her jacket and hat, and accompanied the other ladies to where a great deal of food had been assembled on trestle tables. Linen tablecloths and fine china and glass gave the impression of a wedding buffet incongruously served outdoors, and the food, mainly cold but with a wonderful hot soup, was very good.

She managed to exchange a few words with Lance – after all, it was only natural to find out how her brother was getting on. Quite well it seemed. He was a pretty good marksman and this compensated for his lack of experience of pheasant shooting. Everyone accepted that he wouldn't have had much pheasant shooting in India. He had also survived much good-natured teasing about his behaviour the night before – and some of his worst shots had been put down to a massive hangover. But even Julian had been friendly.

In the afternoon, she changed into a loose-fitting dress of Alix's, and, given the nod by Lady Anne, experienced the release of a few hours without corsets. The gardens were indeed lovely, and Lady Anne talked about them with infectious enthusiasm. Elli racked her brains for convincing information about Indian gardening and had spoken of the dry season, the monsoon, and wonderful herbs and spices.

Dinnertime came round again, and again Ward helped her into a beautiful, if restricting gown – this one of white with navy trim. "Will you need my help tonight?" Ward asked. "I would feel happier if I discharged my duty to you – my lady is very good, but I don't like her imposing her ideas on her guests."

Elli thought. Would Lance visit her? Should she expect it? Would she go to him? She realised how lucky she had been, that Ward had not come to help her last night. But tonight she had the benefit of a little forward planning. "I tell you what, Ward. If I retire before eleven o'clock, I'd welcome your help. But I don't know what will go on tonight, so don't wait indefinitely."

Dinner was earlier that night – 7.30 – as it was assumed that the men (and the one woman) would be ravenous after the day's shooting. And it seemed to Elli that it was simpler fare – fewer courses, and hearty ones. She decided to trust Lance not to overindulge and spent her time having a most interesting discussion about, surprisingly, Shakespeare and Gilbert and Sullivan with the elderly man she was sitting next to. He worked in the City, and spent his leisure time in London visiting the theatre. Only once did she hear Lance's voice: "I know about campaigns against people who know the land better than I do. I'm sorry, sir, but I think it'll take more than a few weeks to quell the Boers!"

"Ha!" thought Elli. "Hindsight is twenty – twenty vision!"

The time when the women were alone together was shorter than was normal, as the men, it seemed, were aiming at an early night, so as to be ready for an early start, for some would only manage the morning shoot before having to return to London. The women, and some of the men, were to attend morning service held for this occasion, in the small chapel attached to the house at the back, through the library – "We usually go to

Chelford, but this weekend is so busy, and the vicar so willing to come here!"

When the men joined them, Elli found herself once more cajoled to play and sing 'that charming, plaintive song you sang yesterday'. As she played, she wondered about the words and Lance's reaction. Now she knew the story of him and his Gwennie, it seemed more explicable.

The party began to break up early, at about a quarter to eleven. Lance came over, held her hands and gave her a chaste, brotherly kiss on her forehead. "When will the coast be clear?" he muttered.

"Give it an hour," said Elli, hope and delight churning through her.

It was well gone midnight, and Elli had almost given up hope. She had drawn back a curtain and was standing by the window, in the dark, watching the rising moon in the east. There was a turning of the door handle, and Lance, resplendent in a silk dressing gown, slipped in. He saw Elli turn toward him, visible in the light from the corridor. She was wearing a long white nightdress, and her hair had been brushed back and tied with a white ribbon.

"A vision in white! It suits you!"

"And you…you look like Noel Coward!"

"If you think I would let you see me in the nightshirt I'm supposed to wear!"

A short, awkward silence fell. How to get over the gulf, Elli wondered. Perhaps I shouldn't have come, thought Lance. He looked round the room for inspiration. "It's the first time I've been in here. It's less Spartan than my room – but the bed's a lot narrower. Do you think the heir has a larger bed for seducing housemaids?"

"Really, Lance, I think better of Lady Anne and Sir Edward! No – it's just that girls require more furniture – larger wardrobe, dressing table etc. So there's less space."

"Sir Edward ... do you realise that in a few years they'll be calling him Teddy Bear?"

Elli laughed, and with the old friendship re-establishing itself, Lance relaxed and went to her, putting his arms around her. She pulled out of the embrace and turned, and went to draw the curtain over again. Then, standing with her back to the faint light that still made its way through, she took a deep breath.

"Lance, why are you here? Is it to prove that last night wasn't just a drunken one-night stand? To show Lyn and Olwen that we're not just following their patterning, their plans? Or is it because, even if I'm not your Gwennie, you still want me?"

"Elli... It was not just a one-night stand. At the moment I couldn't care less about any patterns or plans. And yes, you are not Gwennie, but yes, I most definitely still want you!"

"Ambiguous," thought Elli hazily, as Lance kissed her. "Am I only wanted because Gwennie isn't here?" He kissed her again, and her last coherent thought for a while was, "But then, do I care?"

Some time later, the moon shining through the gap in the inexpertly drawn curtains woke her. She turned and brushed the hair off Lance's forehead, and he woke too, reaching out and holding her close. She found the music from earlier that night was in her mind, and she asked: "'The Carnival is Over' – was that your song? Yours and Gwennie's?"

"Yes," he said with a grimace. "It seemed ...appropriate."

"And 'Plaisir d'Amour'?"

"My song. I think I've played it almost every night since...since I came to Cheshire. Sometimes, time after time, for most of the evening."

"Really, Lance!" said Elli, sternly. "How very...self-indulgent... of you!"

Lance laughed. "Yes, it was, wasn't I? You give me a wonderful sense of proportion, young Elli!"

"You said you wouldn't call me young again. I bet you never called Gwennie young!"

His reply was interrupted by his kisses. "Do not...keep bringing her... into the conversation...I do not aim...to think of her...now!"

"More ambiguity," thought Elli. And: "So what?"

This time, Lance did not allow himself to sleep. "I must go before the meanest servant is about. Did Lyn warn you of the unacceptability of incest?"

"He did. Did he tell you his plans for tomorrow? I've no idea what happens."

"Yes, a little. They involve a mid-afternoon departure, an omnibus toward Macclesfield and leaving our bags on it, to go there without us. But he *has* thought it out. Just follow my lead at breakfast. I'll see you then, my dear."

They were both down in good time the next morning.

Lady Anne cast a concerned glance in their direction. "You look tired, Elli. Did you not sleep well?"

Elli did not dare to look at Lance. "I was a little...disturbed... for some of the night." Lance seemed to be having a coughing fit. "I think I may have overindulged a little. Your cook is excellent, and the food rather too tempting."

As she said later – not a word of a lie in any of that!

Soon Sir Edward appealed to Elli. "Your brother says you aim to continue your journey from Macclesfield. He and his man have researched it – best times and so on. Trouble is, I'll be stretched to get you there – you'll need to go when the London party make for Chelford and we'll also be shooting then – and on top of all that, we've had a message saying that one of the Bromley-Davenports is unexpectedly at home and could he join the shoot – and we must keep in with our neighbours, you know!"

"That's no problem, Sir Edward. Sayer informs us there is an excellent omnibus which stops just opposite your gates."

"But I don't like the thought of a young lady like you on an omnibus!"

"With an army major and his batman to protect her? Besides, I loved riding them in London, as well as the underground trains – and the hackney cabs, of course. Such experiences for someone straight out of India!"

Lady Anne interposed. "Stop fussing, Teddy! If I didn't have guests to see to, I might go with them myself: it sounds fun!"

"Very well," said Sir Edward, reluctantly. When she turned away, Elli noticed Lyn standing quietly near the door, a blank, concentrating look on his face.

She had to wait for the lunchtime break in the shooting to hear the details of the plan from Lance.

"Sir Edward is insisting that one of the footmen carry our few bags and see us on the omnibus. So, we get on, and get off at the next stop, near Olwen. Lyn will tuck our bags under the seat, having put labels on them to wait for collection at Preston."

"And the purpose of that?"

"To take as little of 1900 with us as possible. Clothes can be burnt, later. And Elli, he says you must put jewellery in your bag."

"That seems fair enough – but I'll be sorry to lose the filigree bracelet I wore Friday evening. I love its design, and, and... well, it was just about the only thing that stayed on, later!"

Lance grinned at her. "So true! But it looks almost eastern. Hang on to it, and when all this is over, and we're back home, I'll say I brought it from Iran and I've given it to you." Elli nodded, unable to speak. So Lance was at least considering them as a long-term item, then? But probably, to him it was all so far in the future that the remark meant nothing.

They bade a fond farewell to Sir Edward as the men who were to shoot that afternoon went back to their guns, and then, later, to Lady Anne, busy entertaining the remaining ladies of the party. Elli felt enormously uncomfortable with the offers to visit again, and the good wishes to Aunt Helen, knowing that soon no one here would remember them. But it was better that way: it would ensure no break of what science fiction writers generally called 'the space/time continuum' – no ripples on the surface of history.

It was James, Lance's supporter of Friday night, who carried their bags, despite Lyn's protests that he should do so. "Mustn't make my Lord and Lady feel guilty, must we? This way they'll feel they've given you a reasonable send-off." A large tip –much of the remaining nineteenth century money that Lyn had given Lance – saw him smiling and waving as they boarded the horse-drawn vehicle.

Lyn used most of the money still left to pay for their tickets. That done, he sat down and let the purse slide between the seats and tucked the bags away. Then he woke Olwen and together they managed to erase from the minds of driver and passengers the strange party who brought tickets for Macclesfield but got off almost immediately at the Monk's Heath stop.

Ten minutes after leaving the omnibus, they reached the green shelter of Olwen's wing, and arranged themselves to wait – and sleep if possible – until the dark of night.

Interlude 2: Causes

Elli woke to a beam of light, as she had in the small hours the night before. This time, she was lying on a blanket and alone, but from outside the wing-cave she could hear the low murmur of voices. She wrapped the blanket round her and joined the men, who were sitting on the other blanket, looking east. Lyn turned as she came.

"I'm glad you're awake – I was just coming to rouse you, anyway. I've been filling Lance in with some background – things you know already. But now you need to hear some more – although my own knowledge is far from perfect."

Lance smiled a welcome and Elli sat next to him. He put his arm round her and she leaned back against his warmth. She found herself teasing Lyn. "Merlin the magician? Merlin the soothsayer? – Oh, I see, Lyn Sayer, how clever! Merlin the wizard? Surely you know all about these things!"

Lyn pursed his lips and shook his head, smiling. "Come, Elli, is Merlin ever in Arthur's court once it is established? In any of the stories?"

Elli thought. "No, he isn't – I mean you aren't. You – well, you disappear – locked in a crystal cave by your pupil, or lover, Nimue, or Viviane. Yet she's supposed to be a force for good, and often advises Arthur, which is strange, when I come to think of it…"

Lyn grinned. "Yes, I've read that too. I don't understand the cave bit, but I have been away from Arthur for the best part of thirty years – and I *have* been with she whom you call Viviane. In Ireland, mostly."

"Why? Did you and Arthur quarrel?"

"Indeed not. But remember, when I said there were certain things I would not do, even to bring about the result I wanted?"

"You mentioned twenty-first century weapons," said Lance.

"Yes, and I have not taken so much as a nineteenth century shotgun. Neither will I use Olwen to terrify the opposing army. I *will* use her to time travel and translate and to guide me, so I can help bring about what is recorded, but not to make things happen the way I might dream of."

"So?"

"So, once I'd helped Arthur to be High King it had to be his rule, his decisions, his triumphs, his mistakes. I left. Viviane visited occasionally, but I knew if I did that, I would find it too hard to leave again. I have only been back less than two years. Olwen, who has been near me, conveyed a message from another old pupil, Arthur's half-sister, Morgan, begging me for help. So I came."

"Morgan la Fey?" Elli breathed.

"Why were you sent for?" Lance wanted to know.

"Yes, Morgan – another ambivalent character in your stories. And this time, she was so, and possibly still is, in real life. But that is her story, and maybe she will tell it to you."

Elli kept quiet, but somehow the thought of hearing Morgan la Fey telling her own life story brought home the enormity of the adventure more than anything else, even flying dragon-back, time travel, and realising Lyn's true identity. Perhaps it was that these had been revealed gradually, with time to anticipate. She dragged herself back to listen to Lyn's briefing.

"I was called back because of the feuds that had torn Arthur's land apart. Even his Circle of Companions – his twelve sworn sword brothers – were fighting amongst themselves. But it was too late for me to do anything, if it had ever been possible, which I doubt. Its roots were too deep, and the man nurturing the chaos for his own benefit, too clever, too determined."

"Who was that?" queried Lance.

"Let me come to that a little later. There were two main problems, but they got muddled. One was the doomed love between Lancelot and Guinevere. The other was the feud between the sons of Pellinore – the father of Elin, your predecessor, Elli, and the sons of Lot, and his wife Morgause."

"I know who she was!" said Elli. "Arthur's half-sister, like Morgan."

"Indeed. Now, there *was* a bad woman – she had cause in her life to be embittered, I suppose. But I think that was just an excuse for her to behave the way she always wanted to.

"You must realise that you are not going to one of your romantic, elegant, chivalric settings, such as I have seen in your books portraying Arthur. It won't be pretty-pretty, I warn you. This is Britain after the Romans, with Arthur trying to impose the same sort of overall unity that the Romans had done. Now, there are smaller kingdoms as well as the remaining idea of Britain. Arthur's family have kept as close to Roman traditions – and particularly army ideas – as has been sensible.

"Morgause, on the other hand, convinced herself that Arthur had usurped her place, that power should pass through the female line, as it does, frequently, in these isles. Crazy though, for any claim she had was because of her stepfather, Arthur's father, King Uther. But for many years the children of Lot and Morgause were amongst the closest to Arthur. You may have heard of them – Gawain, Gaheris, Agravaine and Gareth."

"Gawain and Gareth, certainly," said Elli, drawn into the tale, and forgetting, for the moment, that she was beginning to feel cold.

"Yes, I know of Sir Gawain," added Lance. "But these others – all the information and all the Celtic names aren't easy to assimilate, even for someone used to army briefings."

Lyn nodded. "Yes – this is a kind of crash course in our recent history, which must seem completely alien to you." He paused, then: "I've an idea though. Wait." He paused and his face took on a blank look for a moment. Then he smiled.

"Olwen is willing to try and send you pictures of some of the events, to help fix them in your mind. They'll be an odd selection, as she refuses to send you pictures of anyone you're likely to meet – she seems to feel this may make you prejudge them."

Elli looked at Lance whose face had a set, stubborn look. She smiled a little, amused by his uneasiness with the great beast. "Come on," she said. "It will really help."

"Yes, I expect it would. But I don't like the idea, and I don't know if I can be...open enough."

Lyn gave a short laugh. "Olwen has just pictured you to me. She sees you surrounded by spears – 'barricaded against her' would be the phrase it translates to. But look, Elli finds rapport with Olwen easy, and you find rapport with Elli ...easy, even pleasurable. Hold tight to her and I will try to use my power to relax you a little – if you don't mind."

"All right," said Lance, somewhat reluctantly, and tightened his hold round Elli's waist. "I'm ready."

Suddenly, in Elli's mind she saw a tall, dark, commanding woman of middle years, holding a squalling baby, and arguing furiously with a sturdy, angry man.

"Ah," said Lyn. "Morgause and her husband, Lot."

"What are they arguing about?" asked Elli, and, to Lance, "Can you see them?"

"Sort of: like a reflection of a reflection. But yes, I can certainly see them, and feel their anger, and hear it in their voices, although Olwen isn't doing her Babel fish act at the moment. What *are* they arguing about?"

"No, no translation," said Lyn. "She is showing it to you exactly. They are arguing about the baby, Mordred."

"Mordred," said Elli. "King Arthur's incestuous son? So all that is true? Morgause and Arthur? She seducing him, him unknowing?"

Lyn was shaking his head. "Mordred is ill-tongued, and warped in his soul. He is the illegitimate son of Morgause, that much is true, but by which of her many lovers no one knows – it may well be that even she did not! But Lot knew that the child was not his – he had been away on campaign – and he took a rather less generous view of his wife's child than he would have expected if the boy had been his by-blow. Mordred was brought up by his aunt, Morgan."

"So where does this incest idea come from?" asked Lance. "Even I have heard that Mordred was the son of Arthur and his half-sister."

"Unbelievably," said Lyn, shaking his head again, "from Mordred himself."

"What?" said Lance.

"Why?" said Elli.

"Two reasons. They may seem to be contradictory, but Mordred has a good understanding of people, and how they will react. Firstly, to strengthen his claim to the throne – he was only the youngest of Arthur's nephews, after all. And, secondly, to bring Arthur into disrepute. It was only whispered at court, to start with, but by the time he, Mordred, left, it was being shouted. And nothing originally about Arthur being unknowing – that seems to have crept in to keep faith with Arthur's character, somehow.

"When Mordred first arrived at court he started to foment the old feuds, especially the one between his brothers and the sons of Pellinore – Elen's brothers and half-brothers. Why, I'm not sure: probably a general love of mischief and an idea of making life difficult for Arthur, and so, perhaps, set himself up as the new leader-in- waiting.

"The feud had withered because of a lack of feeding – Arthur proved wise in peace as well as war. Then, about four years ago, two things happened. Pellinore died – Lot was long dead – so Arthur decided that this meant he could draw a line under the feud, and invited Pellinore's sons – at least some of them, there are many – back to court. And indeed it might have worked. But for the other happening: the arrival in court of Mordred. Perhaps I do him wrong – he was young (he must have been conceived shortly before Badon) and, remember I wasn't there." But his voice held vast doubt.

"Then Morgause, although by now a mature woman – in fact if it were not for some faerie blood in that family she would be considered old – well, she took a young lover."

"A toy-boy," said Lance amused.

"Is that your term for it? Yes, a toy boy, if you like. Disastrously, it was one of Pellinore's sons, Lamorak. Fresh meat for her. Then Mordred found out, and, always one to push others into action, got the brothers to see for themselves."

Olwen was 'sending' again. This time Elli found herself sucked into the scene and felt like an unseen participant, the more so because it was being enacted as silently as possible, with no speech.

She seemed to be standing in a corridor, in what appeared to be a Roman villa, but with the walls hung with very un-Roman woollen hangings, brightly coloured like the blanket of Lyn's that she was wrapped in. Back along the corridor, a man stood in the shadows, and four young men were pushing at a door on the left. It gave suddenly, and the men stumbled into the room, drawing their swords as they did so.

Now Elli could see what was inside. By the light of brazier and oil lamp, she saw quite clearly the same woman, Morgause, sitting bolt upright in bed, clutching the bed-furs to cover her nakedness. She looked older, but not much, still a mature, attractive woman. At her side a naked young man was leaping out of the bed, embarrassment writ large on his reddening face. Suddenly it changed to a look of complete horror as one of the intruders, white-faced and with weeping eyes, raised his sword and beheaded Morgause. Then the others used their swords to kill the defenceless youth.

"Oh my god," said Elli, pulling back to the present, shaking her head to free it of the images. "Lance, did you see that?"

Lance, tight-lipped, nodded. "I did indeed." Then, to Lyn: "This must have led to chaos, surely."

"Indeed. Arthur was horrified, and his court divided. Mordred tried to suggest that as a newcomer, he was the only one of Arthur's kin to be trusted. He wanted Arthur to follow Roman practice and adopt him as his son and successor. Arthur would not – he has always been a good judge of people, and he felt, instinctively, the *wrongness* of Mordred.

"So Mordred sowed further strife. I gather from Cai and Bedwyr that this was when the rumours of Mordred being Arthur's son were first heard. His mother was dead, and could not refute them – I think she would have: lustful and deceitful as she was, this would have shocked her – and shamed her, if it was believed.

"Then he started on Arthur's other weakness – Lancelot and Guinevere."

Another picture, a brief one this time. It was the back view of a man and woman, much of a height, he dark and she with shining auburn hair. They were standing side by side, not touching, looking out of a window at something Elli could not see. The feeling between them was palpable, even to Elli. She heard Lance draw a sharp breath, but he said nothing until Lyn said, "Known about by many, but never mentioned." Then Lance said, remembering Elli's comment of two nights before, "Like the elephant in the room."

Lyn threw him a startled glance. "I suppose you could say that. But Mordred mentioned it – all shock and rural innocence he seemed, according to Cai and Bedwyr. Sorrowful too. He urged Arthur to prove the rumour wrong, to go and see for himself. Of course Mordred knew they were together, that this was one of few times over the twenty years or more that they had loved each other that they *were* together. Circumstances, and the need for secrecy, and the reluctance they felt about betraying Arthur, all stood in their way."

Lance had turned away, so Elli could not see his face, but she thought she heard a muttered, "Oh, I can understand that!"

"And," said Elli, to dissipate the charged atmosphere, "there they were."

"There they were, indeed. Arthur became ice-cold, and banished Lancelot. He confined Guinevere to her rooms. He set his nephews on guard. And so, for some months, it rested."

Again, a vision filled Elli's mind. Another corridor, another old Roman villa – or perhaps the same one. From behind a door came the sound of weeping. In front of the door, two of the sons of Morgause kept guard. As Lyn continued talking, the scene carried on: servants went in and out the room, with food and other necessaries, each of the brothers took his turn before the door, which, except for allowing the servants passage, stayed locked. "This went on for months," Lyn said, "until Mordred managed to let Lancelot know that Guinevere was about to be executed. False, of course. Arthur, like a wounded animal, had gone to hide himself in the mountains, and nothing could be done till his return. But Lancelot believed, and came, and tried to rescue his lady."

A dark-haired man in the corridor, sword drawn. With a cry, he killed the nearest guard – Elli thought it was Gaharis – before the surprised man could get his sword more than half drawn. More armed men came behind the intruder, who must surely be Lancelot, just as a third brother, leading a group of soldiers, came round the opposite corner. The vision faded to the sounds of sword on sword, and cries of anger and pain.

"The sons of Pellinore," said Lyn sadly, "were those helping Lancelot, of course. They would join in any action against the family of Lot and Morgause, and Gaharis was killed outright, as you saw, and two others died of wound-fever later. Of Morgause's brood, only Gawain – and his half-brother, Mordred – remained.

"Lancelot freed Guinevere, you know, but she would not go with him. When Arthur returned, on top of all the horror he had to deal with, there was the fact that she had gone, leaving a dignified message that she would be the cause of strife no longer, and would go and do penance among the holy women.

"Arthur had been considering re-instating Guinevere as queen and wife. Almost unheard of – but when was Arthur ever conventional? And it might have worked, have healed Britain – and he loved her greatly, of course. But Guinevere had left.

"Gawain, a man mad with grief, had gone after Lancelot – once his closest friend amongst the Companions. Mordred tried to get Arthur to name himself, as the only nephew left, as the King's heir. He might have done so too, but he heard the dreadful rumour that Mordred had been spreading about his fathering and threw him out.

"And then Gawain found Lancelot and forced him to fight. Lancelot, horrified at his own actions, was reluctant, but he was ever the better swordsman, and killed Gawain. Then he bade farewell to Arthur, and left. And this was when Morgan, quite newly returned to court and aghast at all this, begged me to return.

"Since then, Mordred has been raising an army amongst the discontented – mainly Lot's men – and adding to its numbers by Saxons with whom he has promised to share Britain. And some fifteen to eighteen months on, we are arrived at the final battle. And you, Lance, are to replace Lancelot – oh, and probably Gawain, and Gaharis, and so many others. Are you up to it?"

Lance looked at him. "I very much doubt it," he said. "But I'm all you've got, and Olwen and you have taken great pains to fetch me, so the least I can do is try."

Elli pressed his hand, and, feeling there was no more to be said on this subject, asked about something she had wondered about since she had first come across the Arthurian legends. "What was Guinevere like?"

Lyn did not answer immediately. When he spoke, it was in a quiet, sad voice. "Very beautiful, it goes without saying."

Again, a sending. Elli saw clearly Olwen's picture of Guinevere – for it must be she – and she was, indeed, very beautiful. It was the woman she had seen moments earlier from the back, tall and with a sweet expression and very striking auburn curling hair. Beside her, Elli heard Lance gasp, and say, "Oh no, no!" Lyn turned to look at him, but as Lance said no more, he carried on speaking.

"She was not a bad woman, like Morgause. Or one who tried to be on the side of right, and sometimes got things wrong, like Morgan. She was…simpler…than those two. She was very young when she became Arthur's wife, and then their lack of children was a great sorrow to them both. But her main weakness was, I think, was loving Arthur too much."

"Arthur?" Elli was incredulous. "But she loved Lancelot!"

"Of course she loved Arthur." Lance spoke in a cold voice, but Elli could hear the edge to his voice – he sounded, unbelievably, as if he might cry. "Of course she did," he continued. "Olwen has just shared that picture with me and I wish I had refused to see any of her damned sendings. Guinevere is my Gwennie – I'd know her anywhere! And yes, yes, she loved her husband."

Now it was Elli who wanted to cry, but whether for herself or Lance, she wasn't sure. She lifted Lance's hand and pressed it to her face, and relaxed slightly when he responded by stroking her cheek with his finger.

Lyn continued without comment on Lance's outburst. "As I said, she loved Arthur. Indeed, from the start she was jealous of anyone too close to him. She disliked Cai – Arthur's foster-brother – and me. Her distrust strengthened my resolve to go. And at first – I saw this with my own eyes – she set out to attract Lancelot so as to separate him from Arthur: for as soon as Lancelot arrived from the land you call France, he and Arthur were like long-lost brothers."

"And then she was in too deep. And so was he." Lance's voice came out of the darkness. "He should have got out whilst he could."

"Perhaps. But then Badon might not have been won, and everything would have changed – as Elli and I were discussing earlier." Lyn's voice became more upbeat, as if to disperse the tension. "But enough of the past. You will see the present state of affairs soon enough. Time to change clothes again!"

Book 3: Camp and Conflict

Chapter 1

Elli found her new clothes very comfortable, if a little scratchy. Lyn had collected several loose tunics and pairs of trousers that he had left at the cave in his own time for himself and Lance, and Elli had one of these outfits on. She thought it must have been meant for Lyn, as the trousers were only a little too long for her, whereas Lance's legs must be a good two inches longer than hers. The trousers and jerkins were in a fine soft woollen weave, hers a muted green, Lance's a russet brown, as were Lyn's.

Lyn looked at her critically. "I didn't know I would need women's clothes, and you're going to cause enough disruption as it is. Oh well, I'll see if I can borrow a skirt for you when we get to the camp."

Elli started to protest.

"Yes, I know you're 'trousers girl', but let's keep surprises to a minimum: there'll be enough for everyone to cope with. Put your 1900 stuff in a saddlebag, but keep your boots on – we'll find you others when we get there, if needs be.

"Now," he said, "we must be away before dawn catches us. I think we'd better get ready to fly."

"Obviously," said Lance, somewhat predictably.

"Well, let's see." Lyn was in mysterious prophet mode, thought Elli, as she climbed up to her accustomed seat.

What happened next was a surprise, and explained Lyn's remarks. Olwen made no attempt to rise into the air. Instead she shuddered slightly, and Elli, recovering some of her rapport with the great green creature, felt an intense wave of concentration.

The darkness rippled and waved around them, and suddenly the sky was covered with cloud, and a persistent rain was falling. It was cold, too.

"Well," said Lyn, cheerfully, "here we are!"

"We haven't moved!" said Elli, puzzled.

"Oh, but we have – in time, right?" said Lance.

"Indeed." Elli thought distractedly that Lyn said 'indeed' as often as Lance said 'obviously'. "I was almost certain that this was where we were, but the landscape has changed so much I could not be absolutely sure. But now it is a cold, wet, February night. Let's climb down and get under cover as soon as possible. We'll wait till dawn to approach the camp." He waved westward, where Elli found she could see the flickering lights of campfires.

For what Elli thought was probably the last time, they sheltered under Olwen's wing with the blankets extracted from the capacious saddlebags. She found she was still bone-tired, and despite everything, slept almost immediately, with Lance curled protectively around her, and Lyn sitting watching the light outside change.

She was woken by Lance some two hours later, when the light of day was filtering in. It was still raining, however, and once more the blankets were called into use, this time as cloaks pulled over their heads. Lyn had a real cloak, and a shapeless felt hat pulled well down.

"Olwen will stay here – we need her near to help translate, but some of the men, and all the horses and mules are wary of her."

"Are there many animals?" asked Lance, as they set off down the hill toward the camp.

"Most of the army fight on foot, but we have cavalry, as well as the baggage animals – mules and horses. Moreover, the twelve Companions and Arthur have their wonderful white horses. Most of the twelve are natural horsemen, but all have become skilled – even the new Companions, who have come into the Circle since the dreadful losses."

"Of course," said Elli, negotiating her way down the rain-slippery slope. "There must be replacements for Gawain and Lancelot and the others."

"Lancelot sounds a very un-Celtic name," said Lance. "I've been meaning to ask you about that. It's not even French, if that's what he was."

"Indeed not," said Lyn. "Olwen and I have not been very consistent, I'm afraid. Sometimes we have 'translated' the names into the versions you know, or the Welsh of your time, or even left them untouched." He stopped, laying his hand on Lance's arm. "But that reminds me of something we should have talked about – what shall I call you and tell others you are called?"

"What's the problem? Oh, I see! In such company, I can hardly be called Lance!"

"Moreover, in the heat of battle, we cannot rely on Olwen making all smooth. She will be further off, anyway. Is there any other name we can use, that you are used to?"

Lance resumed walking slowly, giving it some thought. Then he said: "All through school I was known by my surname – how does Poole sound?"

"Pwll is a name of Celtic legend – a powerful warrior that ventured into the underworld, and returned unscathed. It may be taken as a good omen, and will be close enough for the others to recognise."

"Yes it is. Pwll or Poole?"

"You can manage the Welsh double l," interrupted Elli, admiringly.

"I've served alongside Welsh Regiments, and my Latin master was Welsh – a Mr Jenkins. He made sure we could pronounce his own tongue as well as the one he taught us."

"Poole will be fine. Or rather, Powell, as that is probably what the Welsh tongues will make of it, anyway!"

As they reached the bottom of the slope, Elli stopped, and said, giggling, "Just as well – otherwise, we'd be Pwll Elli!"

Lance laughed. "Even worse than Teddy Bear!"

Lyn looked puzzled. "What's so funny?"

Lance recovered and said: "It's a town – Pwllheli that is, in North Wales – not far from our cave, I imagine. No, definitely Powell– I don't want to start laughing at inappropriate moments!"

On the plain beyond them they could see a large encampment becoming visible as the day lightened. A small turf bank separated the camp from the countryside, and rows of tents, surprisingly regularly set out, disappeared into the mist of drizzle.

"That looks almost Roman," said Lance, approvingly.

"Arthur's family have always tried to stay close to Roman ways. Wisely, Arthur has adapted them to the new life, and mixed it with the best of Celtic ways – much more use of horses, for example. But he tries for efficiency in the army: in the setting out of this camp, for example. Many of these tents, especially the eight-person ones for the foot soldiers, are old Roman ones, or constructed on that pattern. You will see bits of old Roman uniform and weaponry – especially the short stabbing sword alongside the Celtic broadside. And Arthur, and those close to his family, speak Latin as well as what you would call 'early' Welsh."

They were approaching the camp. An earth ramp led over the ditch, and the way was blocked by a rough gate of poles.

Two men, wrapped in cloaks, stood on either side and challenged them as they approached.

"Not that we expect trouble," said Lyn. "The enemy is still days away, I think. He pushed his hat to the back of his head, and was rewarded by excited greetings from the two men.

"Merddin Emrys," said one, "you are returned! And quickly, too!"

"Indeed," said Lyn.

Of course, he's not absolutely sure how soon he's back, thought Elli. Although I expect Olwen's done what he wanted.

"You have not been absent more than three days," said the second, "but you've had time to shave your beard!"

"And find companions." The first soldier was too polite to question the High King's Advisor openly, but could not resist a questioning tone.

"Indeed. I have brought the High King a tactician, a planner, a fine soldier, to help fill the place of him who has gone. He is Powell, bearing a name of repute. And with him travels Elli, a woman of knowledge and wisdom."

The soldiers looked at each other trying to hide their surprise. Then they made the Roman soldier's gesture of greeting, striking clenched fist to opposing shoulder.

Lyn bowed his head in return. "It is full early to see the High King. Can you take us to a quiet tent and provide us with some refreshment?"

At a low-voiced summons another soldier came from one of the nearer tents, and replaced one of the guards, who then led them further into the camp. The tents seemed to be of leather, neat squares sewn together to make larger areas, but otherwise they looked remarkably like old-fashioned ridge tents thought Elli. Occasionally there was a small round structure, and some that seemed to be made of an unidentified fabric. There were many iron braziers, a few of which still had small fires or smoking embers from the night before.

Eventually, they came to a circle of somewhat smaller tents in what was probably the middle of the encampment. In the centre was a larger, walled, tent, more like a small marquee, with two guards outside and a banner on a tall pole. The banner hung limply in the drizzle, but seemed to have red and gold embroidery on it. Their guide made no attempt to approach this, but turned and walked round the circle and stopped at one of the tents. As he did so, he turned to Lyn and said, " We have put aside this tent for you, Merddin Emrys. You departed so quickly, and spent your last night with the High King, that you may not have realised where we had placed it. I will light you a brazier, and send for refreshments."

He held open the tent flap, and they entered. The smell of leather was strong, and mixed with the smell of crushed grass. The soldier pulled out two collapsible stools for Elli and Lance whilst Lyn sat on the truckle bed, which was the main, indeed, the only other piece of furniture apart from a small table. Elli huddled into her blanket. "I hope he lights that brazier soon," she muttered. "I'm frozen!"

"Indeed," said Lyn. "What possessed Mordred to campaign in winter, I do not know. Generally, campaigning is from late March to harvest. Perhaps he thought he would catch us unprepared, but to move an army through the mud and cold and wet, even using the old Roman roads, is tedious and tortuous. Food and shelter and warmth are all real problems. And now the melting snow water, and the streams it overfills, have made the ground even soggier."

Lance said, "Why are you camped here, waiting?"

"That in part is the fault of the season as well. The travelling is exhausting, as I have said, and we do not want to lengthen our supply lines, or have them running through regions where we cannot count on absolute loyalty. And to the east lies a people that have ever put their first loyalty to Lot's kin. We risk them joining Mordred and swelling his numbers, but better that than have them at our back. And we hope the long journey will tire him too, and that the people he passes through maintain enough loyalty to Arthur to remain uninvolved in what they probably see as a squabble within the High King's court. I do not think many will join him."

At that point, the guide reappeared with a lighted brazier.

"Thank you," said Lyn. "It's Merion, isn't it? From Ynys Môn?"

The young man grinned widely. "You were with us for such a short time and yet you remember me! Yes, that is who I am. You may also recall my father Eynon, who was with the High King at the beginning."

"Indeed," said Lyn. "Does he still live?"

"Yes – old and crotchety, now, but in good health, apart from his poor eyesight. But I'm talking too much – a fault of mine, many tell me! Food will be coming soon – and I must get back to my watch."

They sat warming themselves at the glowing coals, saying little. Although Elli and Lance both felt there was plenty they should ask, they were too weary and cold to formulate it. After about a quarter of an hour, while warmth was beginning to seep back into their bones, the tent flap moved again, and the opening was filled, unexpectedly, by a figure in skirts. The woman was carrying a wooden tray, and on it a jug, with steam rising gently from it, a loaf of bread, and a hunk of cheese. Small cups were attached to her belt. Lyn relieved her of the tray, set it on the small table, and then embraced the newcomer.

"Morgan! How good to see you! And how good of you to come yourself."

"Call it curiosity – I couldn't wait to hear your news – and to meet those you have brought to us," the woman replied with a hint of laughter in her voice.

Lyn turned to the others. "This is Lance – to be known here as Powell – and this is Elli. This..." and he gestured toward the woman, "is Morgan, Arthur's half-sister." As Morgan turned toward them, Elli suppressed a gasp of surprise. It was the woman – shortish, with dark hair streaked with grey – that Olwen had showed her back in the clearing. She was not so elaborately dressed now, and her hair was braided, in keeping with the place and the weather. But it was undoubtedly the same woman. Elli remembered her manners, and tried to bob a curtsey. Lance stood up, bending slightly to avoid contact with the slope of the tent, and offered his seat.

Morgan bowed her head to Lance and took the seat. "So you are the one Merddin Emrys has been seeking. I am so glad he has found you. Do you know, Olwen convinced him that I must learn your language so that we may talk with very little help from her? He took me to a wretched cave on the coast deep in Gwynedd and gave me lessons! But now," she said, turning to Elli, "I suspect she had talking to you in mind – always easier woman to woman. Did Merddin say your name was Elli?"

Elli nodded, wordlessly. Whatever she had expected of the legendary Morgan-la-Fey, it was not this gossipy woman, seemingly friendly, but with an edge to her. "Ah," said Morgan, "we might have expected you, I suppose. A replacement for Lancelot – and for his faithful Elen. No Guinevere?" she asked, almost bitterly, of Lyn.

"No, indeed," said Lyn. "Thanks be!"

"Now," said Morgan, "eat before we talk more. There is warmed wine in the jug, and bread and cheese. Then we will sort tents and so on."

They ate in silence until there was no food left. Then Lyn said, "Which of the Companions is sharing Arthur's tent this week?" He turned to Elli and Lance. "Arthur always has three of the Circle with him – as guards, for company, and so he can stay in touch. This will free up some space in the circle of tents – if you don't mind sharing, Powell?"

"Not at all," said Lance. "But where am I supposed to come from?"

"A far country," said Lyn. "Don't bother them with the idea of time travel, unless it becomes difficult not to."

"If I, a mere woman, may be permitted to answer your question," Morgan interrupted. She's a bit touchy about her status, though Elli. "Owain, Hwyel ap Cai and Taliesin's son, Afaon, are with Arthur this week. Of their tent-mates, I think young Gareth, my great-nephew, would be the best person for Powell to share with."

"A good idea," said Lyn. He explained. "Gareth is the son of Gawain's brother, Gareth – a gentle son of a gentle father. He and his immediate followers are the only ones of Lot's faction to stay with Arthur – the others blame him for the slaughter of that family. However, Young Gareth said that his half-brother, Mordred, was 'black of soul', and that it was all his – Mordred's – fault. But he is deeply saddened at the rift in his family."

"Two misfits together," said Lance. "I'll gladly share with him."

"Unless," said Morgan suddenly, "you and Elli wish to share?"

Elli felt a wave of embarrassment flood her. How should she answer? What were the rights of the matter, regardless of personal desires? She decided to say nothing.

Lance thought. "Do any of the others – the Companions, or ordinary soldiers for that matter – have wives, or, indeed, any women with them?"

"No," said Morgan. "There are some with the baggage train. Some craftswomen – cooks and herbalists, for example – and some whose skills lie in a less respectable direction. But Rhianwen and I are the only women here, in the central camp. We are here as we are part of the king's Council of Advisors, along with Taliesin the Bard and Merddin Emrys, here."

"Then," said Lance looking at Elli with what seemed to be an apologetic smile, "I will share with Gareth. I will not be seen to have privileges denied to others."

"Well said!" Lyn nodded approvingly. "But as three of the Circle always lodge with Arthur, it will be possible to arrange a quiet tent for you two to see each other occasionally."

Lance was irresistibly reminded of his university days. "Can you keep out of the way tonight, I'm hoping Sarah/ Rachel/ Kate will come back with me?" Or: "I may not be in tonight – with luck I'll be staying over at Sarah's/ Rachel's/ Kate's." His lips twitched, but he gained control, and bowed. "Thank you," he said, and reached out and took Elli by the hand. "If it does not cause trouble, we would appreciate that."

Morgan looked at Elli. "And you, I think, had better lodge with us – Rhianwen and me. One more wise-woman will cause little comment. At least, that will be so, once we dress you more…conventionally. I will go and find you some skirts and jerkins. You are between the two of us in height, but my hems should just about reach your ankle, which is no bad thing in this weather. Rhianwen's skirts would soon be mud-draggled, and she has far fewer of them anyway." Without more ado, she gathered up the remains of the meal and went out.

"She talks almost as much as Lady Anne," said Lyn, "but don't be fooled. Like Anne, she is intelligent, and also she has Power – magic, if you like – from her mother's family. Only the women of that kin possess it – Arthur, of course, has his own power, but it is wholly human – nothing people would term as magic. His is the power of character, and wisdom – and intelligence, although that is perhaps less than his instincts, which is, in part, why he misses Lancelot so much."

"I thought Morgan was no friend of Arthur," said Elli. "At least, she plots against him in some of the stories."

"I touched on that last night. They have had their differences, and if Morgan wishes to tell you their history, you will perhaps understand why. Until then, well, just remember all that is in the past. At least, I hope so. Whilst I remember to tell you, she is one of the few who know that you are from our future."

"Who else knows?" asked Lance.

"Arthur, of course, and his Council of Advisors – myself, and Morgan, and Taliesin the Bard, and Rhianwen."

Elli was on the verge of asking about the mysterious Rhianwen: who was this woman – an advisor to Arthur, one of only four? And why did she have fewer skirts than Morgan? – but Lyn was continuing.

"I expect Arthur will have told the two Companions who often join the Council informally, Cai and Bedwyr. In past days, Lancelot was … a full member, if you like. Always consulted. But Arthur has ever valued the advice and thoughts of his two oldest friends, whom he has known since they were all boys together – Cai and Bedwyr. Cai is his foster-brother."

"Sir Kay," said Lance.

"And Bedevere," said Elli.

"Yes. I doubt anyone else knows. Try not to tell them, as it will just complicate matters. They need to keep their minds and wills focussed on today."

Conversation lapsed. Elli found herself dozing, with the warmth from the brazier, the food, the wine and her disturbed night. Lyn had stretched himself on the bed and was, as far as Elli could make out, asleep. Lance sat staring into the firelight.

It was not long, however, till Morgan returned, with two soldiers carrying a wooden chest.

"Here are your things, Merddin, returned from the stores. I've put a skirt in there for Elli. When she's put it on, I'll take her to our tent."

Elli slipped on the green wool skirt and pulled the ties to make it fit. By letting it settle on her hips, it was almost to her ankles. Then she stepped out of the trousers and handed them back to Lyn.

"Oh – and there's a shawl to cover you against this foul weather," said Morgan, giving one to her.

As they left the tent, they could hear Lance's voice: "Who precisely are the Companions?"

"Yes," said Elli to Morgan, "will you explain the Companions to me?"

"Willingly. But let us wait until we're out of the rain."

Chapter 2

The tent she was to share with Morgan and the mysterious Rhianwen was at the far side of the circle of tents from where they had approached. Beyond it, she could see a few more neat rows of tents and then a more disorganised area where the smoke of campfires was rising.

"Yes, we're near the non-military area," said Morgan. "Cooking, hospital tents, stores, horse pickets, and the like. It's just as well – we women can form a bridge between the fighting men – who seem to think that all these comforts are produced by magic – and those doing the work."

The tent was the same size and shape as the one Elli had already been in, but more cluttered, with two beds and a few chests, as well as a couple of stools. Morgan looked around. "These are really two-person tents," she said. "And we're lucky to have these two beds. I'm not sure if we can fit in another, even if I can lay my hands on one. But a mattress should be possible, and Rhianwen is not always here: she has been on a hunting trip since Merddin Emrys left, and has not yet returned, for instance."

"That would be fine," said Elli. "Thank you."

Morgan gestured for her to sit on one of the stools. "I'll search out some clothes for you, and then you look as if you should rest. I expect you will be meeting the King as soon as Merddin Emrys sees fit to tell Arthur that you've arrived. But you were asking about the Companions."

Elli nodded, without speaking. The dislocation caused by being in her fourth world in less than ten days, the lack of sleep, the astonishing, marvellous situation between her and Lance, all these were being crowned by the casual mention of her forthcoming meeting with King Arthur. She brought her attention back to Morgan.

"Ever since he became High King, Arthur has chosen twelve men to be his inner circle. They are called the Circle of Companions or simply the Companions – it doesn't sound quite right in your Saxon-based tongue – we would say the 'Cymry'."

"Oh," said Eli, suddenly enlightened. "That is what the Welsh – those in our time who count themselves as coming from ancient British stock – that is what they call themselves and their land!"

Morgan looked up with a smile on her face. "I will not ask you about your time. I do not want to know – unless I could spend time there and see for myself. It might even be dangerous. But you warm my heart to say our race is still there, and that the Companions are not forgotten!"

"Yes," said Elli. "I won't say there have been no problems, but on the whole, in our time, Saxon and Briton – English and Welsh as we would say – live together comfortably enough. I have both in my family tree – my ancestry. And Lyn – Merddin Emrys – says that what happens in the next few days may be crucial in making sure that that comes about."

"Enough! I beg you, tell me no more! To return to the Companions: they are selected from the best warriors, with an eye to balance so no faction can feel slighted, and so the King can gain as wide a view as possible. Over the years, some have been killed, or died of fever, or left through old age or because their home circumstances demanded it. Arthur has tried to balance their ages too! It has been a fine line to walk, and since the disasters of the last years, heartbreakingly difficult."

"In our stories," said Elli, rushing on before Morgan could protest, "King Arthur's close followers are called the Knights of the Round Table. The Knights – mounted warriors – are usually, but not always, of high birth."

"Undoubtedly, that is an elaboration of our Circle! For the Companions too are mounted, and not just on any small mountain horses. They have fine large white horses and train to be worthy of them. And finding white horses is not easy – some families breed them and we even have a few with us that do not belong to the present Circle, but it is not easy."

"Who is in the Circle now? I know that Gawain and his kin are gone – and Lancelot."

"The names won't mean much to you until you meet them, but may help when you do. You have already heard of Young Gareth, and the present tent-mates of the King, Afaon, Owain and Hwyel ap Cai. Hywel is the son of Cai, who is one of three original Companions remaining. Cai is Arthur's foster-brother, and another of his sons, Mabon, is also in the Circle, as is Bedwyr, the friend of Arthur and Cai and from their boyhood. He was the son of a servant in the family, but now he is probably the closest of all to Arthur.

"Then there are two of Elen's brothers, sons to Pellinore – do you know about him and the feud?"

Elli nodded. "I had read of it and Lyn – Merddin – has told us the tale recently."

"One is Tor, the only other man who has been in the Circle from the beginning. He is also of Arthur's generation, and is actually half- brother to Elen, and the second is Algovale, much younger, and her full brother, the youngest of all that large family.

"Also, there is Palomides, who is dark-skinned and comes from the far reaches of the old Roman Empire. My brother met him when on campaign in Gaul. He is close friends with Penawr

– whom Arthur likes to call Chief Centurion – my brother loves Roman trappings. He is a man of very humble origins, and middle years. He is a soldier through and through."

"What Lance would call the Senior NCO," thought Elli. Aloud, she said, "And who else?"

"I've mentioned the young son of Taliesin, our king's bard, Afaon. And there is Gwalchmai, some sort of cousin of Arthur's, on his father's side – which makes him no kin to me."

"That's eleven I think," said Elli. "Who is the twelfth?"

"Ah," said Morgan, with a small, sad smile, "that is my son, Owain!" Another time, I will tell you our story, if there is opportunity to do so. But I think you should rest now. I will just say this: with all the losses, there are still fine young men anxious to prove themselves, so they can be considered worthy of being admitted to the Circle, should there be the need. There is Cadwr of Cornwall, from our mother's kin, for example.

"Now, rest. I will find you a trunk for these clothes," and she indicated the ones she had selected. "And a mattress. I will wake you when you are needed."

Elli slept dreamlessly and woke to Morgan's gentle shaking. She stretched, and, opening her eyes, smiled with surprise at what Morgan held out to her. She sat up and swung her legs over the bed.

"How wonderful! My handbag! Where on earth did you get it?"

Morgan smiled in return. "Merddin Emrys asked me to bring it to you. He said you might need it before you meet the King."

"Lyn is a marvellous man," said Elli fervently, taking the bag.

"He is. He is seer, wizard, wise counsellor and no mean warrior. He travels in time and is friends with a dragon. But you come to this conclusion because he sends you a *bag*?"

"It isn't just that. With all the calls upon him, he realised I would feel better if I had it, and took time to send it to me. It's understanding, and attention to detail, and kindness."

"True. I was not being totally serious – a fault of mine, I fear. But what is in this magical container, that it will help you face my brother, the High King? Not that he is that fearsome, in actuality."

Elli smiled back. "Girl things. Specifically my brush, my comb, a mirror and make-up – they'll make me feel so much better!"

Morgan nodded. "And I will be intrigued to see them! First, though, I have provided some warm water and a suitable outfit. There is a chamber pot, too. I'll return shortly."

When she did, with a small woman who removed the two basins and the towel, Elli was feeling fresher and confident. Her new skirt and tunic were of the same soft green wool but with fine deep red stripes on the jerkin and some red braiding edging the neck. A belt of soft leather, also dyed red, completed the outfit, and there was a dark plaid shawl, vaguely resembling the Black Watch tartan, to help keep off the rain.

"Now," said Morgan, "show me your treasures!"

Elli extracted her mirror and propped it against the bedding, so that, kneeling, she could see it and leave her hands free. Then she brushed out her hair vigorously and tidied it with the comb. Morgan nodded approvingly and admired the quality of the mirror. "Although I'm not sure I like what it reveals about the wrinkles on my face!" she said wryly. "But you, my dear, look charming. There is a light in your eyes that hardly needs embellishment," she added, as Elli applied mascara and a little eyeshadow. She kept it minimal, partly out of habit, as her father felt make-up unsuitable for a farm, and partly because she felt, in a military camp on the eve of battle, understatement would always be sensible in any society. A little lipstick and blusher completed her preparations, and made her feel enormously better. She sighed contentedly, and turned to Morgan.

"It is strange how much groomed hair and cosmetics make us women feel better. Some things obviously do not change over the years," Morgan commented.

"No, it must be inbuilt. If only I could wash my hair as well!"

"At this time of year? In this camp? How very Roman of you! Well, perhaps I can arrange something later on, or tomorrow. But now, if you're ready, Merddin and Powell are waiting."

They were, under a canopy extending in front of the main tent. The rain had eased somewhat, but the day was still damp and grey, and underfoot the ground was churned and muddy. Lance smiled a welcome and squeezed her hand. "Here we go then!"

Lyn said, "Wait just inside the tent until I call you forward. I will try to leave Lance – Powell – till last, because, if all goes well, he and Arthur will not welcome interruptions once they meet – there will be too much to discuss."

Morgan nodded to two men who were on guard. "I will announce myself," she said. The men stood aside, sweeping up the tent flap for Morgan to enter. Elli heard her voice: "High King, brother, as I said earlier, Merddin Emrys is returned with those he went to seek. Here they are."

Elli followed Lyn and Lance into the tent. There were several men standing near two or three braziers, which were making the air smoky. The men had turned at the sound of Morgan's voice and now made way for Lyn who walked past them. Near the centre of the tent was a tall man with hair had once been red but was now mostly grey. He rose from a carved folding stool and held out his arms.

"Merddin Emrys, how good to see you!" The voice was strong and warm. "Welcome back!"

King Arthur, for it was surely he, walked forward and embraced Lyn, who responded in kind. Then Lyn turned and said, "May I present to you a traveller from afar: Elli, daughter of Marged."

"I can't remember telling him mum's name was Margaret," thought Elli, irrelevantly, as she walked forward. She found Morgan had joined her and walked up with her. Just as well, for she saw from watching the other woman that a bow was more acceptable than a curtsey.

Arthur reached out and grasped her arm. "You are truly welcome," he said, and smiled at her. In that moment Elli understood at least some of the King's power. He had the knack some people possess, of making you feel that for that moment you are the one person they want to be with, and that you are totally absorbing. But it was more than that. There was something in his eyes and his demeanour, in the smile and the handclasp that would make you want to follow him, regardless, to hell and back. She remembered some lines from King Lear: 'You have that in your countenance which I would fain call master...What's that?... Authority.'

If she, a twenty-first century woman, felt this on first acquaintance, how much more would his men, his soldiers, of his own time! And what a responsibility for Arthur, to make sure they followed him on the right course. No wonder he surrounded himself with advisors, from powerful counsellors and his best warriors. No wonder he missed Lancelot, needed Lance.

At the time, all this overcame her more as feeling than thought. Then she sensed Lyn's approval, and Morgan's, and Olwen's, as she said, "I am proud to meet you, sir, and will help in whatever small way I can." Then Morgan touched her shoulder and indicated she should move.

But Arthur held her arm a little longer. "I'm sorry that my affairs press so. I would dearly like to talk with you, and hear your story – and what you think of our life here! Perhaps this evening, after supper. But my sister wants me to move on! Welcome, Elli."

Morgan drew her aside and Lyn spoke again, loudly, so all would hear. "Here, as I promised you, is the man I went to find. Powell, son of Siôn, or John as he would say."

Lance came forward. To Elli's surprise, he halted a few feet in front of the king and gave the soldier's salute they had seen earlier, and said in a clear voice, "Salve, Rex Magnus!"

And that, thought Elli, had nothing to do with Olwen! That was presumably down to Mr Jenkins, the Latin master – oh, the advantages of a public school education!

There was a ripple of approval and Arthur smiled broadly.

"Poole, dicas linguae Latine!" he said.

"Paulus...paulum...?" Lance decided that discretion was the better part of valour, and returned to relying on Olwen.

"A little. I write it better, for I had more practice of that in school."

"Oh, excellent, Powell. It will ease Olwen's load – and she has never been able to translate the written word. Dragons, I am informed, don't read!"

Despite all his worries, the King smiled, not just with his mouth, but with his eyes, and, it seemed, his soul. As Elli had, Lance felt the man's power and magnetism, the instinctive ability to say the right thing, hit the right note. If, in addition, he were anything near as good a commander and soldier, he would be worth his legend. Something of the hollow, that had been inside Lance since he quit the army, shrank.

"It is almost time for the noon meal, such as it is. We are on short commons, being in camp at this time of year, but join us and talk."

"That is our dismissal, I think," said Morgan, with a touch of acid in her voice.

They bowed to the King, who bowed back, and started to walk to the tent doorway, when the flap was drawn back and one of the guards said loudly, "The Lady Rhianwen is returned!" Morgan drew Elli to one side.

"Merddin Emrys!" a clear voice rang from the entrance.

Lyn, who had been in conversation with one of the men, stopped mid-sentence and turned toward the newcomer. "Rhianwen!" he said, smiling broadly, and taking rapid steps toward the tall woman who came quickly to meet him.

In loose trousers like the men wore, and a tunic of a deep red colour, belted with plaited leather, she was a striking figure. She loosened the cloak from her shoulders, tossing it on to one of the low stools. But the most striking thing about her was her hair. Although her face was one of a woman verging on middle age – an attractive middle age to be sure, but without the softness of youth – and although her stride and carriage was that of a younger woman, her long hair was a shining silver, caught back in another leather plait. She and Lyn met and embraced in a fashion which was halfway between a salute between comrades-in-arms and a long awaited reunion of lovers.

"Did he say Rhianwen?" Elli asked Morgan. "*That's* who belongs to the name – but it's not a name I recognise from the writings."

"Rhianwen is not her real name. She is Irish – and not quite human. She is one of the Sidhe…"

"Not another seepage from a different world?"

"No, no – in Ireland, mankind and the Sidhe folk have always existed side by side, in a way that is unique to them. When Lyn brought Rhianwen to us first, we tried to say her real name, but even fellow Celts find Irish names difficult. So we translated it – Rhianwen means White Maiden, and her real name Beibhinn means White Lady, so it's close enough."

"Bey-Vin? Oh we know her as Viviane! Merlin's Lady, with magic powers to match his."

"Indeed! But tell me no more: to know too much of a story when you are in it is dangerous – for you and for the story! Now, we really should leave…"

Chapter 3

As they walked through the camp toward the cooking area, Elli said, "You wouldn't let me wear trousers. Rhianwen does!"

"Ah, but we need you to be unremarkable – you will be the centre of enough gossip and rumour. They are used to Rhianwen – and make allowances for a woman of the Sidhe. Moreover, she has just been hunting: we might even let *you* wear trousers, if you showed talent in that direction!"

"Hunting is necessary?" asked Elli.

"It is indeed! This time of year is not good for food, without trying to feed an army. But we have dried meat and root vegetables, and grain and cheese. We've found a way of baking bread – I will show you that sometime. But, yes, hunting is necessary. If Mordred does not arrive soon, we may not be able to keep waiting for him. But his army must be in the same straits, and with longer supply lines."

Their meal was indeed bread and cheese, washed down with what Olwen translated as 'small beer' – and it did seem all too free of alcoholic content.

As they were finishing, Elli asked, "How can I be of help? I'm obviously not going to be a part of the King's discussions, and quite rightly, too. But as for some reason I am here, I need to do something."

"Perhaps you can help in the medical area. We can show you how to make ointments and tinctures, and we can, as ever, use extra hands to prepare dressings. Unfortunately, soldiers always need plenty of those."

Elli spent the next few hours rolling bandages and stirring mixtures, under the supervision of a large woman and a small man. She said little, to ease the burden on Olwen, who must be busy translating for Lance. When Morgan looked in on her, she said, "I've done a first aid course – emergency treatment – recently. At least I can bandage well and know how to try to stop bleeding. I've even tried the kiss of life – not on a real person of course, that would be dangerous, but on a dummy."

"Kiss of life?"

"How to breathe into a person to start them breathing again. Of course, it's no use if they're beyond help, but it can sometimes buy time for help to come."

Morgan sounded impressed. "That sounds almost like magic."

"No, anyone can learn it: if I had time, I could teach you – the theory, anyway."

"But not now," said Morgan. "For I have other duties to attend to."

Whatever they may be, thought Elli, as the older woman left.

It was not long after that Lance found her. "Can you leave what you're doing, Elli? I need your opinion."

She looked round and tried with gestures and expressions to explain to her mentors. The woman smiled and nodded, and the man took over stirring the liquid Elli had been occupied with. No problem, she thought, when you have been introduced by the great Morgan La Fay!

They walked through the tents toward an open area at the back of the camp, where a group of men were practising sword fighting under the eye of a man wearing what looked like most of a Roman soldier's uniform.

"That's Penawr," said Lance. "The Chief Centurion – rather like…"

Elli interrupted. "I know, the Senior NCO." She laughed at Lance's surprised look. "Morgan told me about the Companions. I can't remember the details of all of them, but him I do remember. However, we haven't come here, on a raw March afternoon, to swap details of our new acquaintances."

"No. Elli, what am I doing here? The weight of expectation is crippling. Lyn searched and located me, and went to all that trouble – kitting Olwen out as a helicopter, for heaven's sake – to bring me here. And for what?"

"To replace Lancelot. Because you are the best," said Elli loyally.

"To replace Lancelot? I'm from a different time, and my knowledge cannot be as good as the least of the Companions, even of most of the soldiers. How *can* I help?"

Elli thought desperately. She must say the right thing, and not just facile comfort. What she said must be valid.

They had slowed to a stop. She turned and said slowly, "Perhaps that's an advantage, not a disadvantage. You may see things differently. You know: 'The onlooker sees most of the game', and, 'You can't see the wood for the trees' – that sort of thing. Listen to what they say, and give your slant on it. See if this could be your... justification."

"You may have a point. God, I'm glad I've got you to talk to! I'd go mad else!" He tightened his grip on her waist, and Elli felt a surge of pride

She had another thought. "It may be that you can be the surface off which Arthur bounces his ideas."

Lance pulled a face. "That sounds very passive – surely I can have a more active role?"

"For whose benefit? The King's or your ego's?"

"Elli!"

"No, listen. Even in the five minutes I was there, I felt Arthur's power – and how responsible that must make him feel.

If he can inspire such faith, he needs to be very sure he's making the right decisions."

"True. I see that. I thought it, even. But what can I do, that the others can't?"

"None of them are Lancelot. I gather Arthur used him to bounce ideas off – he – Lancelot, that is – had the more analytical brain, like you. He has known all the others for years, and they all already have a relationship with him, and this alone must stop them replacing Lancelot – because of what, if I wanted to be horribly modern, I'd call 'baggage'. You can do it: it will be difficult, but... clean. Also, no one should feel resentful that it is you, not them."

Lance looked hopeful, then almost excited. "You may have the right of it. To see things with a fresh eye, to replace a sounding board as cleanly as possible, it is at least a useful function."

"And there may be more to come. Don't try to prejudge and outguess the future – or Lyn and Olwen. *You* may not know. Perhaps *they* do!"

"You're not good for my ego, Elli! You remind me that I can't know and judge everything! But I've just had a thought. Something I may be able to bring from our time to help. No, I won't tell you, not yet, anyway. But you've cheered me up enormously. Elli Tollet, you're a marvel!" And he lifted her off the ground, kissing her as he did so.

"No, Lance, the soldiers may see!"

"So what?"

"They have few women here, remember. Don't... flaunt me. Put me down!"

They turned and walked back to the main camp. Elli said, "You spent the whole afternoon with the King. Is he as impressive as he seemed to me?"

"Oh, yes," said Lance enthusiastically. "He outlined the position to me and introduced the others. By the way I'm glad I'm sharing with Gareth: he seems a pleasant and sensible young man – ten or twelve years younger than me. He usually shares with Owain, who is his uncle, or, rather, his father's cousin, I gather. Anyway, Arthur got them all to contribute, and by the end of the session I already felt part of the group – in itself, a real skill of the King's. Tomorrow, or the next day at the latest, will probably be the last chance we'll have to plan the battle, because scouts say Mordred's army is drawing close.

"So now, my love, I must go and join Gareth and Bedwyr who have promised to show me the lie of the land. And that's where my idea may be of help," he added. Then he kissed her swiftly, and left her at the medical tents.

That evening, they ate in the large tent. Elli and Lance found themselves in the company of the King, his Companions, Lyn, Morgan, Rhiannwen, and a man in his late middle years, not a soldier. Just a few more than at the Bairstows' a few nights ago, she thought, and sternly quelled the giggle that rose up at the contrast – although she suspected that Sir Edward and Lady Anne might just take it in their stride.

Whether, when not on campaign, they used a round or an oblong table, or even a Roman arrangement of couches, when they all ate together, she had no idea. Here, a rough arrangement of benches and folding stools were drawn up in a circle, though, and she murmured to Lance, "Look, the Round Table!"

A trestle table in the centre held large pots of stews, bowls, spoons, several loaves of bread, with beakers and what turned out to be jugs of mead. Arthur asked Lance to sit on one side of him and Elli on the other. Lyn sat next to Elli, and Morgan next to Lance – to ease Olwen's task, Lyn explained, and enable her to focus on the King's conversation. Otherwise, people sat, as far as she could see, anywhere they pleased, and got up to help themselves to food. No one waited on them.

At first, Arthur talked mainly to Lance, so Elli found she was free to talk to Lyn. He felt like an old friend, she noticed, although she had known him for less than a fortnight, or, it seemed, slightly over half a lifetime.

"Well, Elli, how are you coping with this rough soldier's life? This is not the view of my time I would have shown you, given the choice."

"I could do with more warmth and less mud – but I remember saying that about Guide camp in my own time! Otherwise it's fine. Morgan has been very friendly, and helpful, and I think, oddly, I am more at ease with her than the girls at college. Arthur, the King, seems…" She looked for a suitable word: "Tremendous."

Lyn grinned. "It's difficult to find the words, isn't it? But he is as good as he seems. His weakness, if any, is that his heart can rule his head – that's usually a good idea as his instincts are excellent, but just occasionally, this serves him ill, such as his deliberate blindness about – ", he lowered his voice, "Lancelot and the Queen, or his refusal to think ill of Mordred."

Elli spooned some of her stew into her mouth and ate appreciatively. "This is good – rather like our cooking in the clearing, but much better."

"No oranges, though," said Lyn regretfully.

"No. Is this food the result of the hunting party Rhianwen was with?"

"Not tonight – they were successful, but the meat wasn't prepared in time to go into this. This is the last of the hunt before. Have you talked to Rhiannwen yet?"

"Only briefly – she came into the tent just as Morgan and I were leaving tonight. We were a little early."

"And she was late, as usual. No matter. I expect you'll meet her properly tomorrow."

Elli was about to ask, "Why not tonight?" when she remembered the relationship between Lyn and the Sidhe woman, and the fact that Lyn had been away. To cover her thoughts she asked about the man she could not place. "Who is he?" she asked, indicating the man with a nod.

"Ah, that is Taliesin, the Bard. His son, Afaon, one of the Companions, is sitting next to him."

"I can see the resemblance," said Elli. "But he's wearing a cross – surely that means he is Christian?"

"He maintains that his faith is for people of all traditions and modes of life," said Lyn. "And indeed, from what I can tell in our future, Arthur's story will be told mainly by bards and poets of the Christian faith. But I wish more of Taliesin's fellow Christians were as …inclusive. One good thing, however – to have such a man in our counsels means that Arthur does not have to have an official Church representative – he usually finds them less than congenial!"

"Is the land officially Christian, then? I know the later Roman Empire was."

"Most people are, at least nominally, and Bedwyr, for example, is genuinely devout. But now that the Roman rule has gone, many, especially in the west, have remembered the old Celtic way – but they often seem to be able to combine both. Palomides," and he indicated a dark-skinned man of middle-Eastern appearance, "Palomides now, follows the old soldiers' god, Mithras, and I suspect his tent-mate, Penawr, might too."

Elli changed the subject before she found herself asking about Lyn's own beliefs: as far as she could see a man with a father who seemed to be from a different world deserved privacy about this aspect of his life. "Morgan said you have found a way to bake bread here – how?"

"We discovered a deserted, half-ruinous Roman villa about a mile away – on what will be Sir Edward's land, I think. It had a wood-store, and we got their bread oven working. With luck, tomorrow we will get their bath house operating as well, for those who are sufficiently Roman to appreciate it!"

At that juncture, the man on Lyn's far side asked him something, and he turned to talk to him. A little later the King turned to her. "I wish I had met you in more comfortable circumstances, Elli, and with more time. However, if we were living in such days, I suppose I would never have met you at all! I'd be most interested if you could tell me about your home, and your life."

Elli thought, trying to pick details that a Dark Age king could relate to. She described her family farm, the animals, the setting, the hard work.

"You obviously love it. Your father, though, must find it hard, with only one child to help him."

"And, although you do not say it, only a daughter at that."

"No. We Celtic races yield to no one in the knowledge of the ability, and intelligence and energy of our women! But physically, it can be hard."

"Yes. I am at college – a sort of school – so I can learn things that will help run the farm better. Then we can hire men to help."

Arthur spoke to her a little more, and then turned back to Lance. Elli sat, catching her breath. The situation was an odd mixture of the ordinary and the surreal. Her head spun, and not totally because of the surprisingly strong, sweet mead. She closed her eyes.

Lance saw this, and spoke briefly to Morgan. "Elli looks very tired. How long will this go on?"

"Not late. This is a war camp, after all. But you have a point – I'll take her back to our tent now."

"Thank you. I could do with sleep myself!"

Morgan smiled reassuringly. "The King will not keep anyone long." She rose, and, murmuring to her brother in passing, leaned over Elli and suggested she should leave.

"I don't know what's come over me today – I keep wanting to sleep!" said Elli, as they made toward the tent.

"You've had a busy few days, filled with surprises, shocks, and new ways of living."

"Lance – Powell – is coping!"

"Unlike you, he is a soldier, and used to violent relocations. It matters not, anyway. Whether or not you should be, you are tired. Now," as they reached the tent, "a night's sleep – a night's uninterrupted sleep, for Lance will not be interrupting it tonight…" Elli blushed, glad of the darkness. "…a night's sleep will put you right."

A small oil lamp gave enough light for Elli to find her way around the tent.

"Take that bed," said Morgan. "Rhianwen will not be here tonight."

Elli slipped off her top garments, and brushed out her hair. Feeling too tired to do more, she crept gratefully under the blankets. She was asleep in less than five minutes.

The next morning, after another meal of bread, cheese and small beer, Elli felt herself again. She remembered reading of nineteenth century porters in Africa who refused to continue on safari after three days, needing, they said, a day's rest: 'To let our souls catch up with our bodies.' She understood.

She felt even better when Morgan told her that she could have the bathhouse, which was now in operation. "You have no more than an hour, for the Roman group of the Companions will be coming then, and after, those of the army that way inclined. I think it strange, but Arthur believes in keeping morale high, and, I suppose if this helps..."

The rain had thoroughly cleared away, and a thin frost had made walking the muddy ways easier. Elli set off with towel and the last of her small soaps, accompanied by a soldier who walked in front, and said nothing, but knew where they were going.

The walk, to the left of the back of the camp, was uphill to start with, then sloped gently toward the stream on which the villa owners had built their bathhouse. The villa could just be seen on the far side, but young woods were already obscuring the view. The bathhouse, of brick, was derelict in some places, but the core looked sound and a trickle of smoke was rising from the far side, presumably where the furnace was.

Her guide, or guard, whichever he was, opened a creaking door and stood aside for her to pass. The anteroom was still full of the leaves of the last autumn, and hung with cobwebs, and there were weeds growing through cracks. Eli's heart sank, but she moved on, and found the second room had been brushed clean and the plunge pool filled with steaming water. Beyond were other rooms, and investigation showed that in one of the plunge pool had been filled, this time with cold water.

"Good enough," she thought, and, abandoning her clothes, lowered herself into the water, luxuriating in the heat. She loosed her hair and ducked under, then used most of her small bar of soap in a head-to-toe cleanse.

She allowed herself to float on the water and relaxed totally, closing her eyes and letting her mind drift as aimlessly as her body. Thus it was that she only noticed the footsteps when they came right up the edge of the pool. Panicked, she opened her eyes, only to laugh with relief when she saw Lance looking down on her.

"Who let you in?" she queried. "The guard should have stopped you!"

"I came with another soldier, who spoke to the one outside. I don't know what he said – I don't speak early Welsh, but if the whole camp doesn't know about your being...my lady, these soldiers are different from any I've known: they're always dreadful gossips!" He started to undress. "That water looks inviting..."

"Shouldn't you be pulling your weight back in camp?"

"I have been introduced to the troops, and it seemed presumptuous to stay for the inspection. Later, I will be part of the 'war cabinet' as you might call it. In any case, the Romanised Companions will be here in about half an hour, after they've finished with the troops: Gwalchmai, Bedwyr, Cai, Palomides, Penawr – perhaps Cai's two sons, but they're more distant from Roman times, and I gather it'll be more a question of pleasing their father if they do come – and perhaps even Arthur, if he can find the time."

Elli marvelled at how quickly and easily Lance seemed to have slipped into the group, knowing not only their names, but their ways of thinking and acting as well. It was what made him the good officer he must have been, she assumed. These musings were interrupted by the serious, responsible officer in question shouting, "Look out, I'm coming in!" and jumping into the pool, inelegantly, with a large splash.

"Can't the talented Major Poole dive?" said Elli shaking off the after-effects of the jump.

"No. Gave up trying when I was eleven. I don't trust water when I'm out of my depth... or water sports: our swim in the sea was about my limit!"

"Come here," said Elli. "I'll use the last of my soap on your hair. I see you've managed a shave – thank goodness!" as Lance kissed her. "Now, hold still!" Lance did his best to distract her as she worked, but eventually she pronounced his hair clean, and allowed him to finish the rest of the cleaning himself.

"Good," he said, "Now we can get down to the serious business – the guards will whistle when the others approach – at least I hope the mime was clear! So, no interruptions. How cold is the surround? Or shall we stay here?"

Later, with Lance gently massaging her back as she lay on a towel on a raised slab, Elli felt sleepily content. Then Lance abandoned the massage and sat beside her, absently stroking her hair. "You know," he said, "when we get back, I think we'll deserve an entry in the Guinness Book of Records for the variety of places..." he hesitated.

"We've made love?" said Elli, pleased at coming up with a polite wording and forestalling any more basic version Lance might try.

"Yes. Made love. A country house in 1900, a Roman bathhouse in the Dark Ages... a pity we missed out on that sea cave in the – what was it – the fourteenth century?"

"It does sound unbelievable, doesn't it?"

"Yes. When we get back, we'll have to settle for an ordinary bed in Cheshire. But the one I have in mind's quite large."

Elli's first reaction to this was one of relief and pleasure. They had a future. Of course, he was wrong if he thought she could just leave the farm, but something could be worked out... a second reaction followed. 'Settle for' – a come-down then. If it referred to the ordinariness of the venue, fine, but if it referred to 'settling' for her, as Gwennie was unavailable...She shut her mind to this, and rolled onto her side, propping herself on one elbow. "That sounds fine to me."

"Don't move like that! It's highly distracting..." A sharp whistle sounded. Elli got up hastily and dressed, scooping up her freshly washed undies. "No time for the cold plunge – thank goodness! And I think I must 'go native' – one set of under clothes just isn't enough!"

Lance was moving toward the cold room. He paused and blew her a kiss. "I'm not sure when we'll coincide again. I'll try not to make it too long, but things are about to get very hectic!"

"Oh, the trials of being a soldier's woman," said Elli, emboldened by the previous conversation. As Lance looked round for something to throw at her, she slipped out of the building and stood quietly to one side as the Companions approached. Arthur was not with them. She watched them in, and then turned, and with her guard, walked back to the camp.

Lance had asked Lyn about their twenty-first century belongings, and, sure enough, when he returned to the King's tent, they were there. So too were Arthur and Lyn, looking at a parchment spread out on a table. Arthur looked up as Lance entered with Bedwyr and the other bathers.

Arthur spoke. "I'm sorry I couldn't join you – but at least I found time to shave! Now, Powell, you saw the land yesterday, with fresh eyes. Anything you feel we should alter or add to the map?"

Lance looked at the parchment and aligned the map with his memories. Bedwyr said, "If we had a sand-table, we could model the land. But carrying one on campaign would not have been practicable."

Lance spoke. "I think I may be able to help – I have here something from my own place. Without taking it back to refresh it, it will only last a few hours, but it may be of use. Shall I show you? I'm afraid I can only show a few at a time."

Arthur looked at those who were there. "How many is a few?"

"You, Lyn, two or three others."

"Bedwyr and Penawr, you stay." The others bowed and went out. As they were leaving, Lance reached out and put his laptop on the table, carefully putting the map to one side. His landscape-building program had better work. The technology had better work. His watch hadn't, since that first flight. He could only hope the fact that the laptop had been switched off all this time had saved the electronics from being scrambled.

He sat on a stool and opened the computer up, conscious of the rapt attention of the four men standing round. "This is a machine," he said. "It works in a way I haven't time to explain, and in a few hours the power will run out and I have no means here to get any more. But it is not Merddin's type of Power – not magic, as I would call it. I am going to try to make a version of this area, which will be both picture and map and, I hope, a bit more than either. It should help us plan the battle, but it will only be approximate. We would need many more measurements than we have on the map. But it should give us some help."

The King thought. "Palomides and Penawr took most of the measurements – there may be more than we have here. Perhaps we'd better have Palomides join us. And Taliesin, as he is trained to remember. Bedwyr, it doesn't look as if there is room for you, I'm afraid. Can you go and get those two? – And ask Palomides to bring any extra measurements he has."

As Bedwyr went out, Arthur turned to Lance. "Will this work with any system of measurement, or will you need to alter ours? These were taken in the old Roman system of miles and paces."

"No, I can work in any – I'll simply call them units. I need to know their relationship to each other, that's all. And presumably you can visualise the scale: you know what a Roman mile looks like on the ground."

With that, he fired up the computer and prayed. The screen flickered into life and his huge sigh of relief was drowned in the gasps from behind him. He forced himself to ignore where he was and to call up the correct program – a present to himself, only marginally connected to his occupation – but from the MOD advanced selection of 'toys'.

While this was going on, Palomides and Taliesin slipped into the tent and joined the group. At the fringe of his consciousness he could hear Lyn explaining what he had already said. He concentrated on pressing the right keys. Green land appeared on the computer screen, to more intakes of breath. "Now," said Lance, "I'll put in some local landmarks. Here's the hill that Olwen is sleeping on." He moulded the sides of the tumulus Elli had called Sodger's Hump. "Now," he continued, "north-east of this is that marshy, swampy area…" and he drew that in.

"More of a lake, at the moment, after the rains and snow melt," said Penawr, who seemed to be taking the wonders of future technology very much in his stride.

Lance marked the marsh with water and tufts of reed. "To the south of us is thick forest…" He placed that on. "What's beyond?"

"The forest drops to the valley with the lake in it – Cwm Llyn, in our language," said Lyn.

"The lake lies in the way of Mordred coming from the south," said Arthur. "We think he will swing to the east to avoid it, and approach us from the south-east. We chose to make our stand here, not only to avoid long supply lines, and venturing into the land of a lord who may well support Mordred, but because we thought the field of battle would be well defined, and of our choosing."

While the king was speaking, Lance was putting all this into the simulation, and then spent some time adjusting and making it more accurate, using the measurements that Palomides gave him. Then he fed in a further instruction and the whole view tilted so they could see it as a bird, or indeed a dragon might, flying low from the west.

"Oh, marvellous," said the deep, rich voice of Taliesin the Bard.

"Yes," said Lance. "Now look at that. Memorise the lie of the land. I will save this, and later, when we've discussed battle plans, perhaps we can try them out on this."

"Thank you, Powell," said the King. "A marvel indeed, and a useful one."

Lyn said in an undertone, "Not twenty-first century weapons, I suppose – just a clearer way of seeing. I'll allow that."

After a while, Lance said, "Have you got it in your mind? Good. I'll close this down for the moment. I can bring it back for a while later on, as I said." He saved the program, and then closed down the laptop.

"Thank you again," said the King. "That was most exhilarating – and very helpful! Now I think we should go and look with fresh eyes at the land. Are you all willing to go close to the dragon? Is she willing to have us close? And how many of us? I would like Cai and Bedwyr to join us, at the very least."

As they donned cloaks and went out, Lyn detained Lance for a moment. "Well done! I hope you have some contributions to make to the strategy, as well – but I hope you can do it without sounding too 'pushy' – you don't want to alienate the Companions."

"Nor do I!" said Lance. "I'll try my best – and anyway, Arthur makes that comparatively easy – he seems to have a real flair for that sort of thing." With that, they passed out of the tent and hurried to catch up with the others.

Elli, coming round the circle of tents, saw them set off. Finding herself at a loose end, she had come, as she admitted to herself, out of curiosity, even nosiness, to see if she could find out what was happening. Now, sorry to see them go, she turned back and sought out the cooking area where the tall figure of Rhianwen stood out. She came toward Elli carrying enough bread, dried meat, and cheese for two. "I saw you coming and collected your share. Morgan will join us at the tent."

They sat outside, and ate their food enjoying the weak March sun. "It's strange," thought Elli, "that, even when you have had to believe six impossible things before breakfast, as the White Queen, and Lance would say, how the front of your mind can be taken up with whether you like dried meat or not." She chewed some more, then half-choked on swallowing it. Morgan passed her a skin water bottle and Elli swallowed gratefully.

"Thanks. But… this is water – is it safe to drink? Oh, sorry: that wasn't very polite!"

"No, it's a sensible question, as it often isn't. Yes, this is safe. It comes from the spring at the deserted villa. Besides, I have checked it myself."

Elli's face expressed puzzlement.

"It is my main skill, my power. All of us who have the Gift have a…speciality I suppose you would call it, which is far more developed than the general power. Lyn was always a foreseer, even before he time travelled with Olwen. I see into things – their physical make-up. I can see, somehow, how they're made, if there is wrong inside, and sometimes what action would put it right. Occasionally, I can even make some changes myself by feeling my way in. I can't explain it any more clearly. But, for example, I know the water is safe, and, although the time involved is short…"

At this point, Rhianwen stood up. "If you are about to expound on the secrets of what you think of as power, I am off! I will see if I can persuade Merddin to persuade Arthur to call a meeting of his so-called Council – and I hope Elli will join us, too, her knowledge of the future being greater even that Merddin's – although I know she must limit what she tells us."

With that, the Sidhe woman got to her feet and walked away, round the circle of tents. Morgan watched her with a half-smile on her lips. "Rhianwen has great power herself. However, it is Sidhe power – Faerie? Elvish? I'm not sure how you would call it. It is not so useful in the affairs of men, and she is reluctant to use it – and she is right. No power should be used without great thought, and this is an alien power."

"Have you always known you had a Gift?" said Elli.

"Since I became aware that not everybody did," said Morgan. "As a child you assume that what is normal to you is normal to everyone."

"Ordinary is what you're used to," quoted Elli again.

"So true. Merddin threatened you with my story, I gather. At the moment we have time, which is a precious commodity. Would you like to hear it? It may explain the tortuous paths, which have led to the present unhappiness, too."

"I would like that. Thank you."

"My family is of the old ways. The bloodline is traced through the female, and although most are nominally Christian, I think many see the Virgin Mary as just one aspect of the Great Goddess. My mother was Duchess of Cornwall, as you know the place, in her own right, and although she was faithful to her husband, she maintained the right of free choice should she so wish. My sister, Morgause, was nearly ten years older than me, and believed in the old ways far more than Ygraine, our mother, who was by nature a compromiser – something that Morgause never was.

"I won't go into the currents surrounding Ygraine, and Gorlois, her husband, and Arthur's father, Uther – and I never knew precisely what part Merddin Emrys played. I was about seven years old when we moved to Uther's Court. My father was dead, my mother was newly queen, and the baby she had borne Uther some months before was fostered out so he could ride out in peace the ill will brought about by his engendering. Uther had placed him with a family as close to the Roman ways as he was: the family of Cai's father, Ector. That arrangement was wholly satisfactory, on all sides, I think.

"For me, too, life was good. Merddin noticed the power within me, and took me as his pupil. For the years that Uther lived, I studied and grew in my craft and power. My sister, sixteen when we moved to the court, was delighted by the society there. She, like our mother, had a little power, but only a little, and preferred to use the power of her beauty and magnetism. She believed, like Ygraine, in a woman's freedom to choose any man who caught her fancy, but, unlike our mother, she found many that did. But, eventually, in the year before Uther died, she fell deeply in love with one of his men, Lot, and even consented to marry him in the Roman fashion – although this was no guarantee of a lifetime of fidelity! Most of the rest of her story, you must know: of Lot's uneasy relationship with

Arthur when he became king, of my sister's jealousy and resentment over Arthur's kingship, of their sons, torn between the King and their mother."

"What of Mordred?" Elli asked.

"Ah. Let me come to him later. When Uther died before his time, after about twelve years, the country was plunged into chaos. My mother, who truly loved him, went home to Cornwall. Arthur was kept hidden, for he was too young to assume the kingship. I begged to be allowed to stay with Merddin, and as I had not been close to my mother for years, since I became Merddin's pupil and she became queen, I stayed. No one pressurised me to marry, as I was a wielder of power – an enchantress, you might say. Not that I had to remain a virgin, but that I might – and men and family would be distracting, after all!

"But all that changed when Arthur became High King. Unlike Morgause, I was at first delighted – I felt his magnetism, and charm, and his essential goodness, although the strong will and determination were even then obvious. And this showed when a certain aspect of his upbringing came into play. He felt that the women of his family could be used to cement political alliances. Not by force, but by persuasion, and a feeling of obligation. He was pleased about the marriage of Lot and Morgause, and soon became close friends with his half-cousins, especially Gawain, who was not much younger than he was. He charmed me into agreeing to marry Urien – and from his point of view it worked. Urien, a loyal lord, was kept so and 'rewarded' by marriage into the King's family. Urien was older than me, a childless widower, but not unattractive.

"At first I was happy, although I missed Merddin – for we were not based at court but in my husband's lands, Gore, in South Wales. When our son, Owain, was born, I was ecstatic. But Urien was always away with Arthur on campaign, and we were, at best, comfortable together, not deeply bonded. I spent time with Morgause. Then, when Owain was eight, Urien took our son with him, to be his body servant – I suppose you could say his page. He also asked me to take over the administration of his lands – oh, yes, he credited me with competence. He was not a bad man, or a bad husband. So now I was alone, away from the court, too busy to practise my art, bereft of my son, lonely and resentful, and an open vessel for the spite and hatred my sister poured into me – she had sufficient power that I could reach her with my mind. Merddin had gone. From time to time, Rhianwen came from Ireland, at his instigation, I believe, to help advise Arthur. But that was no good to me.

"Then Lot refused to house Morgause's son by one of her lovers, and she sent him to me. Mordred. And I loved the boy. I was alone and frustrated, and he has much of his uncle's charm and instinct to move people's hearts. It is only recently I realised that from his infancy he has used this power not for good, but for his own advancement. Now Morgause had an even stronger hold on me, and, yes, I admit it, I plotted against Arthur, helped her in Mordred's schemes. I was seldom at court, so I didn't see the real Arthur, just the distorted one my sister showed me. I tell you all this in explanation, not in justification – I was foolish, to say the least, and wrong in what I did.

"Later, widowed, I appointed a competent steward, and came to court and wondered. I saw the harm Morgause was doing. I came to know my son, although he has been away from me too long for him to be close to me. I found it hard to believe that Arthur was the monster Morgause and Mordred made him out to be. When Morgause was killed, I was horrified, but not really surprised. I started to see, too late, how everything was unravelling. But still I loved and believed in Mordred. It took the rumour he spread of his parentage – that he was Arthur's son by Morgause – to show me finally how wrong I'd been. And although I felt my soul was tearing apart, I threw in my lot with my brother, and called for help to Merddin Emrys, who came back."

Elli heard the faltering voice and saw tears running down Morgan's face. Moved, she hugged her and tried to find comforting words, but all she could manage was: "Oh, poor Morgan. I'm so sorry!"

Returning from the medicine tents later in the day, Elli found that there was to be no large gathering for the meal that evening. The King and the Companions – and that included Lance, it seemed – were eating with various groups of soldiers throughout the camp. She was called to eat with the unmilitary 'Council of Advisors': Lyn, Rhianwen, Morgan and Taliesin the Bard. From them, over another meal of stew and bread washed down with mead, she learnt that the King had spent the afternoon with small groups using Lance's 'box of power', trying various options for the coming battle.

"But now it will work no more," said Taliesin. "It has been very useful, however. Tomorrow we will decide what to do – as far as one ever can for a battle. We believe that Mordred's army will be here by late tomorrow– or early the day after at the latest, and that means the battle will be fought in the next two or three days."

Rhianwen said, in her slightly edgy way, "So does the great High King require his Council of Advisors?"

"Not yet," Taliesin replied. "However, he is hoping to come to us after he has finished with the men. So we wait."

"As ever," said Rhianwen.

Morgan touched her arm. "I know what you mean – it seems like that. And truly, I know my brother is not faultless. However, this is not a deliberate slight."

"You are right, of course," the Sidhe woman acknowledged.

Elli spoke. "I really feel that I won't stay. I might be tempted to say too much about what little I know of events. What I will say is that the battle must be fought with every ounce of strength, to the last. Secondly: I know this battle as Camlann. I think it may be named after the valley with the lake you mentioned: Cwm Llyn. Taliesin might like to use the name in his account."

"Thank you," said the Bard. "But do not go yet. Stay for the music."

With that he took a small harp out of a soft leather bag and started to play. Morgan and Rhianwen hummed quietly. The music was gentle and melodious at first, and when he started to sin, the bard proved to have as rich a singing voice as had been promised by his speech.

Elli was enraptured. She found that she could no longer understand the words, and realised that Olwen had withdrawn from translating for her at the moment. Other, more pressing calls on her, presumably. So she sat, sipping her mead, full and warm, letting the magnificent music enfold her.

A few scraps of conversation still seemed to be comprehensible – it was significant, perhaps, that they were between Lyn and Morgan, whose brain patterns she was used to. Under the now rousing music, she sensed an argument, or, at least, a disagreement. Morgan seemed to want to tell someone something, and Lyn did not see the need. Gradually, it occurred to her that she was the person under discussion. But before she could discover anything else, the tent flap was pushed aside, and the King, followed by Lance, entered. The music and talking stopped and they all rose to their feet.

"Your Majesty," said Rhianwen. "We are delighted and honoured that you have spared us some of your time."

"Rhianwen, do not mock! I have many calls on my time, as you know. Being of my Council does not give you liberty to be sarcastic to the King."

"I apologise. Sometimes I find deference difficult – and I am not one of your subjects, remember!"

"Indeed not. And I value your advice. Which is why I am here. I have brought Powell with me, because it was his 'machine' that we used this afternoon. Taliesin and Merddin were there, as well, and between us, we can inform you and Morgan of our planning, based on the machine. Then, perhaps, we can refine our ideas."

Elli said, "If I may, sir, I will leave you to your discussions. I have little to contribute, and, as I have already mentioned here, I might say more than I should."

"Very well. Powell, escort your lady to her tent – but don't be too long. We all need to sleep in the not-too-distant future!"

Lance slipped an arm round Elli as they walked the few yards to her tent. He ushered her in, and on following her in, turned her round and kissed her, running his hands down her back. "My dear, you heard that. I cannot stay long. It would be wonderful if I could stay, but…"

"Morgan and Rhianwen might object!"

"If we could find an unoccupied tent, then! You know perfectly well, what I mean: I would dearly love to wake up in the morning with you beside me and not have to rush off – or sneak out. But there's no hurry. Soon, when we're home, we can try it often." Another kiss, a quick hug, and he was gone.

Although he was obviously eager to join the King, it was still an improvement, thought Elli, as she prepared for sleep. No mention of 'making do', or 'settling for'. But still the unspoken presence of his commander's wife, his Gwennie, shadowed her mind as she drifted into sleep.

Chapter 5

The next day, Lance was called early to the King's big tent. Soon a small group had gathered: as well as Arthur and Lance there were Taliesin, Cai, Bedwyr, Penawr, Palomides, and, representing the younger generation, Gareth.

It was not so early, however, for the King, who had already been awake for two hours, and had already received the scouts' reports on the progress of Mordred's army. He spoke clearly and concisely.

"It seems that their army has found it harder to come north towards us than they thought. They swung north-east to avoid Cwm Llyn, and then they found the densely-wooded hilly area, too hard to march an army through. They are having to go further now, and will so be approaching from the east. As most of you know, we are camped over a minor road of the old Romans – that is why some of our main way is less muddy than might be expected." This last to Lance, in explanation. " Further east there is more of it, as the area is less susceptible to floods, and that is the way they will now come. It means, almost without question, that they will not now arrive until tomorrow. So, what does that imply for us?"

Palomides produced a new map, based on all the measurements taken, old and new, and on Lance's computer program. They spread it out on several tables and anchored it with various objects: a stone, a plate, a book, a bowl. They crowded round it and spent some time making sure they understood it.

"As we discussed yesterday," said the King, "we need to impose ourselves on this battle, not just react to Mordred. Which of our plans still seem good to you, in the cold light of a new day? But wait – we have warm ale and bread to break our fast: consider the map and think – discuss, even – for a few minutes while we eat."

Lance spent the time acquainting Gareth with the map, as he had not been one of yesterday's group. He soon grasped it and asked pertinent questions: "How many horses do they have? How good is the surface of the road? And what about Olwen?"

Eventually, they were all round the map again. Arthur asked Bedwyr, "as one who knows Latin, and writes clearly," to take notes. Lance hoped devoutly that his command of written Latin would carry him through, although, with luck, he may not be called on to read the notes.

"We need to squeeze them between the marsh lake to the north-east, and the forest to the south," said the King pointing. "But unfortunately, the land is too wide to constrict them utterly."

"We must surely use the barrow – Olwen's hill – to our advantage," said Cai, thoughtfully.

"How many horsemen does Mordred have?" asked Lance. "Gareth asked me, but I didn't have the answer."

Arthur looked at Palomides enquiringly. "You collated the scouts' reports – not many, as I recall."

"No," said the Syrian. "The Saxons prefer to fight on their feet, although they revere horses greatly. Perhaps that is why – they don't feel they should be beasts of burden."

"And Mordred's men?" Gareth asked.

"Some small bands on smallish mounts. But nothing like our white beauties – or Cadwr's great black beast!"

Gareth explained to Lance: "Young Cadwr of Cornwall is not yet a companion, but he has a magnificent ebony horse, equal in size to ours."

"Your white horses," said Lance, "give you, as far as I can see, two advantages. Firstly, to intimidate by the mere look of them. I think we should build on that. And secondly, they give you height and speed in attack – but they are as vulnerable to stabbing as any flesh."

"Yes – we have given them leather protectors at the front, but too much would be too heavy and unwieldy, and destroy their advantage."

"How about maximising the effect of their appearance, and then saving them to help turn the battle our way later?" said Lance. "Olwen's hill – Elli calls it 'Sodgers' Hump', which means, I believe, the hill of the soldiers. I think we should place the King's standard there and array the King and the Companions on the top to look as formidable as possible."

Arthur took up the idea. "More. Let us make it a hill of Power. Merddin Emrys, Taliesin, and, yes, perhaps the women of the Council too – many will recognise them and, with luck it will strike fear. What do you think, Merddin?"

Lyn smiled. "I think it is quite like old times, with you two striking fire from each other. But maybe there is even more…"

"There is indeed." Rhianwen's voice came from behind them. She had, thought Lance, Lyn's trick or skill of being unnoticed when it was required. "You awe the Saxons with your white horses, symbols of Power to them. Many of Mordred's followers are yet followers of the old ways. We need three women to be the three aspects of the Great Goddess: Maiden, Matron, Crone.

"Who better to be the Matron, the Mother, than Mordred's own kin, his foster mother, Morgan? And although some few, Mordred amongst them, will recognise me, many more from afar, will see my silver hair, and believe me to be the Crone – and indeed I am old enough," she added in an undertone. Lance caught her words and wondered again about the age of this 'immortal'.

"And the Maiden?" asked Arthur.

"I gather it may be stretching a point," said Rhianwen, looking at Lance, who, half-guessing what was coming, quickly looked away, "but the Lady Elli is the right age, and not far removed from that station. Think of the sight of us. What will they see? Silver, black and chestnut hair: Crone, Matron, Maiden."

"You aim to put *Elli* on a battlefield? No!" Lance's indignation overcame his embarrassment.

"Morgan and I can protect ourselves and have sufficient power left over for her, I promise you," said Rhianwen earnestly, and, although Lance was unhappy with the idea, he believed her, and said no more.

Arthur spoke. "I think this is a good scheme," he said. "But Elli must be asked, and agree willingly. We do not coerce people – especially not visiting ladies! I will not start now. But if she agrees, you will not stop her?" he added to Lance.

"I, too, would not force my will on her. I trust the power of Rhianwen and Morgan – but it's not something I can be happy about."

"Then I will go and ask her – and Morgan, for you would be foolish to assume *her* consent: she has too many conflicting emotions here," said Rhianwen, and departed without more ado.

"So," said Lyn, moving on, "we have, on the summit, the High King on his white charger, and, slightly lower down so as not to mask him, his Council. Then the rest of the Companions. It is impressive, so far."

Arthur spoke. "My standard, the Red Dragon, will be by me…planted at first, but carried when we charge. I feel that this should be done by young Cadwr – he has his black beast to stand by me, and is a skilful rider. As usual, the standard bearer will not be able to wield his sword, but the press of Companions will protect him," he added, in explanation to Lance.

Taliesin spoke in his slow, deep, voice. "At Badon, we raised a cross alongside the other emblems. Many of your men are followers of Christ – as indeed are plenty of Mordred's. May we fashion a simple cross and raise that as well? To inspire, and to cow?"

Arthur laughed. "If we're not careful, this small hill will be somewhat overcrowded! But yes, if it proves feasible, it is a good idea. Palomides, are you going to ask for the Bull of Mithras as well?"

Palomides shook his head, smiling slightly. "There are too few of us, on either side, to be inspired – or frightened – so. Those of us in this camp will make our own pact with our god in the dark of the night before. No need for a visible sign, to overcrowd our hill."

Something stirred in the back of Lance's mind. It was hardly a new idea, but he couldn't quite place the particular resonance. However, the idea itself had merit. He spoke.

"You will choose your moment, and sweep down?"

"Yes," said the High King. "It is often the hardest part, to stand and watch your men fight – and die. But we can only charge the once, and we must wait for the best moment."

"Would it help, if, at that moment, a distraction, an attack from an unexpected quarter, were to occur?"

"It would indeed! But we cannot risk putting men in the wood to the south: it is too obvious and their scouts are not fools – they will search it, before, and during the battle."

"No," said Lance, slowly, "But if a small band were to go where their army has already been – the hilly wooded area that they could not move a full army through... Look," he said, turning to the map. "If such a force were to go through *these* woods," he pointed at the wooded, undulating ground to the east of the route from the south. "And if they could receive a signal, they could fall on Mordred from behind, just as you attack from the hill..."

"Powell, you have it! What sort of force have you in mind?"

"You have mounted men? Men who are used to uneven ground, hills, and forests?"

"Indeed – some of our wilder followers, from the mountains of Gwynedd, answer that description. They ride hill ponies or small, sturdy horses. Some have especially made leather boots, so they can communicate through them in a complex way with the horses' very flesh."

"No stirrups, then," said Lance. "Yet I saw some on your horses when I was at the picket lines."

"No stirrups. Although it is perhaps our use of these new devices on the Companions' mounts that has given us the advantage in many skirmishes and battles. But these hill men are happy and skilful in their own style. Besides, we could not provide so many stirrups at short notice: metal is precious and takes time to work."

"Have you any spare? I cannot ride without them."

"You?"

"Yes. I am not trained for your type of battle. I am not used to riding your great beasts, and, despite Lyn's best efforts, I would cut a poor figure as a foot-swordsman. But this..."

"Are you then more skilled on ponies, or mountain horses?"

"Oddly, yes. I played polo."

"Polo?"

"A game soldiers use to while away time, and to keep them fit and alert. It is played on small horses – with one hand on the reins and the other clutching a mallet, with which to hit the ball.

I reckon I could wield a sword like that. But I would need stirrups!"

"We do carry *some* spares! Those we can provide. How many men?"

"Can you spare between thirty and fifty? More would be difficult over the terrain: fewer, and they would be ineffective."

"That will cause no problem. What about language?"

Lance asked Lyn, "Can Olwen translate for me, from such a distance? You said she would move some way away."

"Yes – to the ridge Elli called the Edge. That should be possible, but don't overtax her. Use words sparingly – it is a..." He searched his mind for appropriate twenty-first century slang. "It is a Big Ask!"

"There is one point..." said Lance.

"I know," said Arthur.

"The timing!" they said together, and smiled at each other. Seeing them, Lyn shook his head, and Bedwyr said to him, "Very different, yet so alike! Arthur has his spark back – something that none of us have quite given him, even Cai, or myself, who have known him so long!"

Unaware of this exchange, Lance and the High King were expanding on their theme. "It will be hard enough for you to decide when to charge: how can we coordinate our attack with it?"

Arthur turned to Lyn. "Can you? Will you?"

Lyn took his time answering. "I don't see why not," he said eventually. "There will certainly be enough power on that hill!"

"You have never used your Power to fight for us in battle," said Arthur.

"Indeed. That is true. But we will not be sending a wave of fire over Mordred's army – just a quick pulse of light. It could even be done without power at all – a fire kindled at the right moment would do it. But, in the heat of battle, this way will be more certain."

Arthur embraced Lyn. "You always walk the fine line of your morality so well – thank you, old friend!" He turned to Lance. "What more will you want?"

Lance thought. "Supplies, of course: minimal, but we cannot fight well if we are famished and thirsty. And if you have any white clay, or something? Our front men could paint their faces, and add fright to surprise."

"It is centuries since we in these islands fought wearing war paint! I'll see what we can do. You are right – white would be most effective if it is possible."

The others had been mainly silent during these exchanges. Now Cai said, "When will you leave? Can you be certain not to be seen? What of their scouts?"

Penawr made his first contribution to the debate. "Far fewer scouts and spies in an area they have already explored, but do not disregard the possibility. Set up your own guards, send out scouts. And, you must be in place as soon as possible. It seems the fight will not be tomorrow, but, in all probability, the day after. I should think that today at dusk would be the best time."

Lyn said, "I will make you fairly unnoticeable when you cross the road. Apart from that, it will be up to you – as Penawr has just said – set guards and scouts on all sides."

Arthur put his finger on the map. "Approach the road under the shadow of these trees to the south of us. Then, over and into the area beyond. It is not really hilly, just full of small ups and downs and thickly treed, which, while very hard for a large force – almost impossible to keep it together – should not hinder you too much."

As the discussion became more detailed, Lance realised that yet again, the plan for spending the whole night with Elli would have to be postponed. As soon as the meeting was over, he must find her, for she must not hear this development second-hand. He brought his attention back to the meeting and thought of something important. "When can I meet the men?" he said.

Behind him, Lyn smiled at Taliesin, who responded, "You did well, old friend. Powell may not be Lancelot, but he will do very nicely!"

When Elli had woken that morning, she found Morgan and Rhianwen already absent. She dressed and made her way to the tents put aside for the women of the camp to wash, and then to the toilet facilities.

Walking back, she realised that she felt more relaxed and also more invigorated than she had for days: no, for weeks – since long before they had started on this adventure. She was, she supposed, not pretending any more to anyone: not hiding her attraction from Lance, not pretending to be the niece of a Victorian woman, not trying to be the son her father had lost, not pretending, even, that she was on the same wavelength as the college girls. In fact, she found Morgan easier to get on with than any of them, and even Rhianwen had an edgy spark which she admired and which amused her.

A spring of happiness and well-being seemed to bubble in her. Despite the prospect of the coming battle, she found that the continuing fine weather, the growing friendships within the camp, the bond with Lance –and the prospect of a whole night with him – all combined to make her feel good. She hummed cheerfully to herself as she approached the tent, and was pleased to see Morgan there, with breakfast.

"No fresh bread today, I'm afraid. Sop-in-wine instead. Soak the stale bread in the warm wine, and you'll find it quite palatable."

Elli ate with a will, sitting on one of the camp-stools. "I know it's silly, on the edge of a battle," she said, "but I don't know when I've felt so relaxed, and so happy."

"Ah, as to that…" said Morgan, and stopped.

'As to that' seems to be her catch phrase, thought Elli, adding: it is indeed. Obviously. Realising Morgan was no longer speaking, she prompted, "You were saying?"

"No matter," said Morgan. "You slept well, then?"

"I did – and long: you should have woken me! But you're doing it again – changing the subject. You were about to say something to me yesterday about your Power, when Rhianwen decided to leave us and so you did not continue. And last night, under the music, although Olwen was not translating, I sensed you and Lyn in a disagreement about whether to tell me something. I think you had better follow your instincts, now I know there's something up. What is it?"

Morgan shook her head slightly, not in denial, but in amusement. "You picked up on our conversation, without knowing the words. You noticed my occasional avoidances. You are shrewd, young Elli. No," – as Elli showed her impatience – "I'm not putting you off again. You're right. Lyn and I disagreed, but I saw his point, that there was no need to add to the …complexity… of the situation yet. Yet I still felt that the more time you had the better, and now, with you asking directly, I am happy to override Lyn. My dear, you feel a certainty of happiness, within you?"

Elli nodded, wondering what was coming.

"Yesterday, when I was talking of my Power, and Rhianwen broke in, I was about to say this: my Power allows me to see into things – for example, even though it is very early days – I know you are carrying your Lance's child: and that it is a boy!"

As soon as Morgan said it, Elli knew she was right. Her mind raced. A boy would go far to reconcile her father to the situation: a grandson to replace the lost son, an heir for the farm; her mother would be supportive as always, and would enjoy a baby round the place. With luck, she would get to take her exams in May...

Lance! She had not thought of him: their relationship was too new, and it was too difficult to see the course of it. For a moment she pictured a wish-fulfilment future: Lance, running his projected trouble-shooting business from the farm, with an office there, assisting them with planning and some financial backing. The farm would flourish, and she would help with both businesses. That was, when she could spare time from their two – no three – children: two boys – one to take over from the farm from his grandfather, one to follow his father into the army – and a girl for everyone to indulge and delight in, one who would be able to choose to be a 'girlie' girl if she wanted, or to be a barrister, or an airline pilot...one who had real flesh and blood brothers to share the weight of expectation...

She pulled herself out of the dream. This might come to pass, but only if Lance decided he didn't feel trapped. There would be time for the relationship to develop when they got home, and, if all went well, she could tell him in two or three months. Earlier, and she might fall way behind Gwennie. She would be the replacement who entangled him, not the shining paragon who so nobly let him go.

"Don't tell him!" she said, and found that Morgan was saying "Don't tell him!" at exactly the same time.

"You feel it too? I might...drive him away?" Elli asked.

"No, indeed. I just felt that a soldier on the eve of a battle needs as few distractions as possible!"

"But I might, Morgan. Drive him away, I mean. This whole thing is so new, and his love for...for his Gwennie, so powerful, it might be too much. He could so easily hate me for trapping him, on top of not being her…look at your Lancelot and Elaine."

"It is a possibility. I would be foolish to say it isn't – human relationships vary so much. But although you are patterned like Lancelot and Elen, you are *not* them. I have seen the way Powell – your Lance – looks at you. But yes, leave it a little until you feel more certain – your very anxiety about his reaction could provoke the one you do not want!"

Elli stood up, and went to Morgan and hugged her. "You are a good friend and full of sensible advice. And although I do not feel sick, I certainly feel different, and all the complications in the world – now or in any future – aren't going to take that measure of content from me!" She paused, then added, "But shouldn't I feel sick?"

"By no means all women do," said Morgan. "I did – and it took as much Power as I had to control it! My sister never did, except with her last, Mordred. I think she did not fight hard to keep him with her because she was so tired – and because, being Morgause, she resented anyone who could make her feel so ill!"

They sat there, with the sun growing stronger, saying little, until they saw Rhianwen hurrying toward them. With little preamble, she announced, "I have been at the King's council-of-war!"

"Oh, were you invited?" Morgan asked blandly.

"Not as such. But they were pleased I came – I am quite up to Merddin's skill at coming and going unnoticed, and once there, I proved useful."

"I'm sure you did," said Morgan. "So might I have, but I had the courtesy to stay away from where I was not invited!"

Rhianwen smiled with good humour. "Annoyed you did not think of it? But truly, my good friend, this is too important to squabble about. It concerns you, and Elli as well." She outlined the discussion she had been part of, and waited for their reactions.

Elli had to take a firm hold on the new calm and happiness inside her. She wasn't sure quite how she felt about Rhianwen's idea. Surprised? Yes. Excited? Certainly. And frightened, and flattered. And, she decided, inadequate.

"You want me, with you two…enchantresses, for want of a better word… you want me on the hill with you?"

"Certainly," said Rhianwen, crisply. "You have the perfect look. We can protect you easily against a flung spear, and we can also make you unnoticeable, should the need arise."

"I don't doubt that…but is my presence that important – to go to those lengths?"

"As to that," Morgan stated, "I think it is a good idea you have had, Rhianwen, and Elli is definitely necessary to it. So: yes, Elli, we need you there."

"Then I will be there," said Elli with determination.

"Moreover, you will view the battle – and be able to keep an eye on Powell," said Rhianwen, only half joking.

"About your idea," said Morgan to Rhianwen, "I have thought of a few refinements we could make."

"Merddin is always very Moral when it comes to how much power we should use," warned the Sidhe woman.

"Don't I know it! But this is only to add to our awe-inspiring appearance!"

She outlined her thoughts, and despite herself, Elli was drawn into the ensuing discussion, and even added a few ideas. Surprises seemed to be coming thick and fast that morning. Again, she was struck by the oddity of her presence, the impossibility of her companions and the weirdness of the subject of their talk. And underlying it all was the alarming thrill of her pregnancy.

This was not the last surprise that morning. Before midday, she saw Lance coming, like Rhianwen, from the direction of the King's great tent. There was a spring in his step, and, as he came closer, Elli could see suppressed excitement in his face, mixed, she thought, with some embarrassment.

"Greetings, ladies," he said, trying for a bow. He looked at Elli, then addressed Morgan. "Can you spare Elli for a while? I have something I must tell her."

"Somewhat abrupt, but to the point," said Rhianwen, smiling. "You have finished your conference, then. Moreover, the outcome concerns Elli?"

"Yes. No. Not directly. Yes, we have finished, and no the outcome does not directly affect her. But I need to speak to her, all the same."

"We are not a royal court, for you to ask formal permission," said Morgan. "Go with him, Elli."

Lance whisked her into the next door tent, conveniently empty. Facing her, he held her hands and again she could see the excitement on his face. "My dear, we will have to postpone tonight. I'm off as soon as it is dusk!"

"Off?" said Elli. "Where?"

Lance explained, waxing enthusiastic about the strategy, what he knew of the horses and men, and about this chance of making a positive contribution to a battle so far removed from his own experience. Elli smiled fondly: it was like hearing a boy describe his first BMX trial, or how he had fared in a robo-wars competition.

When he finally ran out of steam, she cast round for encouraging words, to mask her disappointment, and fear. "My Lord Aragorn," she said eventually. Seeing the blank look on his face, she said, "You remember. *Lord of the Rings*. The Battle of Pelennor Fields. Aragorn sails up the river and attacks from behind – 'Thus came Aragorn, son of Arathorn... out of the mists of morning..."'

"Of course!" Lance dropped a kiss on her forehead. "I knew the plan reminded me of something. Not that there haven't been plenty of battles that turned on an attack from an unexpected quarter. But it felt literary – suitable for this whole set-up!"

"Glad to be of service!"

"But it does mean that I will be away until after the battle. I'm sorry."

"If it is only until after the battle, I can put up with that! But Lance, it is a literal battle, not a literary one. You could be injured or killed. People do die – oh, not the heroes in most books. But this is real: it will be bloody, and nasty, and no respecter of persons. Especially someone not used to fighting in this way."

"I know. But I think the mere fact that I'm here suggests that I might just have some protection – after all, the circumstances are rather exceptional."

"Yes," said Elli, who doubted the logic, but thought it wise not to challenge it.

"Anyway, I can't do anything about it. I will, of course, take care – as much as I can, without risking the scheme. But for now, my love, take this as a promise." And he pulled her to him.

Not for long enough. Soon he was away, hastening out of the tent. Elli found tears blinding her eyes, and the words of the song from Lance's past running in her head: 'The Carnival is over, we may never meet again.' After a few minutes, she scrubbed her face with her sleeve and tried to compose her expression. But still, as she went out to rejoin Morgan and Rhianwen, she found herself singing softly:

> *"Though the Carnival is over,*
> *I will love you till I die."*

Chapter 6

The rest of the day passed quietly: at least there were no more surprises. Internally, Elli thought, it was far from quiet: if she had been a Victorian maiden in what her grandmother had called a 'novelette', she felt she would have been described as nursing 'a maelstrom of conflicting emotions in her bosom'!

At dusk, Morgan took her to the south-east corner of the camp, and, looking southwards, she saw dimly a line of some thirty or so horsemen, quietly dressed in brown garments and riding small dark-coloured horses, fade silently into the trees. "There goes Powell, your Lance," said Morgan. "You may yet catch glimpses of him over the next day or so, if Olwen is not too busy to send you some images."

Even as she spoke, a noise from the direction of the small hill made them turn. The dragon was rising into the air. Once she had gained some height, she turned and with slow wing movements moved north and slightly east toward the barely-visible outline of the abrupt hill of Alderley Edge. There she landed, merging into the dark shape of the ridge, so that, to a casual eye, there was nothing out of the ordinary to be seen there.

"Another of Lyn's 'Noble Ideas'," Morgan commented as they moved away. "We must not upset the fabric of history by frightening the enemy with a dragon – especially as the future accounts do not mention one!"

This made Elli think of something. "Morgan, in many accounts of our day, it is said that Lancelot fights in this battle –

can you make sure, afterwards, that Lance is known by his real name, not Poole, or Powell?"

"If I can, I will."

Elli went early to bed that night, and, surprisingly, went straight into a deep, seemingly dreamless sleep. In the morning, she wondered if it had been simply because she had exhausted herself with the varying emotions and events of the day, or whether Morgan, aware of this, had 'helped' the sleep in some way.

The day proved grey and overcast, and it had obviously rained overnight. Poor Lance, she thought, in the forest amongst the dripping trees... She was rewarded by a sudden vision, vivid in her mind, of leather sheets stretched between the trunks of trees. Men were rolling them up and tying them to the saddles of their horses. She felt relieved that they had been dry overnight and was mentally thanking Olwen, when, in the corner of the picture, she glimpsed Lance, helping with the last cover. Then all was gone. She redoubled her thanks, and went out to face the day.

There was an added air of excitement and expectation in the camp that day. The news soon spread that Mordred's army would indeed arrive by dusk, and Cai had organised a band of soldiers to dig a ditch and barricade it with stakes. "Mordred will have them pulled up as soon as he arrives, of course," said Morgan to Elli, when she asked about it. "In the dusk tonight, or at first light tomorrow, if necessary. But it will slow them down, and no army, on foot, or mounted, will cross that ditch in the dark. So we keep some choice about when and where we fight."

The King spent time that day encouraging the diggers, inspecting the horses, laughing with some of the soldiers. He also absented himself from the busyness of the camp for long talks with Rhianwen, Taliesin and Lyn, to which Morgan and

Elli were not invited, although, for short whiles, Cai, Bedwyr and also young Gareth were all called in. Elli was surprised that Morgan was not offended, but instead seemed quite content. "I have some idea what it is all about," the older woman said, "and I feel it would not be right for me to be there. I am too involved." She would say no more.

In mid-afternoon, the king and the others emerged from the tent. Elli happened to be passing, and Lyn caught her by the arm. "My dear girl, it seems a long time since I spent time with you – and we saw such a lot of each other only recently! But we have no time to right that, now: we have received news that Mordred and his army are about an hour away. The ditch will ensure they do not come upon us today, but tomorrow will be the battle. You and I know something of the outcome – but also how vital it is that it is fought to the last breath. Arthur is aware of that last, although not the outcome, of course. It will give extra form to his speech – for he would address the forces now. Can you find Morgan and come, both of you, to the open area, the practice ground?"

Elli hurried to the medicine tent, where she knew Morgan was. The paths of the camp were crowded with soldiers, walking briskly toward the area at the rear of the camp. The sound of hammer on anvil and the sharp smell of hot metal came from behind the horse pickets where the smiths were replacing cast horseshoes, and making last minute repairs to harness, armour and weapons. Finding Morgan, Elli gave the message and Morgan nodded briskly, dried her hands on a cloth, shrugged on her cloak and together they left the tent.

"I hope you will follow what the King says," she remarked, "for Olwen is further off now, but she will exert herself to the utmost to ensure you do. And I am now glad Merddin Emrys made me learn your tongue sufficiently so that I need only a little help from Olwen. Life would be even harder than it is, otherwise!"

They had arrived at the edge of the practice ground. Here the land sloped away slightly, so that they would be able to stand and be seen by all the men. Arthur alone was mounted, on his great white stallion. On one side of him stood his Council – Merddin, Rhianwen, Taliesin, Morgan – and, to her consternation, Elli, as well as Cadwr: on the other, the Companions were ranged.

Arthur spoke. He had a loud, clear, resonant voice, remarkably young and unaffected by the hard years just behind him. Elli suspected that Lyn might be amplifying it slightly, for the benefit of the men near the back, but it was still impressive.

"My friends," he said. "We stand here on the edge of doom. For what we do tomorrow will ring down the ages, will affect those who live in these islands for hundreds, no thousands, of years. This battle will shape our lives, and how we think of those who now come against us – for don't forget that we have lived in relative peace with the Saxons as neighbours for these last twenty years. Now, an ill-wishing one of our own has stirred them up against us and we find ourselves fighting for our very way of life, our beliefs, our peoples and our families. We must fight – even in this cruel season. Do you think that I would have asked you to leave your farms and forests, your wives and children, to slog over mile after mile in the wettest, coldest weather, if this were not so?

"But of course the risk is great. We must fight and fight, through the day, through pain and through weariness. I cannot pretend that every man will come safe home to feast his neighbours with tales of glory..." Elli shot a startled look at Lyn, who avoided her eye. He had obviously read some Shakespeare on one or other of his time journeys, and shared it with Arthur.

The King was continuing, "No, some will die. And in case I am one of them…" A gasp went through the assembled troops. Cries of "No!" and "Never!" rose above the general intake of breath.

Arthur laughed. "Come, my friends, I'm flesh and blood, like you are. If you tickle me, I laugh and if you stab me, I bleed…"

More Shakespeare, thought Elli.

"And I would not leave the succession unprovided for. It is no simple matter, for there are at least three systems at work amongst us. Those who follow the old Roman ways would have me – lacking an heir of my body, as I do – you would have me name an heir, or heirs, and adopt them as my sons. Others believe that the kingship should pass through the female line, and still others, that the Council should choose from amongst my kin.

"Before I continue, I would like to tell you of a conversation I had today. I talked with Gareth, my great-nephew here" – and he indicated the young man with a sweeping gesture – "We decided that, although I love him dearly, I would not include him in any succession. We go to fight his uncle, his father's half-brother, and although I will personally vouch for his absolute fidelity, he feels that this circumstance leaves too much room for later dissent."

"Besides which," Gareth spoke up, unexpectedly, "I would not desire to be king – nor would I make a good one! Perhaps, when I am older, I may gain enough wisdom to be an advisor, a counsellor."

Applause, cheers, and foot-stamping greeted this. Arthur waited for the noise to die down, then leant from his horse and embraced the tall young man, causing the cheers to break out again. Finally, Arthur straightened up and raised his arm, and the hubbub ebbed away.

"Now for what I – and the Council – have decided. I hope to please all three traditions: I have chosen three heirs, and my Council –and, I hope, Cai and Bedwyr – will choose from them. From those who survive, I mean, for of course, they are as mortal as I am – and this is an additional reason for naming three.

"From my father's kin, I name Gwalchmai, who knows both the Roman and Island ways. He is of middle years; a wise and faithful friend and a Companion of many years…" He indicated the tall, dark-haired man, who stood forward and bowed.

"Secondly, I name Owain, my sister-son. His mother, Morgan, is even now here, a member of my Council, my advisor and my friend. She it was who called back Merddin Emrys to my side. And Owain's father, Urien of Gore, was my father's faithful aide, and one of my first Companions. His son has taken his place, and I have felt myself honoured as well as delighted by his support and companionship, and, I make bold to say, his love. As all my Companions are, he is skilled with sword, spear and horse."

He presented Owain, a stocky, sturdy, dark-bearded man in his thirties, who shot a startled look at Arthur – the news was obviously a surprise to him.

"Finally," said Arthur, "it may be that circumstances seem to suggest a younger man, suitable for a new start, one who knows me, but is capable of judging my ways in a more detached manner. So I offer you my kinsman on my mother's side, she who was Ygraine, Duchess of Cornwall. Cadwr of Cornwall is not yet a Companion, but he has the same skills of warfare that have Owain and Gwalchmai, and experience of ruling his own land of Cornwall. Like the other two he has a cool head and mature judgement. So, for those of you who do not yet know him, I give you Cadwr of Cornwall!"

Cadwr, too, was obviously surprised, but he kept his composure, and following the example of Gwalchmai and Owain, he bowed to the King and then to the troops. Elli looked at Morgan, who, despite her protestations of lack of feeling for her son, had a smile on her lips and tears in her eyes.

"So, my friends, my warriors, you see we have tried to think of everything. I aim to see you after the battle, and have you tell me that the matter of the succession was – premature. But it will be need to be settled sometime, and now it is.

"To return to the present. Eat well, sleep well. Your centurions, chiefs and commanders know where you are to fight tomorrow. Some of you, I know, fought with me at Badon. Others are their sons, or sons of those who fell there. We have a fine tradition to look back on and to maintain. Fight so that I will be proud of you, and, more importantly, you will be proud of yourselves, and future ages, even in a thousand years time, will say, 'This was their finest hour!'"

The troops stamped and cheered. The Companions and Council and all beside the King joined in, only slightly more decorously. Elli was amongst them and tears blinded her eyes, despite her mind saying in a detached voice: Churchill as well! Lyn *has* been busy! But it was not just the words: the voice, the delivery, the stance, the sheer charisma of the man, was overwhelming, even to her, a stranger from a strange time. And yet…and yet… whichever version reflected the reality more, by tomorrow evening Arthur, High King of Britain, would be dead, or taken way, gravely wounded, never to be seen again. Oh, to fight to the end, 'To bear with unbearable sorrow… to dream the impossible dream…' (Damn it, must she, too, think in other people's words, and worse, in popular songs?)… Oh, it was noble enough, and would leave the most splendid stories for telling and retelling, but the waste and the sadness were almost overwhelming.

Just then a quietly dressed man appeared from the tents and spoke to Cai, who in turn said something to Arthur. The King raised his arms, and said with a loud voice, "We have news. Mordred and his army have arrived. Seeing the ditch and stakes, and in this growing dusk, they are not moving on us now, but settling for the night. Our fate is upon us. As I said, we stand on the edge of doom. Tomorrow, let my faith in you buoy your hearts and guide your swords. Tonight, sleep well!"

With that, he turned his horse and moved off. The Companions and the Council followed, as did Elli. She, too, wanted to settle for the night as soon as possible. The knowledge she had about the outcome weighed upon her, and she was reluctant to talk to others, innocent and even hopeful. She took her supper to the tent, and then readied herself for bed.

As she pulled the covers up and put her head on her pillow, she heard Lance's voice, close at hand saying, "Goodnight, my love. Sleep well." She sat up abruptly and stared into the shadows cast by her oil lamp. But there was nothing there. She felt a wave of warmth and amusement wash over her. She smiled, and replied softly, "Goodnight, Lance." Olwen was still showing interest and kindness to herself and Lance. She sent a heartfelt thank you to the great green creature, lay down again, and was soon asleep.

Before dawn, Elli woke with Morgan shaking her. "Time to rise! We must look our best to play our part today. Rhianwen is already decked in splendour, and has gone to fetch us food and drink."

Elli's eyes gradually focussed on Morgan and saw that she, too, was 'decked in splendour' – the red and gold over-tunic she had been wearing when Olwen had first showed her to Elli. I was thinking I had no close female friend, thought Elli, And Olwen let me glimpse Morgan. She was right – I feel closer to her, after a few days, than to any other woman – in some ways, closer even than to my mother.

Then she saw that Morgan was holding a dress out toward her. It was of fine white wool with touches of gold embroidery. Where had she got that from, Elli wondered, but said nothing. "For the Maiden," said Morgan. "We must all look as glorious as we can, to dazzle everyone!"

As they were brushing their hair by the light of the oil lamp, Rhianwen returned. She looked stunning. Her dress was black, as befitted the Crone, with silver embroidery reflecting her silver hair. She brushed aside Elli's "You look wonderful", and subjected her to a close inspection.

"Good," the Sidhe woman said finally. "Here we are, the three aspects of the Great Goddess – and very impressive we look, too!"

"I only wish my hair was as long as yours," said Elli, tugging at hers, which had now grown to just below her shoulders, but couldn't compete with the waist-length hair of the other two women.

"It looks well enough," said Rhianwen. "Now, since we are not truly Goddesses, here is some sustenance: it will be a long day."

As Elli ate the standard breakfast of stale bread and warm wine, she wondered how she would cope with the long day ahead. Fearful of even thinking of the greater issues, she concentrated on her stomach. No food, obviously, but no drink? This worry, at least, was answered when Rhianwen furnished them with leather water bottles to hang on their belts. Then she ushered them out. At the last minute, Elli dived back into the tent and found the long knife that Lyn had given her, and fastened it, in its sheath, to her belt.

It was still dark, but not the thick darkness of true night. There was a hint of brightness in the sky to the east, the faintest hint of sunrise and there were no stars to be seen. The fine layer of cloud would have stopped that, anyway, thought Elli. As they rounded the circle of tents, they could see a steady stream of soldiers in front of them, heading to the eastern gateway, and beyond, to the flat land between the marsh and the forest, where the battle would be fought.

They turned aside, and entered the King's Great Tent. There, Arthur was waiting, with Lyn, Taliesin, Cadwr and the Companions. They, too, looked splendid: Combed hair, cleaned faces, and with the metal and leather of the armour polished till it shone. They looked vaguely Roman, thought Elli, but not quite. Lyn and Taliesin had fine flowing robes over workmanlike trousers and belted tunics. From the belts hung their swords, in worked leather sheaths.

"Good morning, sister," said Arthur. "And good morning to you, my Lady Rhianwen, and my Lady Elli. It looks as if it will be a fine day to fight – neither too hot, nor too cold, nor yet, I hope, wet! Thank you for your offer of help: I hope you will not be too… uncomfortable… on our hill."

"Nothing like as 'uncomfortable' as you – or, indeed, any of the soldiers," Morgan said dryly.

"True. But we – and they – expect that in a battle. You might reasonably remain here, in some sort of comfort."

"To 'weep and wait', bind up wounds, and prepare the dead for burial," said Rhianwen, dismissively. "This suits me better – and, I believe, the others, too."

"Enough conversation," Lyn broke in. "Go, and fetch your horses. We will wait for you at the gate."

They stood, shivering in the dawn cold, as the last of the soldiers filed out. To the left and right they could dimly see the small contingent of mounted troops who would, Rhianwen said, be stationed, out of sight, on the far wings of the army. Elli waited for the Companions to join them, but no white horses glimmered in the half-light.

Then, behind them, there was a clattering and a wild cry. Through the centre of the camp, past the older serving-men who were already dismantling tents, rode Arthur, sword raised. Close behind him, Cadwr on his black charger carried the King's banner, flapping against its pole in the still air. After him came the Companions. Their speed was necessarily slow through the camp, but the sight was still enough to make Elli's heart lurch and her stomach turn over.

Lyn and Rhianwen looked at each other and smiled. Then, breaking eye contact, they looked ahead and suddenly the mist was back, as white and dense as it had been in the fourteenth-century Peak District. In the midst was a clearer area, and through that the horsemen rode, slowly now, and silently, followed by the small party on foot. The ground sloped upward, and then, through the mist, Elli saw in the growing daylight the rough wooden cross that had been fashioned the night before. Arthur and Cadwr stayed near it, while the companions crested the hill and moved swiftly down the far side.

As they left the mist, they shouted again, and a mirroring shout from the troops below echoed and re-echoed. It must, thought Elli, look magnificent – a great piece of theatre, with the white horses appearing out of the mist, and taking their places on the lower slope, halfway between the King and his men.

Lyn gestured them to stand on the King's left, slightly lower down the slope, whilst he and Taliesin stood to the right. Then he brought his hand down, and suddenly, the mist was gone and the banner was lifted by a gusty breeze – could he arrange a wind too, Elli wondered – and it streamed out, displaying the great red dragon and its golden fire. A stray glint from the rising sun found its way through the clouds and the embroidered gold shone as if it were fire indeed.

There was a gasp, which came not only from their own troops but also from the army on the other side of the ditch. Elli saw them for the first time, and quailed inwardly. She had known the fight would be hard, but now she saw it and felt it.

She turned her head again and took in more completely what had caused the gasp. Arthur on his white charger, backed by Cadwr on his black one. The cross, the ensign. Lyn – no, in this context surely Merddin Emrys – and the great bard Taliesin. Belatedly, she realised that some of the wonder must be because of her group as well: clothed in black, red and white; silver, black and chestnut hair; Crone, Matron and Maiden. She stood tall, and looked east, at Mordred's army, and, specifically, at the men leading it.

It was surely, she thought, that Olwen was lending her vision: this was far clearer than she would otherwise see. In the middle were an army largely and disconcertingly like Arthur's: men on the whole narrow-boned and dark. Many were short, although height and red hair were not uncommon. Their clothing, too, was similar with remnants of Roman armour. But on either side were tall, blond Saxons, armed, it seemed with the curved swords or seaxes, from which Morgan had said they got their name. Others wielded axes, and the clothing, although similar to the Celts', seemed generally of brighter colours.

Centrally placed were three horsemen, the only ones she could see in the whole opposing army. The middle rider must be Mordred, she supposed, but she was unable to make out his features even with her enhanced vision. He was a tall man, not unlike his uncle, Arthur, in build. The other two were, surprisingly, Saxons – obviously leaders and thus accorded the honour of being on horseback, of riding the sacred beasts.

As she looked, she caught a movement to her right, and, turning, saw Cadwr plant the banner firmly in the earth. Arthur must have spoken to him, for now he took a shorter white flag from his saddlebag and, unfurling it, galloped down the hill. Rhianwen spoke, "It is of course useless, but I suppose we must try."

"Indeed," said Morgan.

Elli said nothing, but watched. As Cadwr reached the ditch so recently dug, one of the two Saxons flanking Mordred moved his horse forward. He also bore a white flag.

Rhianwen spoke to Elli. "Each will give the terms under which they would consider not fighting – but it is just empty ritual."

"Not on Arthur's part," said Morgan sharply. "He would love to avoid this encounter, even now. He still harbours a hope of reconcilement with Mordred."

"Then he is more of a fool than I thought him," said Rhianwen. "He cannot keep his feelings under control in his private life, as we all know to our cost, but surely in this matter of state, he should acknowledge that Mordred is power-hungry and will not stop until he is High King – or exiled – or dead? Better dead, for he could plot and cause havoc if he were half a world away!"

Elli had turned her head to listen to all this, and so missed what was happening below. But then a shout arose from both sides and the two horsemen turned and moved quickly away from each other. With a roar, swords were drawn, and axes swung. Men were leaping over the ditch, and, where Mordred's men had managed to bridge it with planks, hastening to be across before the enemy reached the makeshift gangway. Battle was joined.

As Cadwr reached the group on the hill, Elli caught some of his words of explanation, and half-remembered the story. It was to be the first of many times that she felt familiarity with events without recalling them exactly or knowing what was to happen. As he had talked to the Saxon, who spoke the Celtic tongue well, one of the men behind him had drawn his sword to kill a snake he thought he saw. Mordred had cried treachery, and all hope of talking further was abruptly over. "And it was only some rope left from Mordred's bridging the ditch," he concluded. "I saw it, clear as clear, but it was too late. And what snake would be fool enough to be abroad on this sort of ground, in this weather, between two armies of noisy men, anyway?"

Elli didn't catch the King's reply, but Cadwr stowed the white flag, and again raised the great banner, holding it high and moving it in slow passes before planting it once more in the ground. Elli turned back to the battlefield, and looked wider, for the first time, taking in the full view, and gasped. The opposing army was so much larger than Arthur's. "Surely there are not so many in the land willing to fight the High King?" she said to Morgan.

Morgan shrugged slightly. "If you look at the British in their army," she said, "I would guess the numbers to be roughly the same as we have – especially if you remember that our horsemen are not yet fighting. It is hard to raise an army at this time of year – and even harder to feed them. But to that army, they have added Saxons, who have the hope of winning land to settle – some have even come from over the Eastern Sea. But they all still need feeding," she added after a pause. "We can hope they are not as fit as us because of lack of provisions, although I do not suppose Mordred will have been as scrupulous in obtaining some as his uncle." She stopped talking and stood looking over the battlefield.

By now, the ground below was covered with a heaving, roiling mass of men. Elli wished that her senses were not Olwen-enhanced, for she could hear only too clearly the shouts suddenly cut off, the screams of agony, the yelling, the thud of sword on shield, the ring of metal on metal. Once or twice she heard what she felt must be the noise of axe splitting bone. She could shut her eyes, perhaps, but not her ears. Indeed, shutting her eyes seemed pointless when all the noises were so clear. So she stood and looked out, seeing men fall and be trampled, axes rising, swords sweeping down, the mass moving this way and that. She noticed that Arthur's men now had red headbands, if they did not have Roman-type helmets, because – obviously, as Lance would have said – they might otherwise turn on each other, there was so little difference between them and the Celtic element of Mordred's army.

Elli shut her eyes briefly, then opened them again. What pleasure could anyone derive from this? Hurt or be hurt, maim or be maimed, kill or be killed? Surely you would only do it as a last resort, to defend family and friend, your way of life, all you hold dear? How could Lance love it so much, miss it so much? For that matter, how could she love someone who felt that way? Perhaps she could excuse him – his style of warfare was different, more at one remove? Perhaps when he saw this hand-to-hand, bloody business, he would change his mind, and his heart? But discovering burnt bodies in a wrecked tank by the roadside must also be shocking. And would Lance be the man she loved if he lost something that was woven into his whole being?

As if thinking of Lance brought him nearer, she was favoured by Olwen with a sight of him: he was on a small horse, under the shadow of the trees. His head was turned away from her, addressing the riders behind, but there was no doubting who it was: she knew the look of him, his head, his way of holding himself, even unfamiliarly, on horseback. As he turned back, he was suddenly gone.

It was now mid-morning, perhaps later. There was a thin layer of cloud, but generally the day was fine and dry, with a good breeze from the south-west. Elli caught with the edge of her mind a surge of Power, of question and answer, although she could hear no words. She saw Arthur turn and say something to Lyn, who nodded, and called to him a young lad whom Elli had not noticed before, but who must have been sitting quietly on the far side of Lyn and Taliesin. The lad ran down the slope to the Companions. As soon as he returned, Elli felt the power surge again, and then withdraw. She saw and felt the stillness of Rhianwen, Morgan and Lyn. She waited.

Suddenly, there was an enormous flash of silver light. It dazzled Elli, and, it seemed, the men fighting, because for a moment the clash of weapons was replaced by cries of wonder. When the light faded, she saw that Arthur was already moving, riding quickly down the hill towards his Companions. He was closely followed closely by Cadwr, who had taken the ensign from the ground, and held it high in the breeze. As Arthur reached the men on the white horses they fell in behind him, the first two on either side of Cadwr, who, as standard-bearer, could not draw his own sword.

Now their pace increased, and a wild war-cry rose from the galloping men. It climbed over the renewed noise of battle, and Elli could sense that most of the fighting men were giving much of their attention to the ride of Arthur and his Companions.

"Good," said Morgan, "for here come the rest of the horsemen, just as Arthur has captured most eyes."

Elli saw that the horsemen were appearing on either wing from behind the hill. Her breath caught as she realised that this must be Lance's moment, too, and she strained her eyes to see what was happening at the edge of the battlefield, where the dark mass of trees edged the horizon.

It seemed that Olwen took pity on her, for she could suddenly see the trees clearly, and out of them burst a band of horsemen, riding swiftly and swinging their swords. At the front was Lance, his face almost unrecognisable, with streaks of white clay painted on either cheek, and a wild wide grin on his face. He was indeed swinging his sword like a polo stick, Elli thought with amusement. She felt, rather than heard, the wild cries issuing from Lance's men rising and mingling with those of Arthur and the Companions. Despite her earlier thoughts, she felt the uplift and excitement of the charge, and was only brought back to earth when she heard Rhianwen's voice. "An attack on all four sides – that should even things up! Although we are still outnumbered, I fear."

Now the neighing and occasional screaming of horses added to the dissonance that was the battle. The fighting seemed to have no clear pattern and neither side had an obvious advantage. Elli thought she saw some of Mordred's army, mainly Saxons, withdraw, but none of Arthur's men came back past her group. It was past midday and the wind was now bringing up clouds from the south-west, making the sky dark and threatening. How long, she thought, will it take for this to grind to a stalemate and then a halt? It did seem as if the number of men fighting was lessening, revealing an alarming number of wounded, dying, and dead, on the ground.

For some time she had thought that she was seeing with just her own eyes, with little or no help from Olwen. She strained to see which of the men on the white horses was Arthur, which of those on the brown ponies was Lance. There was the banner, but was that Arthur near it? She drank some more of the leathery tasting water from her bottle and shifted from foot to foot. How could Rhianwen and Morgan stay so still? Then, suddenly, she heard, louder and more clearly than she had ever done, the dragon inside her head.

"To Arthur – go – you are needed. Go now!"

"Me? Why me?" Elli threw back in her mind to the dragon, but no answer came. She looked despairingly down at the battlefield and found her gaze drawn to a riderless white horse on her far left, not too far from the marsh, and just on their side of the ditch. She felt the approval of Olwen, and paused only to draw the long knife from its sheath. Then, holding up her skirts with her other hand, she set off.

The ground was uneven and she nearly tumbled once or twice before she decided that whatever this was about, her ending in a crumpled heap of broken bones at the bottom of the hill was not going to help. She slowed, but kept going as fast as she could, trying to keep her eyes open for danger. The hill must have some from of protection from Lyn and the others, she reassured herself, as there was no one on it, or approaching it.

Once she got down, it was different. Almost at once a large blond Saxon loomed up, with a look of astonished delight on his face at the sight of a young woman in the middle of a battle. She slashed out with the knife, and perhaps taken off guard by her aggression as well as her presence, the Saxon fell back, clutching at a deep slash on his arm. Shaking, Elli ran on, cursing her skirts, longing for her jeans. She saw two men engaged in swinging heavy swords at each other, and, horribly, felt the clutch of fingers round her ankle, and heard a faint "help me" before she tore her foot away. Then, mercifully, there seemed to be a thin mist round her. Perhaps Morgan or

Rhianwen had seen her descent and were now protecting her. Soon she saw that others didn't notice her, and realised that Lyn must have conjured up his 'unnoticing' spell again. Nearly stumbling again, she paused and looked back, and was horrified to see men swarming up the hill: the protection that had been there had gone – to protect her? She said crossly in her mind: "Olwen, can't you and they manage a bit of protection for me and the hill both?" and ran on, leaving the others to sort the problem.

The mist thinned in front and she saw the horse, head down, nudging at a still body on the ground. There was a black horse, too, and the kneeling figure of Cadwr, his banner lying on the ground beside him. As she approached, he looked up, with tears in his eyes. "He doesn't breathe," he said. "I fear he has left us."

"Breathe for him," the voice in Elli's skull said. Bemused, she just shook her head. The voice grew insistent, even impatient. "Give him your breath. You have said you can do this."

In her mind she saw herself and Morgan, talking near the medicine tent. "Oh my God! Mouth to mouth! Olwen wants me to do mouth to mouth on King Arthur!" She saw Cadwr looking at her oddly, and realised she had spoken aloud. "I may be able to help," she said to the young man, "But don't get your hopes up."

She knelt on the muddied ground and regarded the King. He lay on his back, helmetless, and he had a shallow cut on one cheek, as if he had almost, but not entirely, avoided the downward stroke of a sword. Otherwise, Elli could see no outward hurt, except for a small seeping of blood near his waist, which suggested internal injury. She turned his head to one side, and, trembling at her audacity, put her finger in the King's mouth, checking there was no obstruction, that his tongue was well forward. She felt for a pulse, listened for his heart, looked for the faintest rise and fall of his chest. Nothing. Nothing.

She breathed deeply, slowly, and tried for calm – and to remember the instructions. Next, she tipped Arthur's head back slightly and with one hand pinched his nose. Then two breaths, her lips forming a circle with the King's lips, cracked and dry. No response. She pulled up his leather jerkin and saw the line of blood and bruising. So little a mark for what must be such terrible damage. She pulled her gaze away and located, first by sight and then by touch, where to put her hands. Fifteen compressions. Two breaths. Fifteen compressions. Two breaths. Fifteen compressions. Two breaths. Fifteen compressions. Two ... Stop! There was the slightest movement, just as she was taking her touch away. She held the back of her hand by the King's lips. Could she feel the faintest movement of warm air? She paused. Yes: there it was again.

Looking, she could see Arthur's chest moving slightly. She put her hands there and felt the barely perceptible heartbeat. Then, to her astonishment, she felt warm liquid splash on her hands and realised it was from her own tears. She drew a deep, ragged breath and sat back on her heels. Someone's arm went round her, and looking up, she saw Lyn. "My dear Elli, that was wonderful." He helped her to her feet.

"We should put him on his side, in the recovery position," said Elli, calmly. "But I think he has serious internal injuries, and moving him could be fatal – in fact, I fancy I have done him no favours, bringing him back. But I had to try – and Olwen told me to." Turning her head onto Lyn's shoulders, she wept noisily and shudderingly.

Lyn patted her head, as if she were a little girl. "There, there," he said. "You have done well, very well." He spoke over her head to Morgan and Rhianwen who had arrived and were standing quietly to one side. "Morgan, will you look into him? See if there is anything to be done."

She nodded and knelt silently by her half-brother, holding her hands out, but not touching him. Elli, her sobs slowing, turned to watch. Lyn still kept his arm around her, and for that she was grateful. After a while, Morgan sat back and then stood up, tears in her eyes. "You were right, Elli. There is much damage, much bleeding inside. I think he took a knock on the head, too. I believe I can slow, and perhaps even stem, the bleeding, but I can do little else. And any movement could start it all again. Undisturbed, the organs might heal, but as he comes to himself he will move, and the pain will make him move more, and he will cause more damage, and it will all have been in vain."

Elli looked round the group: young Cadwr, Morgan, herself, all with tear-stained faces; Lyn dry-eyed but grief-stricken. Only Rhianwen, the Sidhe woman, the immortal, looked unmoved and calm. But her voice was warm with concern as she said, "Is there nothing we can do? We can make the pain less, certainly. But anything more?"

Elli spoke. "In my time they would probably put him into what they call a medically-induced coma – a deep sleep, whilst the body heals itself. It can last for days, weeks even. But we do not have the means, here."

Lyn spun her round and kissed her on both cheeks. "Elli, my girl, you may have the answer! Let Morgan stem the bleeding as best she can, then we will give him this sleep. We can, you know!" Morgan with a brief, bright smile, went back to her brother's side, and knelt again, hands out, as before.

"Are we safe here, on the battlefield?" asked Elli, embarrassed by Lyn's praise, and seeking to control the hope within her.

"The battle is almost over. Soon terms of disengagement will be arranged," said Lyn. "I have put an unnoticing spell around us for the moment, but I will need all my Power soon – for Arthur's sleep to start with. Even now, a keen observer might find us. But Cai and Bedwyr and their men stand guard." Elli noticed for the first time some men, including two on white horses, a little way off. "But the fighting has all but stopped. Too many dead, too many wounded, and now no cause." He swept his hand out, indicating Arthur, and then, further to his right, another still form on the ground, with a black horse standing guard. Elli looked, then back to Lyn, puzzlement on her face.

"Go, see," he said.

She walked the few yards and looked down at the man. She felt her skin crawl and the hairs on the back of her neck lifted. For she was looking down on what at first sight seemed to be Arthur. A younger Arthur, now she looked more closely. One that was unquestionably dead, with a great wound in his chest, and a huge amount of drying blood surrounding it. The sword that had caused this lay nearby, as if pulled out and then thrown down, either by its owner or his victim. She looked back to where the true Arthur lay, and understood...Mordred. Arthur's nephew – why had they not told her that they were so alike? It made the whole mess more explicable – how easy it would be to believe the two were father and son – yet more tragic. A voice spoke behind her. It was Cadwr.

"Yes," he said. "I saw them. Mordred sought the King out, and challenged him. They fought, at first on horseback, and then on foot. And Mordred wounded the King badly, but then my lord Arthur gathered all his strength, and struck Mordred. And killed him. Then he howled, with despair, it seemed, and wrenched his sword out, and flung it on the ground, staggered a few yards and then collapsed into my arms. I laid him on the ground, and the rest you know."

Elli could not speak, but touched Cadwr on the shoulder, feeling his grief and helplessness. She moved toward the other group, where Morgan was still on her knees by Arthur, and Lyn and Rhianwen stood ready to help when the healing sleep was required.

Something stirred in her mind. Was this why there were two versions of the end of the last battle? Arthur dead, or Arthur carried by water to Avalon, 'to heal him of his wounds'? There was something else in her mind too, and, as she looked out over the marsh to the hill of Alderley beyond, she almost retrieved it. But then everything else was driven out of her mind as she saw another figure join the group.

She knew his walk and the very way he held his head. Leaving Cadwr behind, she ran over the uneven, muddy ground stumbling over her skirts. Lance stood there, with torn jerkin, muddied, bleeding from a cut on his forehead and with the remnants of white clay still on his cheeks, but, as far as she could see, whole and virtually unharmed. "Lance, oh Lance," she said and flung herself into his arms.

He kissed her forehead. "I told you I would be back," he said and then found her lips with his.

Book 4: Caverns

Chapter 1

They did not return to the camp that night, but stayed where they were, because of Arthur, now deep in the sleep of enchantment. Men brought tents, and a makeshift stretcher of wood and leather. Very cautiously, Arthur had been lifted on to it, away from the damp ground. Morgan had accompanied him into the tent, and gently washed away the grime of battle, then covered him with blankets.

Taliesin had joined the group, profound relief shining in his eyes, for his son, Afaon, had come through unscathed. Lyn, Morgan and Rhianwen were taking turns to sit with Arthur. Elli and Lance were side by side, the same blanket over their shoulders, keeping them warm. Completing the circle were Cai and Bedwr, Arthur's childhood friends, Owain, Morgan's son, and the new king, Cadwr.

Cadwr had been chosen late that afternoon, when the light was fading. Before the whole group was assembled, and fearing to use the mist as it might attract attention, Lyn had once again used his unnoticing spell until a protective arc of men was in place. No sooner than that had happened, a Saxon and one of Mordred's men approached, with a white flag, asking for a parley. Lyn nodded to Cadwr, "Go, then, and arrange terms."

"Me? Why not you? Or Gwalchmai? Or Owain?"

"It is not my business. Owain and Gwalchmai are not here, and you are Arthur's heir, as much as they are. Go now." Cadwr squared his shoulders, retrieved his own white banner and walked off. Lyn looked after him thoughtfully.

"What to do, with Arthur neither dead nor fully alive? To choose a new king? A regent? And who? Well, let us see how Cadwr manages this."

Impressively, it seemed. Half an hour or so later he was back, and reported that the two from the opposing army had come to call an end to the fighting, now that Mordred was dead. "They want to send their dead into the next world," he said. "The Saxons wish to burn their dead, as there are so many. It would take days to bury them, and those left are eager to be away."

"What did you say?" asked Lyn.

"I said, yes, we would stop fighting. You may have heard the trumpets. Each army is back on his own side of the ditch. Where we started. To what end?"

"There has been some gain," said Lyn. "Mordred has been stopped from letting his poison infect the entire land. The Saxons will go back to where they have lived for the last twenty years. We are all too tired to go on fighting. Small gains, perhaps, but gains."

"True," said Cadwr. "I said that the king – I didn't say who – would send messages to arrange a meeting of all parties. I do not know who, if anyone, will represent Mordred's men. I hope, now Mordred's madness has gone, they will come back to the High King. The Saxons will send their leaders. It may be we can find some land for their brothers who have come from over the sea."

"For that meeting," said Lyn thoughtfully, "we will need a king, fully empowered, not a regent."

During the time Cadwr had been away, Cai, Bedwr, Taliesin and Owain had joined the group. Lyn turned to those behind him and nodded, saying, "You see?" He said no more, but faced Cadwr once again and asked, "What did you say to the burial question?"

"I said that I would have to ask the King's Council," the young man answered, "but I thought that many of the British, whether Christian, or of the old religion, might find burial by water acceptable. We have a flooded marsh here, and it is the old way into the afterlife. I know, too, that we Christians have words for such a ceremony. Then, a small burial mound might be possible, alongside the Saxon's pyre."

"It was well done," said Lyn. "A least, I think so." The others nodded in agreement. "Come, sit down. Refreshments have been brought. We will talk when we have eaten, and when the High King is more suitably placed."

It was some time later that they were ready to talk. Lyn led the discussion. As he spoke, Elli looked round at the group: all looked weary and worn. Cai in particular seemed to be in deep shock: but then, thought Elli, he was Arthur's oldest friend, his foster-brother. She herself did not feel the euphoria that her mind told her she should feel, for surely their mission was over, and soon she and Lance would be on their way back home, back to their future. In a couple of months, with any luck, they would be an established couple, and she would tell him about their baby... she hoped by then that Gwennie would be at most a fond memory at the back of Lance's mind, and then, and then... But life here seemed too real, too close, and this future vision just a dream. In addition, there was a heaviness in her, a feeling like that on a sultry day, with a distant rumble of thunder.

She brought herself back to the discussion. Owain, Morgan's son, was speaking. "Gwalchmai is dead. I found his horse not an hour ago, standing over his master's body. And my uncle, the High King, lies somewhere between life and death. How do we proceed?"

Lyn spoke. "So one of Arthur's heirs lies dead before the King. He was a good man, and a loyal. When we have time, we will mourn him – and all the other brave men who have died today. But, right now, Owain has asked the vital question – how do we proceed?" There was silence.

Taliesin was the first to break it. "It is difficult. It would be difficult anyway, for we have before us two fine men, both approved by the High King as a possible successor. But with our dear King lying as he does... a regent is perhaps the obvious answer, but we need someone to act as himself in the situation we are in. And who knows how long Arthur will remain as he is?"

Lyn smiled sadly. "You have summed it up well, Taliesin, old friend. I feel we must choose a king, and, perhaps, give out that Arthur is 'at the point of death'. If he recovers, we will deal with that when it happens."

Elli thought: Lyn knows he won't. He knows the legends that have come down through the centuries. And I know other things, too, if I could only clear my mind enough to think of them.

Owain pushed himself to his feet. "I am honoured to have been chosen as an heir of the King. If he were dead, I would be more than willing to be considered by you all. But I have been Arthur's man since my father took me to court when I was a young boy. I have been a Companion for over fifteen years. I do not think I can be king in his place, and act as if he were dead. I would be trying to guess his thoughts, wanting his approval. But perhaps it is not my decision to make."

"This is not a task to be undertaken half-heartedly," said Lyn. "Reluctantly, yes, for who would willingly be king with his land in such a state? And with his lord lying helpless but alive? But what you have said, Owain, goes beyond that."

Bedwyr spoke. "Cadwr is perhaps less of Arthur's man. Not in loyalty, but because he has been duke of his own lands, and has come but fairly recently to court – and he is not a Companion."

"Certainly," said Morgan, speaking for the first time, "he has done well this last hour or so. I do not think anyone could have done better."

Lyn looked around the group. "Are we agreed? Cadwr, given all that has been said, will you take on this task?"

The young man sat still for a long while. Eventually, he nodded. "If you all wish me to, how can I say no? Yes, with reluctance, I will try to be king."

Chapter 2

So here we are, thought Elli, and still the talk goes on. Now it was of replacing and renewing the Companions. For not all had survived. They had already heard the news that Gwalchmai, one of the heirs of Arthur, had died. Then, once Cadwr had accepted the kingship, and all rose to take him by the hand, or embrace him, Cai had barely touched the new king when he broke off and walked away from the group. "Let him go," said Bedwr, sadly. "His son, Hywel, lies dead, and it is only his strength and loyalty has kept him here this long."

Finally, one of Arthur's first supporters, Tor, son of Pellinore, and the brother of Elen, had also been found dead.

Elli dozed against Lance's shoulder. When she woke, Cai had rejoined them, and the decisions had been made. In the end, it was quite simple – brother was to replace brother. Another of Cai's many sons, Gwyn, would be offered a place, and Maldwyn, half-brother of Tor, and Gwalchmai's brother, Emyr, were to be given the same chance. Partly, Elli gathered, it had revolved round what Lance called, in a muttered undertone, 'The White Horse Question'.

"For the horses of Tor and Hywel were also killed. But these are the families who breed the white horses, and the only two extra ones in the picket lines are the two that the families have brought. It's not the only factor, of course, but it helped. I gather it is important that the Companions have their white horses, their badge of office, right away – especially in such doubtful circumstances as now. It's a question of morale."

Elli said, "And the third new one – Gwalchmai's brother?"

"Gwalchmai's horse survived. His brother now inherits it."

Elli felt unutterably weary. The oppression in her mind seemed to be growing rather than easing, and the day had been long, and full. She found herself yawning. Morgan noticed and said to Lance, "It is time for your lady to sleep – and you too, by the look of you."

She looked at Lyn, who nodded, and gestured for her to carry on. "You have both done so well today, and we are deeply in your debt. On behalf of the King's Council, I thank you. And I, myself thank you too – especially Elli, for the saving of my brother, of Arthur." Her voice broke.

Elli shook her head, wordlessly. She was still unsure of the benefit of what she had done for Arthur, although Olwen had impelled her to act, and all the others had praised her. She got to her feet, and Lance scrambled after her, putting his arm round her waist. They bowed to the others and, leaning on each other for support, made their way to one of the recently erected tents.

During the night, Elli was disturbed by a vivid dream. It seemed nonsensical and harmless, but felt threatening and even distressing. She was tucking white horses into bed, covering them with blankets, stroking their manes, and saying, 'Goodnight, sleep tight, sweet dreams'. Obviously, she thought, as she woke in the dark of the night and listened to Lance's steady breathing. Obviously, as Lance would say, I'm muddling up The White Horse Question and the joys of motherhood – if he knew the latter was relevant. She went back to sleep, and the dream reoccurred, but this time she did not wake, but passed into a dreamless sleep.

She woke the next morning to find that the night had not cleared the feeling of oppression from the evening before. Nevertheless, she opened her eyes and turned with a smile to where Lance was. But he had gone. She must have slept soundly

– and late. She hurried to make herself ready for the day, grateful that someone had brought her a set of the woollen trousers and tunic, and that she did not have to put on her incongruous dress.

Coming out into the bright day, she felt that the sun and mild air were out of sympathy with recent events. Everywhere was quiet, and she was puzzling about this when she saw Morgan emerge from the tent where Arthur lay sleeping, guarded at the entrance by two soldiers.

"What's happening, Morgan? Where is everyone? How is the High King?"

"Everyone has gone to the main camp to announce and invest Cadwr as king, and to do the same for the three new Companions. I am late for the ceremonies, for I wanted to check on Arthur."

"And?"

"I have looked into him, and he is healing, but slowly, oh so slowly. That is partly the effect of the Sleep, of course, which has all but suspended life in him. It is probably a good way to heal, as well – but, human as I am, I could wish him to be well now! However, if you are ready, let us go to the main camp."

"And leave the High King?"

"My dear, my instincts are to stay. But this sleep is nothing like the coma you mentioned – I had your Lance explain it to me earlier. My brother needs no food, no drink, has no need of bodily care in any way. There are two men to guard the tent in case anyone tries to do him violence. But, otherwise, left to himself, he could sleep for a hundred years – or longer!"

Elli stood absolutely still, and put her hands to her head, to contain the thundering in her skull. The oppression of the last twelve hours or so, her dream, and Morgan's words coalesced to show her what it was she had forgotten. Following the revelation she felt a wave of approval from Olwen, as if the great Beast had been willing her to remember.

"Morgan, I have thought of something, something I know from my own time, that may be vital. But you told me to be wary of telling things from the future."

Morgan stopped walking and looked at her, then withdrew her gaze, and seemed to be listening. Then she said, "Olwen seems to approve. I don't communicate easily with dragons, but this I *can* feel."

"I can feel it too. And it *is* vital – what I've remembered, that is. It makes sense of so much…but I don't understand about the missing horse," she added to herself. Morgan looked at her, quizzically, but said nothing. In silence, they walked rapidly to the main camp.

They arrived to see the new king invest the last of the three new Companions. Under the cheers and applause, Morgan spoke with Lyn and Cadwr. They bowed to the men, then turned and walked to the Great Tent, followed by the rest of the Council, the twelve Companions, Lance and Elli.

Cadwr spoke to them all. "The Lady Elli has something of great moment to say to us. I do not know what it is, any more than you. Merddin Emrys?"

"All I know is that the Great Dragon knows – and I have a feeling that it may be something I came across on my travels, but gave no consideration to. But let us hear."

"Lyn, have I permission to speak freely?" asked Elli.

"But certainly."

"Very well." She addressed the whole group, voice raised slightly. "Some of you know, but many do not, that we have come to you from your far future."

A collective intake of breath, but nothing more. They were in control of themselves, these men.

"With help and guidance from the Dragon, Merddin Emrys sought us out – although I think I was a bit of a surprise to him. He brought Powell to help the High King, in place of Lancelot. And it may be that the Dragon wished for me to come, precisely that I may tell you of this matter.

"In my time and for many centuries before, there are tales of your High King. One persistent story is that he did not die but went somewhere 'to heal him of his wounds'. He sleeps, the stories say, in an enchanted sleep under a hill, from where he will come to rescue the land at its moment of greatest peril, when it is faced by unimaginable danger. One of the hills about which the story is told is the one on which Olwen, the Dragon, sits at this moment – the sharply outlined hill you can see from this camp."

Again the intake of breath. Lyn had a look of enlightenment on his face, and one or two of the others turned to look at each other.

"But this is not all. Surrounding the king are his knights, his closest companions – some say a hundred of them, but I think that is an exaggeration, a useful round number, like twelve…Each also sleeps, and has by his side his white horse, and I think, I think, that this must apply to…to…"

"The company here gathered," said Lyn. "I had heard the tale, but paid it no heed. But now, you are saying, with the king already in an enchanted sleep…"

"That is not all the story – at least not as it applies to this hill – to the Edge…" Elli broke in. She still experienced the heaviness within her, and felt impelled to speak on, immediately, in case she lost courage and kept the rest to herself, although its significance eluded her.

"It is quite enough to be going on with. Men, you have heard the story. This 'magic' I, and the ladies Rhianwen and Morgan, could do. To enchant a room, or in this case, a cavern, and hold people within it is easier than working on an individual. However, first we must see what our new king, Cadwr, says. You have loyalty to him. Then you must consider your own circumstances. Each may decide differently, for, as the Lady Elli says, one hundred or twelve, may be just round numbers – they are not necessarily precise.

"Finally: you were prepared to die for the High King Arthur – are you prepared to stay alive for him, to sleep and wake in the far future in a strange world, at the time of greatest peril?"

He stopped. Cadwr said, "For my part, I would not, could not, stop you, should you decide that way. If I were Companion, not King, I know what I would choose. Moreover, the world has changed, and it is a new one we face. I will, if needed, face it with a completely new Circle of Companions. Or," he added slowly, "perhaps with none so known. The Companions, the Cymry, may pass into legend."

Elli suddenly couldn't stand it any longer. "May I go, my lord?" she said to Cadwr. Receiving his nod, she made her way to the entrance. Seeing Lance make to follow her, she said "No…there's more, and I feel it's the important part – for me, anyway. You being with me'll just confuse the issue. I'll go and pack – we shan't be here long now."

"Besides," said Cadwr, hearing some of this, "it would be good of you to stay, Powell. You are, after all, an honorary Companion, so to speak."

Rhianwen found her some forty minutes later, sitting on her bed, one of Lyn's rucksacks stuffed untidily beside her, staring into space, and trembling slightly. Elli looked up, and said, "I know the rest of the story, but it doesn't make sense, nor does the terrible effect it's having on me. Which of the Companions doesn't have a horse?"

Rhianwen said, "But all of them do. Why?"

"It doesn't matter...I expect I'll find out what it's about. You came for me?"

"Yes. The discussions are over. We felt you should hear the results."

They slipped into the tent, as Cai rose to his feet. "For my part, I am weary. My son, Hywel, is dead. My younger boys I have hardly seen, for always I have been with Arthur. Now I could lose Mabon and Gwyn as well. More, I have loved Arthur ever since he was brought to our house as a mewling baby. I, for one, will go with him." Mabon stood by his father and nodded his agreement.

Gwyn spoke. "And I will go with my father and brother, so they have kin with them. Also, I was willing enough to take the glory of being a Companion and there is now no war in which to prove myself. I will do it this way."

The other new Companions, and then, one by one, all the remainder, in their own ways, pledged themselves to Arthur, to lie asleep until they were called to wake. Last to speak was Bedwyr. "Like Cai, I have known Arthur since I was a young boy. I have felt honoured to be with him, to call him friend as well as King, to have laughed with him, and feasted with him, as well as planned with him, and fought alongside him. How could I do else than stay with him now?"

Elli listened with a puzzled frown on her face. Surely Bedwr was Sir Bedevere of the later stories, the one knight left after the battle, the one who remained to tell the world of Arthur and his fate? The thunder in her head had returned, intensified, and was pounding away. Why? What was it she had still to remember? To work out?

Lyn was speaking. "I am honoured to know you all. I spoke only part of the truth when I said that twelve was merely a round number. It is a round number because it has Power. Your sacrifice will be so much more effective because the number will be complete. The King and his Companions will wait until the future…"

"No!" The word seemed wrenched from Elli and echoed round the tent. She looked at them with tears in her eyes and said, "It isn't Bedwyr. It can't be. He always remains behind in all the stories. It isn't him. It's Lance."

The response was not what she expected. Lyn, Rhianwen and Morgan seemed shocked, but, possibly, enlightened. She did not dare to look at Lance. But the others looked merely confused. One of them said, gently, as if to one with little grasp on reality, "But, Lady Elli, Lancelot is become a Holy Man. He has left us; he will not return."

Seeing Elli for the moment incapable of speech, Lyn answered, "Elli means Powell. In his time his name is Lance, and his second name is Poole. We chose Powell as one he would respond to: we avoided Lance because, as you see, you think of Lancelot first."

Elli had barely listened. In her mind she saw the bright bubble of her future: she and Lance and three children living in harmony with her parents on the now prosperous farm, Lance fulfilled, with a flourishing business. Like all bubbles, she thought, it didn't last long. It burst, and left her desolate for its bright, brief beauty. Her only consolation was that the pounding in her skull was gone. In its place was the swell of approval and enthusiasm and relief that the Great Dragon was communicating.

She looked up and saw Bedwyr advancing towards her. He took her hands and said, "Lady Elli, it seems you have knowledge which is necessary, even vital, for the success of this enterprise. Merddin Emrys has only this moment spoken of the importance of the number of the Companions. What you say could leave both you and I desolate – bereft of ones we truly love. So it must be considered carefully. Will you tell us?" he led her to a camp-stool. She walked with her head down, still not daring to look at Lance.

Sitting there, she recalled the day not two weeks earlier, although it seemed centuries past, when she had recited legends for Lyn. Then it had been exciting, almost unbelievable, and mixed with the thrill of her new, uncertain, love for Lance. Centuries later, centuries earlier, she now had to repeat more legends – not for her own enlightenment, but that of others.

"Bedwyr, all I can say is that in all the legends, you are the one who is left. You see Arthur safe on his last journey. You are the symbol of the great High King. I feel you must work with Cadwr and Taliesin in this. The black horse and the white. And this country becomes Christian. It must be right that you, and Taliesin, are of that faith."

"As is the new king," said Cadwr.

"And as to the other, listen, this is the tale: Once upon a time, a farmer from Mobberley – a village near here – went to Macclesfield market to sell his white mare. Macclesfield is to the east, over the hill, the Edge. As he went over the hill, he was stopped by a man in flowing robes, who offered to buy the white mare. 'No', said the farmer. 'How do I know that I won't get a better price at Macclesfield market?'

"'Very well,' said the stranger. 'You may try, but no-one will buy her.'

"And so it proved. Everyone admired the animal and said it was perfect, but somehow no one offered to buy it. The farmer, tired and deflated, set off home. When he reached the spot where he had met him, the stranger was still there, waiting. 'Now will sell me your horse?' he asked.

"'Certainly,' said the farmer, 'if you will give me a good price.'

"The wizard – for so he proved to be – turned and led the farmer over the hill, and down the rocky path, till they came to a cliff face. Then the wizard struck the rock with his staff, and suddenly there were iron gates embedded in the rock face. The wizard opened them and took the team into a stony passage, with small openings on each side. It was not a long passage, and it ended in a large cavern. There was a still, silver light filling the space, and by it the farmer could see, to his amazement, the sleeping form of a king, surrounded by his knights, also sleeping. Even stranger, by each man slept a white horse. Looking closer, he saw that he was wrong: one knight did not have a horse.

"'Now you know the reason why I want to buy your mare,' said the wizard.

"The farmer, being, as farmers are, careful with his money, asked again what he would get in exchange. 'Come,' said the wizard. They left the mare in the king's chamber and went to one of the side openings. This led to a small cave, stuffed with shining gold and precious jewels.

"'Fill your pockets,' said the wizard. When the farmer had done so, he was led up to the light of day. He stood blinking the sunlight, and when he turned round there was no sign of either wizard or the iron gates.

"He went home, grew prosperous, and often searched again for the Iron Gates. But he never found them."

Elli stopped, drew breath, then said, "One of the king's men did not have a horse. The wizard waited centuries for one. In our time a soldier like Lance, does not have a horse. You all heard Cadwr call Lance 'an honorary Companion'. Bedwyr, I know, must not wait with Arthur – who else to take his place?"

The roar of approval she felt from Olwen was obviously felt by many, if not all, of the others, for they clasped their heads and looked in wonder at each other.

Blinded by tears, Elli rushed from their company.

By the sun it must be just past midday, Lance reckoned as he hurried from the others. His first instinct had been to rush straight after Elli when she ran from the Great Tent, but Lyn had laid his hand on Lance's arm.

"Let her go. You need to think what you will say. Empty words of comfort would be cruel."

Lyn had been right, as so often, Lance thought. He had talked to the others, and then spent a little time with Lyn, in silence and with speech. He had a clearer idea of his path now. However, as he looked for Elli, he realised that for the first time since he had known her, he was reluctant to find her.

He found her sitting on the outskirts of the camp, looking toward the Edge. He sat beside her, silent. Eventually, Elli spoke. "So how soon do you all go?"

"Oh, Elli, if it were not for you, this would be the easiest decision I've ever had to make, not the hardest. A chance to belong again, be with my own kind, to make a contribution, to help change, perhaps save, my own land, to claw back some honour – the feeling of shame I've carried, you can't imagine! To 'chicken out' because of the mess I'd made of my life, because it was the only way to stop things getting worse – you've no idea how bad it made me feel! There was nothing to hold me in the twenty-first century – I told you I was a dinosaur. There are things, situations, I would love to leave. But now…oh, my dear, how can I do this? How can I do it to you, to us? Especially…" He stopped.

Elli bit hard on her lip to stop herself telling him of the other reason he should stay with her. She would not mention his child, she would not… "How would you feel if you stayed with me? In a year? Ten years? You know what a mess you were when I first met you – and yes, you missed Gwennie, but I think you missed your army life more. And yes, you were adjusting to being without it, but now you've got the chance to have it back. I don't know if I could live with your resentment."

"I wouldn't resent you, Elli," said Lance, but even he could hear the lack of total conviction in his voice.

"You won't get the chance to – you'll be with all the others, in that cavern! You know it, I know it, and all your fine words can't hide it!" She got up and ran to her tent, so he would not see her tears or feel her anger. Lance was not the only one who could feel resentment.

Some time later, when Morgan brought food and ale to her, Elli seemed composed and only the whiteness of her face and the redness of her eyes told otherwise. To stop discussion of Lance before it started, she thanked Morgan for the food, then asked, "What happens now? This afternoon? Tonight?"

Morgan, reading the signs, said, "Soon we have the funerals – both sides will hold ceremonies, and honour the dead, in various ways. We will use earth, water, fire – and when the smoke rises, air – all four elements. Tonight I, Lyn and Bedwyr will dress the High King as befits his status. Rhianwen will help keep him from further harm as we do this. We think we had better sleep in the tents surrounding him tonight. Bedwyr and Taliesin will join us, and the new King. The twelve Companions are to stay together, in the Great Tent."

Both thought, but neither said: so Lance will not be here tonight. Elli also thought that it might well be a relief for them, and felt sad because it was so.

"Tomorrow, we women are to take Arthur across the marsh. It will be the smoothest journey, thus the safest. We have asked one of the local fishermen to steer his boat for us. Scouts will go to find a safe, dry route round from here to your hill."

"I think," said Elli, breaking in, "that there must be gravel or sand ridges or something, across the marshes over there." She gestured in a semi-circle south-west to north-east. "That's where the roads run in my day. And perhaps that's why the farmer was going – will be going? – over the Edge in his journey – it was the dry route."

"That will be useful. Thank you."

"What will the others – the Companions – do?"

"They will see off the last of the troops, and make sure the remnants of Mordred's army have gone. Then it is suggested they recoup their energies. Some may hunt – for pleasure and to ensure that all of us eat well the next day…"

Elli thought, but did not say: the condemned man ate a hearty breakfast.

"It is suggested that then they all go to the Roman villa and bathe, and rest and relax, and even sleep, as well as they can. They are all, I think, exhausted."

"R and R," said Elli.

"R and R?"

"Rest and Recreation. What soldiers in our day get between two spells of duty."

"That describes it well. When the scouts return they will all be able to plan their route and will ride to join us the next day. The new king will be with them of course, but Bedwyr and Taliesin are talking of setting off earlier. However I think they may well stay to provide a fitting escort for Cadwr."

"But..." Elli hesitated, then forced herself to go on, "but Lance has no horse – how will he ride with them?"

"There are spare ponies, of course. However, Arthur's horse has no rider. Lance will take it round the marshes."

Elli smiled. "It's a much larger horse than he's used to."

"Oh yes. But he needs to practise for his white mare, although mares are usually easier to handle. There have been jokes about how he will manage if he is riding a horse he cannot stop by putting his feet on the ground!"

270

"Unfair…but not unfunny," Elli said, reluctantly smiling again.

"Come, if you have finished eating, it would greatly please us if you would join us for the funerals. Then many will depart, although it is late in the day, because they are so anxious to get away from this place. In two days all that will remain will be a small party, striking the remains of Arthur's mighty camp. Then the winds will blow, the seasons pass, and there will be nothing to show it was ever here."

"Except," said Elli, "a whisper, and a local legend…and me, living not so far away, knowing, remembering…"

Morgan touched her on the arm, then gathered up the dishes and left the tent. Slowly, Elli followed.

That afternoon, dressed again in their flowing robes, they stood with Rhianwen on the hill and watched the funerals. They had been at the edge of the marsh for the three Companions entry into their next life by water, then retreated to stand by the cross and the new king to see the rest. "So much waste," said Rhianwen. "So much sorrow." Apart from that, no one spoke.

Food that night was sparse, as was conversation. Elli determinedly sat between the other two women and avoided looking at Lance. But as those spending the night in the camp of the High King departed, Lance moved quickly and caught hold of Elli as she left, drawing her to one side in the dark of the night.

"I'm sorry," he said.

"So am I," she answered. "You will go, you must go, I realise that. I'm the one who saw it, even. But that doesn't help, although… although I know you wouldn't be the person I love, and I do love you, if you didn't go. You have, after all, an old-fashioned idea of duty."

"The dinosaur, that's me."

She went to kiss him lightly, in forgiveness. But he pulled her close, and in the fervour of his kisses, she forgot, for the moment, everything else.

Elli viewed the boat with misgiving. It was more like a punt, shallow and flat-bottomed, she thought. She was wearing her comfortable trousers and tunic, but 'for the look of it' as Morgan had said, wore over them a skirt and shawl. The morning wind blew cold and the sky was clouded. Bedwyr, Lyn, Cadwr and Taliesin lifted the corners of the leather stretcher and carefully, slowly, and reverently, raised the High King Arthur and carried him toward the marsh. He now looked like a storybook king, thought Elli, dressed in his finest, with the great Pendragon banner draped over him. A thin circlet of gold had been placed on his head.

Now the pall-bearers had reached the water's edge. Gently, they took hold of the ropes attached to each corner, and lowered the makeshift bier into the boat, where the boatman steadied it.

When it was safely lodged, he held his hand up and helped the three women into the boat. The other men stepped back and lowered their heads. Then Lyn, Cadwr and Taliesin withdrew, but Bedwyr seemed unable to move, unwilling to break the bond. The boatman cast off, and stood up, gently poling the punt away from the shore. Rhianwen and Morgan raised their hands in farewell, then turned, Morgan bending to straighten the banner, Rhianwen to look ahead.

Suddenly Bedwyr became even more still, his gaze fixed on the sleeping king. Then he turned and ran into the tent, where the King had been lodged. The boat was some thirty yards from the shore when he reappeared, bearing the King's sword.

"He will need this – it has been forgotten," he shouted and threw the sword over the widening water.

Morgan was on her knees, Rhianwen facing the other way. They responded, but not swiftly enough. Elli found herself reaching up and catching the sword by the hilt. She smiled, and bowed to Bedwyr, who bowed back, then turned and walked rapidly to catch up Cadwr, Lyn and Taliesin. Elli laid the sword by Arthur's side, her heart pounding as she realised her luck in catching it safely.

Only later did she realise that this was a scene that would resound down the years.

The boat moved silently, the boatman skilled in finding the deeper channels and knowing the ones to avoid. At his request, the women sat, to make the boat more stable, and they spoke little, each busy with their own thoughts. One of Elli's surfaced as a question: "Where will the gold and jewels for the farmer come from? I have seen nothing like that with you."

"Oh," said Rhianwen, almost dismissively, "there is gold enough in Ireland – and plenty of it belongs to the Sidhe. It seems I will have a great deal of time to move some here, and trade some for jewels."

More silence. The boat's progress was not swift, but gradually the hill of Alderley loomed larger, through the channels, although the marsh did not take a direct route but wound round small islands of tussocky grass. Elli had been told that it was at this time of year that the marsh most closely resembled a lake, because of the rains and the snows' melt-water, but even now there was much firm, if not dry, land within it. Perhaps it was at this same time of year that the farmer would travel to Macclesfield, over the Edge, thus avoiding the marshes – mosses they were called – which were plentiful in these parts. How long in the future would it be? She had no idea. And Lyn – he was obviously the wizard – how old would he be then?

Into the silence, she risked another question. "How long will Lyn live? Can you be sure he will be there for the farmer?"

Morgan spoke this time. "We have thought of this. Knowing nothing of Lyn's father, we cannot tell his lifespan. We already know he ages more slowly than the normal run of mankind, and that he will live longer. But it is a risk we cannot take. After the main cave is sealed, Rhianwen will seal Lyn in one of the side ones, and wake him when she judges the time of the farmer and his mare to be near."

"Yes," said Elli. "That fits with another legend – when Merlin's lady traps him under a stone, but is still considered worthy to be Arthur's advisor."

"The story is tangled," said Rhianwen coldly, "but something of the truth is there."

As the firm ground of the edge came into sight, Elli risked a third question. "If Rhianwen wakes Lyn then, will it be she who wakes Arthur and the Companions in the far future?"

"That," said Morgan, "we do not know. It may be Rhianwen; it may be the cry of pain from a suffering world. We have no guidance here, so we must leave it to the future."

Now Elli wondered about a more immediate problem. How were they to get the king up the Edge to the caves? These were mainly over the far side, she thought. The boat grounded gently, and the boatman got out and pulled up a little. Then, with less elegance and ceremony than the four previous pallbearers had managed, he and the three women lifted the stretcher and laid it on the ground. A man of few words, he bowed a little awkwardly, and got into his boat again, steering it back to collect the necessaries for their overnight camp and –Morgan had said – a couple of Cadwr's men as bodyguards.

Elli knew that the three of them were waiting, although she did not know what they were waiting for. Then there was a susurration of sound, and from her place on the crest of the Edge, Olwen swooped down, and hovered. Then she extended neck, and smoothly, slowly, looking, Elli thought, a little like the traditional picture of a stork with a baby, the dragon carried the High King Arthur toward his resting place.

By mutual, unspoken consent, they made their camp a little lower than the cave complex, although they gave themselves more work that way. "These caverns will have occupants soon enough," said Morgan, "and we have a day or so before the others come, so we need to have work to do." Elli felt very calm, as if her emotions had been shut away, in a room she dared not enter. It occurred to her that perhaps Morgan was enspelling her, but it didn't seem to matter at the moment.

They ate that evening round a fire, reminding Elli of the time she had spent in the clearing below Lud's Church, but, again, as a distant memory, with no power to disturb. Then they retired early, and she slept long and peacefully.

The next morning passed similarly, in a state of numbness. There was little to do but wait. Even if the king and his company had set off early, it would be afternoon by the time they arrived. The only point of interest came about halfway through the morning, when Elli realised that Morgan's command of English had deteriorated and she could not understand the others at all. With a feeling of panic which came close to opening the closed door of her emotions, she realised it was because Olwen was no longer with them. The evening before Rhianwen and Morgan had expressed their opinion that the great dragon would not be staying in this world for long, but would follow her brothers back to their own place. "But not without taking me home!" Elli felt like shouting. "Not leaving me here, without Lance and Lyn, with no hope of seeing Mum and Dad and the farm!" Suddenly, she felt homesick and weary of all the adventuring. If only Lance could go home with her. But then, she suspected, Morgan noticed her distress, and calmed and quieted her once more.

It was afternoon when she realised Olwen was back, and soon after that, outriders on sturdy Welsh mountain horses arrived, heralding the arrival of the rest of the company. At that moment Elli felt her emotions rush in on her again, breaking down the constraining door. Anticipation pushed to the fore, reducing the rest to a low dread, an undertone that she could do without, but that it was almost possible, at this moment, to ignore.

They rode in almost cheerfully, talking and laughing. They checked this out of respect to the sleeping King, but the feeling of a band of brothers – to quote Shakespeare once more, she thought – was strong, as was her feeling of exclusion. She spotted Lance, almost unrecognisable in fine clothes, laughing at something his tent-mate, young Gareth, had said. But before resentment could win out, he dismounted from the High King's horse and came toward her and swept her off her feet. While the others were busy pitching camp a little further down the slope – Elli suspected it was so they could renew their joviality from the sobering influence of the sleeping King – Lance pulled her away from all the bustle and busyness and walked her out of sight, and more or less out of sound of the camps. In their day, the Edge would be covered by beech woods, and before that, almost bare of trees. Now it was more like the landscape that would give it its Saxon name – Alderley, the clearing in the alders – with some trees, and also grassy spaces, as well as signs of old copper mines.

They sat looking over the view of the plain to the north-east, to where in their day would be the urban sprawl of Stockport and Manchester.

Elli, fearful of saying the wrong thing, said nothing. Lance pulled from under his tunic a fine chain, and unpinning the clasp, let something slide into his hand. "I can't marry you, Elli, not in these circumstances, but I would have…if you accepted me. And I want the world to know. Will you wear this for me?"

He dropped the object he was holding into her hand. To her astonishment, it was a heavy gold ring set with a large, deep red stone – could it be a ruby? "Where did you get this?" she asked, avoiding deeper issues.

"Morgan offered it to me, yesterday, when she heard of my need. It is beautiful, and no doubt valuable, but it is no more than I would wish to give you."

Elli said, in a measured tone, "Thank you. I will be honoured to wear it."

"Third finger, mind. It's an engagement ring."

Torn between delight and sorrow, Elli searched for some other topic to talk about, as she slid the heavy ring onto her finger, where it sat, emblem of a promise that was impossible to fulfil. Lance was saying, "I hope it will make things easier for you, especially…" when she broke in, realising with horror that she had not considered what to tell people about Lance's disappearance.

"What will I tell people – about you not being there, I mean!"

"Lyn and I have worked it out – and put some of it into practice. You will tell people that I've been recalled to the army: something urgent and secret. And in a few months you – as my fiancée – will get a letter, informing you that I am missing, believed dead. Lyn went with Olwen today, to arrange it." He paused, looking almost embarrassed. "He did something else as well. I put a text on your phone, and Lyn took it and sent it to your mother – he had to work hard, I gather, to make Olwen 'unnoticed' even for the little time it took!"

"My mother! Why? What did it say?"

"Why? So Olwen can have leeway as to when she drops you off. This time, Lyn says he arrived before he met us, so to speak – strange, isn't it? As to what it said: what I've just told you: I've been recalled, and you've taken me to Crewe station. Obviously."

Elli's sense of humour overcame her and she laughed, weakly at first, then more and more strongly, until she subsided, and said, between splutters, "I'm sorry – but the contrast: here we are at what Arthur called the edge of doom, at the point where legend and history meet, surrounded by amazing and incomprehensible forces, and facing…facing…personal loss, and you talk of Crewe station!"

Lance hugged her to him. "Oh, Elli, you are wonderful. And yes, it does seem silly. But it won't tomorrow." The word tomorrow sobered her and she fell silent. Lance kept her close and spoke over her head, not looking at her.

"Don't laugh at me: all this preparation has some point – I'm trying to make things a little easier for you, ungrateful wench! There's more: I want you to take my laptop with you. I'll have no use for it. In the case you'll find my car keys, the keys to my flat, and two envelopes – lucky I had them and my cheque book in there." Elli twisted and tried to look at him, but he carried on, speaking over her head.

"They're part of the preparation: I don't know if it'll work. One envelope is addressed to your father. In it is a brief letter that says, to show I'm in earnest about his girl, I've written him a cheque: it's about the most I felt my bank manager wouldn't query. For investment in the farm."

"Oh Lance, how thoughtful – how clever!"

"The other envelope is my will. I fear they'll make you wait, perhaps the full seven years – as I'm 'missing, presumed dead'. Even then, my third cousin might contest it, as otherwise it'd all go to him. But I've left everything to you."

Elli could think of nothing to say, so she sat, overwhelmed. Eventually, trying for lightness, she said, "It would be wonderful if it came off. Especially..." Oh my God, she thought, nearly mentioned our child!

"Especially?"

"Nothing. But who did you get to witness it? Surely Taliesin the Bard and Cadwr the King will arouse suspicion?"

"My good friends from the Welsh regiment I served alongside: Lyn Sayer and Gwyn Kay."

"Gwyn Kay? Oh, Cai's son. My dear love, you've thought of everything. I only wish it wasn't necessary. And I bet Gwennie would have no need of your...your...posthumous financial support. She surely has her own money and could be quite self-sufficient!"

"Gwennie? Why bring her into it?"

Because, thought Elli, surprised herself at the welling up of feelings she had thought dead, because I'm still not sure. I won't have time now to erase her completely. In the Sleep you may dream of her. Now, if you knew about the baby...perhaps, perhaps, it would be different!

"I'm sorry. Take no notice. Let me thank you properly." She kissed him hard on the lips to stop her mouth from betraying her, and soon she lost the desire to tell in quite a different desire.

Returning, they found that decisions had been made in the short time they had been absent. Morgan told Elli of them, as Lance hurried to help with the lower camp, receiving much good-natured teasing for his absence.

"Tomorrow we will seal the cave. Lyn, Rhianwen and I will have to work hard – we dare not rely on Olwen overmuch, though we will use her, of course."

"Dare not?"

"What if we used so much of her other-worldly power, that when the time comes, it can't be undone without her? She will be long gone. But that should work to your advantage."

"My advantage?"

"She will not be too weary to return you to your own time late tomorrow – just after dark, we were thinking. You will not want to linger here, I feel."

"No, I don't think I could bear it, although it will be hard to part from everyone."

"Indeed, as Merddin Emrys would say. He will not be sealed till the day after tomorrow: we will need to recover our strength. I think that sealing will be up to Rhianwen and myself alone, for I would not be surprised if we do not see Olwen again, after she takes you home. Indeed, I think it probable."

"So it really is the end – for me, that is."

"Yes, indeed – for your sojourn here, anyway. And I will miss you. But let us not be maudlin: come and help me with the supper."

Later, Elli looked at the company gathered round the fire. In the camp below them there was another group, the contingent of Cadwr's men who had accompanied him, and most of the Companions. Conversation and occasional laughter floated up to the smaller group where Lance and Elli sat.

She was alarmed by the resurgence of uncertainty she felt: would Lance have left Gwennie so easily? But it was, it seemed, necessary for him to go, so perhaps that was a good thing. She shook herself, and told herself that now was no time to be self-centred. Round this fire the mood was more sombre than in the lower camp. As she looked around, she realised that everyone, except perhaps the new king, would be losing someone close to them. Cai had left his sons in the lower camp and sat with his lifelong friend Bedwyr; Morgan, by her long-estranged son,

Owain, and Taliesin with his son, Afaon. On Elli's left side sat Lyn, and next to him, Rhianwen. Hers would not be the only sorrow.

As if he knew what she was thinking, Lyn said, "Your loss will be the greatest, I think – the rest will have others left, who are part of the same loss, with whom they can share their sorrow. But you will be alone: and your happiness is so very new – we are all conscious of it."

Elli, finishing her bowl of the ubiquitous stew, did not know what to say. Eventually, she found words. "I will miss you, and Morgan very much – and the others, of course, but you have been my mentor, my father-figure if you like, since the start. And Morgan is the closest thing to a friend of my own sex I have had since I was a little girl."

"We can do little to ease your pain. But we have thought of a small …treat, you might call it."

Lance, finishing his food, put his arm round Elli and moved, so he could see Lyn more easily. "A treat?"

"We heard of your wish to spend one uninterrupted night together, so we have arranged it – we didn't think the night after the battle counted. If you look, you will see a fire in the mouth of the cavern system above us. Up there, you will also find water heating, for washing, blankets to warm you as you sit by the fire, your clothes for the morning. There is even a flask of wine and two cups. Further in, we have prepared a bed-chamber for you – and left lamps to show you where. Go now – enjoy the moment!"

They looked at each other and grinned. Wasting no time, they rose to their feet and Elli dropped a kiss on Lyn's head – much to his surprise, and, it seemed, embarrassment – saying, "Thank you, my good friend. I will always remember you, and your kindness."

Then they turned and made their way up the slope.

An hour or so later, Elli was lying with her head in Lance's lap, watching the dying flames of the fire, and beyond that, the night, now thick with stars. The wine flask was empty, and she felt warm, inside and out.

Lance ran one of Elli's curls through his fingers, noting how the fire struck light from the dark chestnut.

"I find I'm growing fond of this colour hair," he said.

"As opposed to? Which colour did you prefer before?" said Elli, a little defensively, deliberately tempting the pain she thought she had relegated to the past.

"Ah. As you know, Gwennie had shining hair, flame coloured. And it drew men, like moths to its flame. So bright: but perhaps a little…one-toned."

Elli kept quiet. She discovered that, much as it hurt to hear him talk of her rival, as she found she still thought of Gwennie, it was better than wondering if he were always comparing them silently, to her detriment. This was the most he had said since those first nights, and it contained a precious 'but'. She waited.

Lance continued. "I've often wondered how Gwennie, as dazzling, and witty, yet sweet-natured and loving as she was …is…will be... how she would have coped over these last few weeks. Probably – no, certainly – not as well as you, my Elli. At first sight you would be outshone by Gwennie. But like your hair," and he extended and straightened a curl, turning it so the fire lit it again, "you, Elli Tollet, have hidden depths. Now, let's find this bedchamber, or rather cave, they have prepared for us."

They walked down the sloping corridor, where oil lamps had been placed on the floor to light their way. The cave was on the left and not large. It had a wide shelf of stone to serve as a bed, and that had been piled with furs and blankets, over an improvised mattress of heather. In the future, a farmer would find this same cavern crammed with gold and jewels, but now, with just two small oil lamps on a high ledge, it looked both exotic and familiar, as the whole of their journey had seemed.

As Elli pulled Lance to her, he resisted, and held her at arm's length, looking far into her eyes. Then he said, "Look after our son."

"You know? I've tried so hard to keep it from you."

"I thought that might be it. Lyn told me, that first day, when you ran from the Great Tent. He felt I should make my choice unblinkered. I've tried to tell you I knew, but the conversation always turned. But I might have guessed, back in 1900, after I heard the full story of Lancelot and Elaine…

"Remember, we're following a pattern. Try to make our son more… rounded… than his predecessor. Oh, and don't burden him with the name of Galahad!"

"Obviously," said Elli, trying for Lance's dry, detached tone of old.

"Obviously," he agreed, with a brief, sad smile.

"He will be named William Lance. William after my father, and Lance…after his." Lance brought her close to him, and after that there was no more talking.

Elli stirred in Lance's arms. Their lamps had long since guttered out, but now the faint light of day was growing in the passageway outside. Soon, high on the Edge above them, it would be possible to see the sun rise over the Pennines.

She whispered to him, without thinking, "High above the dawn is breaking…" then caught her breath as the next three lines sang in her mind. Perhaps there was one crumb of comfort: perhaps now it would be their song, not his and Gwennie's.

The unheard music echoed round the cavern, but Lance said nothing about it. "Time, or almost time, to go and face the world, my Elli," was all he said, turning her to him.

The sun was fully up, making the remaining leaves shine glistening gold, when everyone came together. Lyn, Morgan and Rhianwen were by the cavern entrance, and Elli could feel the presence of Olwen, strong in her mind. She herself stood a little apart, near the new king, Bedwyr and Taliesin, as the Companions lined up. Arthur, the Once and Future King, had already been taken into the inmost cavern, his pall-bearers those who had placed him in the boat. Five minutes earlier, Lance had kissed her swiftly, told her to take care for her own sake, and that of their child, and hurried off to stand by Gareth. Was this all? Was that it? Unexpectedly, anticlimax seemed to be Elli's overwhelming emotion.

As the column approached the cavern entrance, Lance broke away and came to Elli, who was turning, ready to return to the camp. "Wait, one last thing I must tell you."

She almost continued to walk away, thinking she could bear no more. But in the end, the desire to postpone the final moment won. She stopped, and waited.

"Yesterday, as we rode here, Lyn asked me something, and I answered without thinking, without hesitation. And my answer showed me that in one respect we are not following the pattern – we are not shackled by someone else's past."

"What did he ask? What did you say?"

"Lyn said, 'Who will you dream of, down the years, in the Long Sleep?'

"And I answered from my heart, without thinking, 'Elli'."

She caught her breath as a ridiculous joy flooded her. "Not Gwennie? Not your shining Gwennie?"

"No, my darling. We are like but not like. I am not Lancelot du Lac; you are not Elaine, the Lily Maid. And down the long years, my heart is yours, Elli Tollet. Not Gwennie's. Now go!"

He would not let her, immediately, though. Not before one long, last, fierce kiss. Then he turned her round and sent her away. Morgan detached herself from the group by the entrance, and walked with her back to the king.

Lance did not look back, but as he exchanged the bright day for the cool, shadowy cave, he thought he heard a thread of song, in Elli's distinctive voice:

"Though the carnival is over,
I will love you till I die."

Late that afternoon, Morgan came looking for Elli. She found her, near the top of the hill, looking over the plain, but with blank eyes. She had changed into the strange garments belonging to her own time, the enchantress noted, and had a large leather coat – surely it must be Lance's? – wrapped around her.

Ell looked up as Morgan approached. "I can still smell him, you know," she said. "Through the leather, I can still smell him." Then, seeing Morgan properly, she said, "Oh, Morgan, you do look exhausted: is it finished?"

Morgan sat beside her. "Indeed. For today, at least. Tomorrow, with my help, Rhianwen will seal Lyn in a side cave that he may wait for her awakening spell, and then, in turn, he will wait for your farmer with the horse."

"And where are they now – Lyn and Rhianwen, I mean?"

"Waiting for us – but do not let us keep them waiting – this is their last night – as yesterday's was yours. Let us give them a long evening."

"No!" Elli burst out. "It is *not* the same. It is *not* their last night. You said it...Rhianwen will wake Lyn up. Lance and I, on the other hand, Lance and I..." Her voice broke, and she turned away. After a moment, she continued. "Morgan, why did Lance have to go? I understand why he came back here: I saw how – necessary – he was to Arthur in the battle. But after, he could have stayed with me. Olwen will take me home today, you said, when she's rested for a bit. Why not Lance as well? Surely they didn't send him to the Long Sleep because of that stupid legend…yes, they should lack a horse, but there could have been many reasons for that. For you to believe my crazy idea that it was because there was a man from the twenty-first century involved, who wouldn't have a horse, … for heaven's sake!" She had leapt up, and would have rushed away, but that Morgan rose as well, and restrained her and made her sit again.

"I think that is part of the reason that we are a horse short," said Morgan. "But I do not believe that Lance has gone with them merely to fulfil the legend."

"What are you talking about? Don't do a Lyn on me and turn all cryptic and prophetic!"

"Stay sitting, Elli, please! That's better. Now listen – as to that…" Morgan hesitated.

"As to that, what?" Elli said bitterly.

"We have been thinking, and talking, last night, when you were …elsewhere. You have a point – I thought of it myself, and when the others stopped to think, they did. The legend has power, but our interpretation of it is not – complete. However, you know yourself that Olwen was most firm that Lance should be one of the Companions in the cave. And, as I said, we have been thinking. Now this is no true foretelling, so do not take it as such, but perhaps it is necessary for the Companions to have a man from your time with them."

Hope, wild and uncontrollable, rose in Elli. "But that would mean…"

"Yes. There would be no point in that, unless they were to wake up in your time. Or in a time not so far removed."

"But…but… we have weathered many terrible things without Arthur and his Companions waking. What could be so unimaginably awful that they would wake in our time?"

"You use the word unimaginable, so your question is unanswerable. But perhaps, in your near future, the world will need our heroes – and one from your own time, with knowledge – and family ties."

"Lance has no family," Elli stated.

"My dear, he has – he has you, and he will have a son. That may well be important. Lyn said that Olwen was determined to – to make your son's existence certain. And what a son! Conceived in one time, born more than a hundred years later – and spending time in the womb some fifteen centuries before! He will be special, Elli, whether or not that other comes to pass."

"But you think it might."

"Do not depend on it. I told you I am not foretelling, just thinking. It may be so. But if you depend on it, build your life round it, bring up your son in its shadow, you will not only blight your own life, and his – you may well ruin the re-emergence, if it should happen in your time." She sighed. "I should not have mentioned it at all, perhaps. But you are so very unhappy, and I do not believe your despair can help either!"

"Thank you. You have always been kind to me. But you said it did not do for anyone in a story to know too much about it – should you have said anything at all?"

Morgan smiled. "But this story is not in the past – it is no more than a hope for the future, a case of what might be."

"True," said Elli. Then a thought struck her. "Did anyone mention this to Lance – to give him a hope as well?"

"No – partly because the thought was not fully formed last night. But don't distress yourself – for him, it is only one night's sleep. It is you who will need a small amount of hope, to see you through the long years."

This time, Elli rose calmly and helped Morgan to her feet. She embraced the older woman. "Dear Morgan, how I shall miss you! You have given me hope, and good advice, and care, and love. Now, we had better stop talking, for Olwen's sake, if for no other reason. Even the minimal amount of help she's giving us must be tiring. And I want her as rested as possible if she's taking me back home today!"

"She may be rested sufficiently already. Are you prepared to go?" Elli nodded. "Come, then," said Morgan. "Let us find the Great Dragon, and if she is ready. But first, come and say your farewells to the rest of us."

Together they walked down the path, two small figures under the darkening sky.

Epilogue: College

Elli settled herself in her car seat and looked about her. Strange but familiar. Familiar but strange. On the seat beside her was her bag, and one of Lyn's rucksacks containing Lance's leather coat. Safe from harm in the footwell was Lance's laptop and, in its case, the keys and envelopes – brought from the past to help with the future. The only other links were about and within, her person: the filigree bracelet, the ruby ring, and young William Lance. For his sake she must move on.

The phone rang. It took her time to realise what it was, and she feared it would stop before she found it, deep in her handbag. Her mother was speaking, "Where are you, Elli? Shall I take your food out of the oven and reheat it when you get here? If you're much longer, it'll dry up. It was nice of you to take that friend of yours to Crewe... but I thought he'd left the army."

"So did I. It was a bluff, I think. Look, I've had to call back in college, but I'm leaving now – see you soon."

The twenty-first century was sweeping her away. But as she drove out of the car park, she saw, silhouetted against the bright moon, the unmistakable shape of a dragon. Then it winked out, and was gone.